THE BAD WIFE

SARAH EDGHILL

First published in 2023 by Bloodhound Books.

www.bloodhoundbooks.com

Print ISBN: 978-1-5040-8626-4

1

As the man sank to his knees beside her, Katie caught her breath; his face was so close she could see the pinpricks of sweat on his forehead, the smattering of tiny freckles across his nose, the way a muscle twitched just beside his left eye.

He was gorgeous.

'What's happened here?' he asked.

'I'm not sure,' the receptionist called across from behind the desk. 'I thought she might have fainted?'

The old woman had fallen with no warning as she walked across the waiting room, her fingers flying out and clawing at Katie's arm, dragging on her coat sleeve. As she hit the floor with a crack, her bag of shopping split and scattered its contents: a carton of milk smashed onto the carpet, an apple rolled away.

There had been a shocked silence, a second of inactivity. Katie had watched milk unfurling in a puddle by her feet, her brain struggling to process what had happened. Then the waiting room was filled with the buzz of murmuring and exclaiming, the scrape of chairs being pushed back as people stood up to see what was happening.

'Can someone get one of the doctors?' the receptionist had called, as she came out from behind her desk. 'Mark's on a call, but Joe should be in his room.' She shrugged off her pink cardigan, and pushed it gently under the old woman's head.

Katie knew she was in the way and ought to move. She had stared down, watching the apple rocking to a standstill; someone was going to trip over that – she ought to pick it up before it caused an accident.

The old woman lay with one leg twisted awkwardly, her coat flung open and her skirt riding up her thigh, and Katie dropped to her knees and pulled the edge of the material back across the old woman's exposed tights. It seemed important to restore her a little dignity. At that moment, the phone rang and the receptionist went to answer it, leaving Katie kneeling on her own. She felt so exposed, at the centre of this crisis, but desperate not to be. She put her hand on the woman's arm, not sure what else to do, but wishing she could shuffle backwards and hide herself amongst the people hovering nearby.

It was then, as she looked up at the sea of staring faces, that the man pushed his way through and knelt beside her.

The old woman was now moaning, low whimpers edged with panic.

'You're going to be fine,' he was saying. 'I'm one of the doctors here. Can you open your eyes for me? That's it. We need to check nothing's broken.'

'Her name is Mrs Burns,' called the receptionist. 'She was booked in to have a flu jab.'

Katie pulled away slightly, her heart hammering against the wall of her chest. She couldn't drag her eyes from him; his fringe fell across his forehead and he swiped it away with the back of his hand. Kneeling just inches from him, she could smell the washing powder on his shirt, as well as something else – moisturiser maybe, or aftershave. His shirtsleeves were rolled up and his forearms were lightly tanned. She imagined stretching out her fingers and brushing the tips across his skin. Her heart was thundering so loudly, surely he must be able to hear it?

But he wasn't looking at her. He was concentrating on the old woman; holding her hand, the paper-thin skin crinkling beneath his touch. He ran his fingers over the base of her skull, down her neck, quietly talking to her all the while. As he moved her leg, the woman cried out. Sitting beside her, Katie flinched.

'I think we ought to call an ambulance, Bridget,' the doctor said, his brown fringe again falling across his eyes. He could have been in his thirties or early forties – Katie had never been good at judging ages – and his eyes were deep blue.

She felt light-headed but still acutely aware that she was doing nothing useful here. She reached out again to rest her hand on the bony shoulder in front of her. Below her, the tangle of white hair was stark against the pink cardigan. The chatter all around was getting louder, bubbling up as fellow patients animatedly discussed the fall and the effect it would have on those brittle bones. There was excitement in the voices: glee that disaster had struck elsewhere.

Suddenly, the doctor was looking up, talking to her, those blue eyes reaching deep under her skin.

'Sorry?'

'I said, are you together?'

She shook her head, took a breath to steady herself. 'No, I was just standing beside her when she fell.'

A few of the other patients were now walking back to their seats, possibly disappointed that the most exciting part of the show was over. 'Poor old dear,' muttered someone. 'I bet there's something broken.'

Suddenly angry at having been forced to play a part in this impromptu performance, Katie glared up at the handful of people who were still gathered around her, hoping they'd pick up on her disapproval and realise how inappropriate their behaviour was. Nobody noticed. One woman had taken out her phone and was tapping furiously, possibly texting the news to her friends. Katie half expected her to lean forward and snap a quick picture.

'The ambulance is on its way, Joe,' called the receptionist.

'Thanks. Can we get her a blanket?' He turned back to the figure lying in front of him. 'It may take a while before we can move you, Mrs Burns, but I'm going to stay right here. There's no need to be afraid.'

Katie suddenly felt she might cry. The old woman's anguished wail rang in her ears: her own mother had sounded the same, when she fell in the hospice. She could still see her, stretched out on the bedroom floor: the smear of blood spreading across the side of her head, red spots brutal against the cream carpet.

A young man was collecting the bits of food that had fallen out of the shopping bag and Katie watched, willing him to pick up the apple.

As the doctor repositioned the cardigan beneath the old woman's head, he accidentally brushed Katie's hand. It was the lightest of touches, the tips of his fingers flickering across hers, but it made her jump. His skin was soft and warm.

'Thanks for your help,' he was saying. 'It's kind of you to stay with her.'

'That's fine.' Her cheeks were burning and her mouth was dry. Those eyes were such a deep blue, so compelling; as he smiled at her, tiny laughter lines spread out from the side of them, white creases cracking the bronzed skin.

'I probably need to get back to work,' she said.

'Of course. We can take it from here. Thanks again.'

Katie pushed herself up and automatically brushed her coat as she stood, wiping away dirt that wasn't there. Forcing her way through those still craning their necks to get a ringside view, she went towards the door. Before pushing it open, she turned, hoping to catch one last glimpse of him. But the onlookers had closed ranks; she could just see the back of his shirt, the material stretched across his shoulders as he leant forward.

Walking outside, she thrust her hands into her coat pockets, and her fingers closed around a piece of paper: Anna's eczema prescription. She'd been about to take it into the surgery's dispensary, but couldn't face going back in there now; it wasn't urgent, she'd do it tomorrow.

Striding across the car park, she took deep breaths to clear her head. That poor woman; what an awful thing to happen – and in such a public place. Although, if you were going to collapse anywhere, doing it in the waiting room at the local surgery was probably ideal. Did she have a family? There might be grown-up children who would rush to the hospital to be by her side. Perhaps a daughter; a woman like Katie, who would soon be receiving the sort of phone call everyone dreads.

The cars on the road ahead of her suddenly became blurry, the tarmac beneath her feet a hazy grey. As she raised her hand to wipe the tears from her cheeks, a sob forced its way up her throat, followed by another. She stopped and tried to control the emotion flooding through her body, her shoulders heaving with the effort, gasping as the cries ripped from her mouth.

A man walked past, hesitating as he moved towards his car.

She closed her eyes for a couple of seconds, hoping he would keep walking. *Ignore me; don't be nice to me.* She took a deep breath and forced herself to start walking again.

That handsome doctor had been so kind.

Those eyes.

Had he left another patient in his consulting room, halfway through an appointment? He might have been called to the emergency when he was in the process of diagnosing an ingrowing toenail or an ear infection. Maybe he'd rushed off during an intimate examination, with the curtain drawn around a pair of quivering, naked buttocks. The thought made her snort with laughter and she wiped away the last of the tears. *Come on, Katie, get a grip.*

As she stood waiting at a junction, traffic thundered by in both directions; the flaps of her coat were slammed backwards by a rush of air as a lorry roared past, accelerating to beat the lights.

Were you born with that natural ability to care and console, or did it come as part of the training? Over the last year she'd met some wonderful people who worked in the health service: the doctors and nurses who didn't just provide treatment, but also smiles, kind words and comfort; the hospital porters who joked with her mother as they wheeled her to X-ray; the girls who delivered trays of food that sat untouched on the bedside cabinet; the elderly ladies from the League of Friends who pushed around trolleys of thumbed paperbacks.

When her mother was admitted onto a ward for the final time, there had been a wonderful man who broadcast on the hospital radio. Katie remembered him popping his head through the curtain around the bed, introducing himself with a flourish. 'Anything you want to hear, my love,' he'd beamed at her mother. 'From Buddy Holly to Boney M. You name it, we'll play it.'

It felt like such a long time ago. But it was just six weeks.

Katie turned down the steps towards the canal. Her boots slipped in the mud on the towpath and she moved away from the water's edge, where plastic food wrappers and empty bottles were trapped in the brambles, the wheels of an upturned supermarket trolley forming a bizarre sculpture in the mud.

Mrs Burns was lucky to have that handsome doctor take

care of her. Katie couldn't get his face out of her mind: the warm smile, reassuring and reliable. Don't panic, it said; I have everything under control.

She looked at her hand. The skin still felt strange where he'd touched it: tingling as if shot through with an electric current. Something in the pit of her stomach lurched at the memory of him next to her. She shook her head: she was being ridiculous, it had been accidental – nothing like a proper caress. She rubbed the fingers of her left hand, her wedding ring strangely tight, digging into the skin.

As she walked on, she thrust both hands into her pockets, trying to think about something else: work, tonight's supper. But the further she walked away from the surgery, the more she wanted to be back there; kneeling close enough to that man to still have the scent of him in her nostrils, close enough to be able to reach out and rest her hand against his cheek.

2

'Hey, you lot – the kitchen fairy is handing in her notice!' Katie yelled up the stairs.

Silence.

'So, from now on you'll have to clear up your own mess after breakfast.'

No one answered.

'You'll have to do your own washing as well, and hoover the stairs. Oh yes, and someone will have to clean the shower and pull the hair out of the plughole!'

She walked back into the kitchen and began to stack the dirty plates, sweeping up crumbs, wiping a smear of butter from the back of a chair.

'Bad news!' she yelled again. 'The self-loading facility on the dishwasher is broken, so your breakfast things can't put themselves inside. But don't worry, the kitchen fairy will do it for you.'

It was pointless: they hadn't heard her. Anna was singing in the bathroom and Suky had the radio playing so loudly in her bedroom that, even down here, Katie could hear the DJ wittering on about issues of international importance, such as whether or not Taylor Swift was pregnant. Having put the pile of plates in the sink, she plonked a mug on top of them and there was a pop as the handle came off in her hand; tea began to leak through the crack in the side and spiral down the plughole.

'Bloody hell.'

'What's the matter, what have you done now?' Pete was pulling on his coat as he came into the kitchen, distracted, looking for something.

'I haven't done anything,' said Katie. 'Nor have you. That's the point, Pete. Why can't you put things away when you've finished with them?' She knew she was nagging, and hated the whine she could hear in her own voice.

'Please don't go on, Katie,' he said. 'It's only few dishes. The world won't end if they sit there until we get home tonight.' He started flicking through a pile of papers on the worktop beside the fridge: bills, pizza delivery flyers, money-off coupons.

'What are you looking for?'

'I'm sure I put it here,' he muttered.

'What?' Katie knew exactly what was in that pile.

He turned and walked out of the kitchen, leaving the papers spread across the work surface as if a blast of wind had ripped through them.

As Katie swept them back into a neat pile, Suky slouched down the stairs, eyes glued to her phone.

'I need to find that form,' Pete was saying. 'It has to go in the post today.'

'Where's my lunch money?' asked Suky, without looking up.

'Please?' added Katie. 'Where's my lunch money, please?'

'The form, Katie – did you put it somewhere?'

'I said please.'

'No, you didn't. And I haven't touched your form. Have you looked in the office? Suky, I gave you ten pounds yesterday. You can't have spent it all?'

'This is ridiculous, I had the damn thing earlier. I'm sure it was in the kitchen.'

The two of them finally slammed out of the front door in a rush of coats, bags and bad temper.

'Have a good day!' called Katie, knowing there'd be no reply.

There was a bump behind her, then another. She turned to see Anna coming down the stairs, dragging her schoolbag behind her so it fell heavily off every step. Katie pictured the bruised spines of the textbooks inside, the shattered strips of coloured lead within the expensive pencils.

'Are you and Daddy getting a divorce?' asked Anna cheerfully.

'Of course not.'

'Olivia's parents are getting a divorce,' said Anna. 'She's going to live with her mum, but her dad will buy her stuff to make her feel better. She's getting her own laptop. So, I don't mind if you get a divorce.'

As they got into the car, Katie felt she might cry again. What the hell was the matter with her? She was cross with Pete, but it was just a silly row: she never used to get so upset about things like that. It was a month since the funeral; she should be feeling better now, but there were still days when misery crept up unexpectedly and kicked her in the gut.

'So,' she said, reversing out of the drive. 'What lessons have you got today?'

Listening to Anna's chatter always cheered her up. Her younger daughter's nine-year-old world was full of so much more excitement, anticipation and intrigue, than Katie's adult one. The class was going on a trip to a museum the following week, and they'd been told they'd be able to try on Roman costumes.

'I'm going to wear a toga,' Anna was saying. 'It's a dress made from a sheet. Mrs Hall says men wore them too. I think that was before they invented jeans.'

Having dropped Anna at the school gates, Katie turned towards town. Traffic was backed up along the main road, the red brake lights of the car in front growing bleary then sharp again as the wipers cleared the windscreen. She drummed her fingers on the steering wheel, glancing at the clock. She had tried hard not to be late recently; she was always rushing to do one extra job before she left the house in the morning, giving herself ten minutes to make a journey she knew would take fifteen.

'You need to be more organised,' Pete had told her. 'You're trying to get too much done.'

'I'm a woman,' she'd replied, laughing at the time. 'It's in the job description.' She didn't feel like laughing now. She wouldn't always be running late if her lazy family bothered to put dirty clothes in the laundry basket and pick up damp towels from the bathroom floor. Her life's work would be complete when they learnt a cloth didn't just sit in a sodden lump in the sink but could also be used – miracle of miracles – to wipe down kitchen surfaces.

A car horn sounded behind her, making her jump. The lights were green, and she shoved the car into gear and moved forward, waving apologetically at the driver behind.

Every now and then, she imagined what it would be like to swap places with Monica. She pictured herself living in her best friend's neat, beautifully decorated terraced house, not having to worry about anyone else in the morning except herself. Monica would be arriving at work right now with plenty of time to spare, in clothes that had been ironed, having eaten a leisurely breakfast in a kitchen devoid of dirty plates, school bags, muddy trainers and piles of scattered paperwork. Katie loved her family to bits, and she knew there must be times when Mon was lonely. But sometimes the prospect of being without all this domestic chaos, was more than a little appealing.

3

When she walked into the office, Fraser swung round in his chair and looked pointedly up at the wall clock.

'Did your car break down, *again*?' he asked. 'Or did you have trouble finding a space in that big, empty car park outside?'

'Hello, Fraser. Nice to see you too.'

The morning trundled by as Katie typed up orders, updated spreadsheets, logged sick pay and dealt with email enquiries. Every time she thought back to their angry start to the day, her heart flipped. She hoped, half expected, that Pete would text to say sorry, but her phone didn't make a sound. Just before lunch, she sent him a message.

Sorry I was grumpy earlier. Bit tired. Love you xx

He didn't reply.

She'd been planning to go to the supermarket at lunchtime, but felt guilty about being late, so made a show of staying at her desk, flicking through invoices while she snatched bites of her sandwich. By 1.15pm, both Fraser and Duncan had gone out, so she closed the spreadsheet, checked her Facebook notifications and skimmed through some Daily Deals on eBay.

A copy of the local paper was lying on Fraser's desk and she pulled it towards her as she opened her crisps. Flicking through the pages, she stopped at a photograph, showing a man wearing a purple and white striped shirt.

It was him: that doctor. He was smiling into the camera, looking relaxed and leaning forward, with his arms folded, as if about to laugh at something the photographer had said. He really was gorgeous. Just looking at his photo, made something tingle in the pit of her stomach.

The caption underneath the picture read: *GP Joe Harvey launches a campaign with a heart.* Smiling out from the page, he reminded her of someone, though she couldn't work out who. He didn't have film star looks, but everything was finely proportioned: perfect cheekbones, good teeth, that warm smile. He was the sort of man you'd be proud to take to a school reunion.

'Joe Harvey. Dr Joe Harvey.' Saying the name out loud, she remembered him kneeling beside Mrs Burns, holding her hand and reassuring her he wasn't going to leave. The tenderness had been so natural.

'Katie, stop it!' She slapped the pages shut, hiding Dr Harvey amongst the local community's horticultural shows and playgroup fundraisers. Turning the paper over, she read a football report; on the inside page there was hockey and rugby. God, she hated sport. She flicked her way quickly back through gardening reports, late-night chemists, film reviews.

It was ages since she and Pete had been to the cinema; the last film they'd seen was the one about space, which had won loads of Oscars. But he'd fallen asleep halfway through and woken with a start as the credits rolled. 'What a waste of £10,' he'd moaned. 'And we've still got to pay the babysitter.'

As she turned the pages, she knew she would eventually find herself back with Joe Harvey. Sure enough, there he was on page nine: arms folded, eyes twinkling. She skimmed through the story beside the picture: he was going to be the main speaker at a talk about healthy living, to be held at the library.

'Heart disease is a major killer in the UK,' says Dr Harvey. 'But some simple lifestyle changes can dramatically reduce your risk of suffering a heart attack.'

She heard his voice in her head – deep and a little gravelly, no trace of an accent.

'We all know we need to cut out smoking, take more exercise, eat a healthy diet. But those things aren't always easy, which is why it's important to...'

She leapt in her seat as the phone rang. 'Triple A Hire, how can I help?'

As soon as she'd put down the phone, it rang again and, while she was filling in the paperwork for the resulting order, Fraser came back from lunch and reached across to drag the paper from under her elbow.

'Thank you so much!' he said, as Katie reluctantly moved her arm. 'Buy your own copy, cheapskate.'

When she shut down her computer, just before 3pm, Fraser had his earbuds in and was logging payments. He didn't look up when she put on her coat, and she didn't ask what he had planned for the weekend. She dreaded to think.

When she reached the school, Anna flung herself into the car, almost hysterical with excitement. 'Mr Scratchy has had babies!' she yelled in Katie's ear.

'Really? Who's Mr Scratchy?'

'The class hamster, Mummy! The one we got last week?'

'Oh, yes. Well, that's exciting.'

'He's had four babies, so Mrs Hall says that means we have to call him Mrs Scratchy.'

'That makes sense,' Katie said, signalling to move back into the traffic. 'Do you think Mr Scratchy knew he was pregnant?'

Anna shook her head and raised her eyes to the roof of the car. 'Mummy, don't be stupid. He's a *hamster.*'

Back home, their copy of the local paper was sticking through the letter box, thrust into it at some stage by the boy on the red BMX, who had eagerly delivered papers at dawn when he first started the job, but nowadays struggled to complete the round before most residents left for work. Slumping onto a chair, Katie flicked through the pages, her heart beating faster as the photo of Dr Harvey stared out at her again.

What was it about this man? She held the paper closer, wondering if she would notice some imperfection that had escaped her when he was feet away in the surgery: some grey in his hair or a blemish on his skin, perhaps a dirty mark on his collar. He might be the sort of bloke who wiped his nose on his sleeve, or bit his fingernails. He could have dandruff and sweaty palms, halitosis and excessive ear wax. Or he might be as near perfect as she remembered.

The front door slammed and Suky walked in, throwing her rucksack on the table. Standing in front of the cupboard she pulled down a packet of biscuits and ripped it open, stuffing one into her mouth as several others fell onto the worktop.

'Suky, please!' said Katie.

'Suky, please what?'

'Don't fill up on rubbish, have some fruit first. Or even a piece of toast.' God, why had she said that? She sounded like her own mother.

'Leave me alone, I've had a bad day,' snapped Suky, emptying more biscuits into her hand, throwing the packet onto the table and walking out.

Screams of protest came from the sitting room, as she changed the TV channel without consulting Anna. Katie sighed as she closed the cupboard door. She lifted Suky's rucksack off the table and dropped it onto the floor.

Joe Harvey beamed up at her again from the open pages of the paper. The talk about healthy living was taking place in the library on November 17th at 7pm, and Dr Harvey was encouraging people to go along:

'Come and find out how to live a long, healthy life!'

By the time Pete got home, Katie had opened a bottle of wine and nearly finished her first glass as she stood frying onions and mince. She saw him glance at the bottle on the worktop as he pecked her on the cheek and took his lunchbox out of his bag.

'Good day?' he asked, emptying the wrappers into the bin.

'Yes fine,' she replied. 'How about you?' He seemed to have forgotten they'd shouted at each other this morning. Or it just hadn't bothered him.

He sat on a kitchen chair and bent forward to unlace his shoes, his hair looking grey under the beam of the spotlights in the ceiling. 'Not great,' he said. 'We've lost the funding for that science trip, and three sets of parents came in to see me about Damien.'

'Oh dear,' she said absently.

'The Carters are threatening to pull Charlie out, unless something gets done.'

A piece of onion was sticking to the side of the frying pan, smoke twisting upwards, filling the kitchen with the pungent aroma of burning. She scraped it off with the wooden spoon and took another sip of wine.

'We need to address the underlying problems, not just cast blame,' Pete continued, sitting back in the chair as he kicked off his shoes. 'But he's an aggressive little bugger and it's not easy to persuade people he wants to change.'

'You've been putting so much effort into this,' said Katie, emptying a tin of tomatoes into the pan.

'He's a good lad at heart,' Pete was saying. 'He lashes out, but if we can work with him and give him some space...'

Katie had stopped listening. She stirred the sauce, watching it splatter across the wooden spoon. Dr Harvey's talk about healthy living was next Tuesday; she was supposed to go to book group at Monica's that evening, but hadn't read this month's choice. It was some historical romance by an academic who'd just got her own TV series; the author photo on the back cover showed a pretty blonde, barely out of college.

Katie raised the wine glass to her lips and the cool liquid slid down her throat.

Maybe she could skip book group, just this once?

4

There he was.

She'd been looking forward to tonight, but was still surprised when her heart lurched at the sight of Joe. He was standing at the front of the room talking to a woman with a flurry of untidy, grey hair. Katie was thrown at first: there was something about him that didn't seem right. Then she realised he wasn't wearing the purple and white striped shirt; he was in a pale blue one, tucked into jeans. For some reason she'd been expecting him to look exactly as he had in the paper.

After cutting out the article, last Friday, she'd slipped it into the side pocket of her bag – pulling it out frequently, to read again the words she already knew by heart. Now she realised the photograph was imprinted on her mind: from the angle of his head and the way his arms were crossed in front of his chest, to the smile playing at the edge of his mouth and the precise width of the stripes on that shirt.

But it was wonderful to see Joe Harvey again, in the flesh.

Katie stood in the doorway. A man in front was taking his time deciding where to sit, and the couple beside her were rolling their eyes at the delay, the wife unintentionally battering Katie's ankle with her umbrella.

She hadn't been to the library for years, but the smell was familiar: a combination of sweaty feet, body odour and musty books. She'd spent hours here when the girls were younger, listening to storytelling sessions and sitting on grubby beanbags in the reading corner. She had run her fingers along spines on the shelves, and hung her head in embarrassment at the desk, when returning books that had fallen into the bath or been scribbled over with crayon.

This evening, rows of chairs had been set out in the centre of the room, facing a table and projection screen at the far end. A poster was on the wall behind it, featuring lithe, smiling models, jumping into the air.

Katie waited for a man with a hacking cough to move forwards and choose a seat, before heading to the opposite side – never mind jumping into the air: some of this lot wouldn't be able to break into a trot if the projector caught fire. They were clearly in need of whatever advice Dr Harvey could give them when it came to healthy lifestyles.

She edged along a row of orange plastic chairs and sat down, watching Joe at the front of the room. He was taller than she'd remembered, more muscular. She couldn't drag her eyes from him, intrigued by every slight move of his head, comparing the breadth of his shoulders with those of other men standing nearby.

A young woman wearing a T-shirt bearing the words *Fit for Life!* clapped her hands. 'Thank you for coming tonight, ladies and gentlemen!' She paused, waiting for conversations to die down. 'If you'd like to find a seat, I'll introduce our speakers.'

Katie put her bag on the floor in front of her, then immediately had to pick it up again to allow someone to shuffle past. Why was she feeling so excited? It was a talk on healthy living, not a film premiere.

'We're delighted to have Julia Gibson with us tonight, from the British Heart Foundation. Beside her is Dr Joe Harvey, who works at our local surgery, Pelham Green, and is keen to encourage us to make small changes that will lead to great improvements in our health.'

He looked at the audience; Katie's heart did a little skip again as he seemed to stare straight at her. She felt her cheeks heating and dropped her eyes, fiddling with her bracelet.

Julia Gibson spoke first, pointing at the screen as it displayed statistics about low-density lipoproteins and high triglycerides. Katie lost sight of Joe behind dozens of heads. She moved to the left, then shifted to the right where she could just see the side of his face. The man next to her turned and glared.

Ms Gibson's grey hair was bouncing off her forehead and it reminded Katie of a Brillo pad: the thought made her giggle and the man beside her glared again. As she joined in the applause at the end, her handbag slipped onto the floor, spewing its contents underneath the chair in front.

The young woman in the *Fit for Life!* T-shirt stood up. 'Julia, thanks for that fascinating insight. Our next speaker, Dr Harvey, is the man at the cutting edge, who not only wants to help those suffering from heart disease, but prevent it happening to his patients. Joe, over to you!'

As Katie scrabbled around on the floor for her keys, tissues and biros, she peered through a gap in the seats and saw him stand up.

'Good evening!' he said. 'Thank you for inviting me here tonight…'

She sat back in her chair and zipped up the bag, short of breath.

'We all know the things we should be doing to stay healthy and protect our hearts. But isn't always easy to…'

His voice was just as she'd remembered it. Low and

measured, full of the self-assurance of a man who knew his subject.

'I'm delighted when my patients tell me they gave up smoking twenty years ago, and now eat five portions of fruit and vegetables a day. But although these things matter, a healthy lifestyle is about more…'

How old was he? Now she had a chance to really study him, she guessed late thirties. She imagined him living in one of the apartments in the new canal-side development at the edge of town: a stylish bachelor pad. He looked like the sort of man who did the washing up and remembered which night the bins had to be put out. His bookshelves would feature novels by Julian Barnes, Zadie Smith and Hanif Kureishi; his taste in music would be wide-ranging but he might – like her – have a secret soft spot for nineties hits. He probably made Spotify playlists in his spare time and was bound to be on social media: he might not be on Facebook, but she could try searching for him on Instagram. If he drove a car, she'd put money on it being a VW Golf, although it wouldn't be surprising if he cycled to work – this was a man with a social conscience, who cared about the world and the space he occupied in it.

She jumped as the people on either side of her began to clap again.

'Are there any questions for our experts?'

Katie felt the man beside her raise his hand. She shrank down in her seat as he spoke. His question was about the reliability of diagnostic tests, then someone else brought up the impact of stress on coronary heart disease. It was another twenty-five minutes before the event drew to a close, by which time Katie had had more than enough of hearing how to improve her physical and mental well-being. As the people around her got to their feet, she joined the slow progression towards the door.

Why not go and talk to him? The thought sent her heart

leaping into her throat again. But why not? Just a quick hello; she could say how enjoyable the talk had been. No, not enjoyable, that was frivolous. Interesting; the evening had been interesting, and the advice useful.

She turned and marched to the front of the room before she had time to change her mind. He was leaning across the table, scooping leaflets into a neat pile.

'Hello!' Her voice sounded too loud.

He turned and smiled, his eyes sweeping across her face, momentarily unsure if he ought to recognise her.

'We met at the surgery, the other day – when that old lady collapsed?'

He smiled and put out his hand. 'Of course, good to see you.'

As his warm fingers pressed against her palm, Katie knew her cheeks were colouring again. Was he being polite, or did he really remember her?

'That was great!' she tried to slow down, steady her voice. 'The talk I mean, so interesting. Plenty of food for thought. If you see what I mean – excuse the pun!'

Food for thought? Katie, stop waffling.

'So, er, I just thought I'd come and say thank you!' She wanted to click her fingers and disappear, have the worn, brown carpet open around her feet and swallow her up. How embarrassing.

But he was still smiling.

'I'm glad you found it useful,' he was saying. 'It's good to see so many people here tonight.' He smiled and put up his hand to sweep his fringe away from his face, like he'd done in the surgery.

She smiled back, left breathless by the deep blue of his eyes and deafened by the sound of the blood racing around her body. She'd just opened her mouth to speak, when something bumped against her.

'Excuse me, dear, I need to ask this young chap something.'

An elderly man, no taller than Katie's shoulder, elbowed his way forward and prodded Joe's chest with his finger. 'Bacon!' he said. 'What I want to know is, can I still eat bacon? It may be making my arteries fuzzy, but the butcher says it's full of protein. I've been eating bacon for seventy-five years and I don't want to give it up now.'

Joe was looking down at the man, nodding and giving the question serious consideration. 'Well,' he began. 'Bacon is…'

'All this healthy eating malarkey gets on my nerves!' he interrupted. 'I'm fit as a fiddle, and I still walk into town every week to go shopping. My arteries don't feel fuzzy.'

Joe put out his hand and rested it on the man's arm. 'Well, in that case I think you should continue to eat bacon,' he said. 'It's obviously not doing you any harm, and the butcher's right, it's high in protein. If you eat it in moderation, I'm not going to tell you to give up something you enjoy.'

The old man gave a satisfied nod and stepped backwards, onto Katie's toe. 'Good,' he said. 'That's all right then. Thank you for your time.'

As he moved away, Katie turned back to Joe. He was staring at her, his smile broad now, those tiny laughter lines radiating out from the edges of his eyes. He raised an eyebrow and she felt her own face stretching into a smile. For a moment she was wrapped in the warmth of his look, as if there was nobody else in the room.

'Joe, that was great!' The girl in the *Fit for Life!* T-shirt appeared and put her arm through his. 'Come and meet Mike from *The Gazette*, he's going to do a story.'

'Nice to see you again,' Joe said to Katie, and she stood staring after him as he was dragged away from her.

5

She couldn't get him out of her head during the drive home: his face, his smile, the gentle rise and fall of his voice, the way he swiped at his fringe without even knowing he was doing it. Katie was pretty sure he hadn't recognised her from the surgery last week, but that wasn't surprising – he must see dozens of people every day. She couldn't help feeling disappointed: they'd been right next to each other, kneeling on the surgery floor for what felt like hours, although it had only been a couple of minutes. How can he not have remembered her? She told herself not to be over-sensitive: he'd been dealing with an emergency – he was a professional and his mind had been on Mrs Burns.

None of that mattered now though, because the way he'd looked at her tonight had definitely meant something. As the bacon man shuffled away, Joe's eyes had met hers and twinkled, almost conspiratorially. There had been something so intense about that look. Her head was light, buzzing, as if she'd been drinking. As she sat waiting at a red light, she realised her heart was thudding almost as loudly as the song playing on the radio.

When she pulled into the drive, the house looked like a fairy castle, with lights glowing in every window. She threw down her bag in the hall and kicked off her shoes before wandering through the sitting room and kitchen, clicking light switches and turning off an unwatched television. Upstairs Anna's door was open, a pair of feet sticking over the edge of the bed. Her daughter was lying on her stomach, playing a game on Pete's phone, tinny squeaks coming from its speakers.

'Does Dad know you've got that?' asked Katie.

'He's not using it,' said Anna, her eyes fixed on the screen.

'Yes, but does he know you've got it?'

'Sort of.'

Katie was about to stride across the room and pull the phone from her daughter's hands, but decided she couldn't be bothered. If Pete had left his phone lying around, it was his own fault.

'Come on, it's bedtime,' she said. 'Where is Dad anyway?'

She found him downstairs in the cupboard-sized room they optimistically called the office, tapping away on the computer keyboard, his shoulders hunched, his eyes so close to the screen that its luminous display was reflected in his reading glasses.

'You're back early,' he said, not looking up. 'Did they bore for England tonight?'

'Who?' For a second, she wondered how he knew about the talk on healthy living.

'Book group!'

She froze in the doorway; she'd forgotten she was even meant to be there, let alone that she'd mentioned it to Pete.

'Oh, it was fine,' she said, backing out of the room. 'It's freezing out there,' she continued, raising her voice as she walked across the kitchen. 'It really feels like winter now.' She knew she didn't sound like herself; her voice was too high, too cheerful. When she'd left the house earlier this evening, she had gone to the library instead of to Monica's – taken a right turn at the bottom of the road instead of going left. She hadn't made any plans, it just happened. Because of that, it hadn't felt wrong. Until now.

'I wouldn't be surprised if we get a frost tonight,' she continued. 'What are you up to?'

It wasn't lying if she didn't say where she'd been.

'I'm putting together some thoughts on Damien,' said Pete. 'We're not going to make progress unless we teach him alongside the rest of the class. Sara wants me to come up with something to reassure the governors we're taking this seriously.'

Katie's pulse was racing, her mouth dry; she could hear his fingers tapping at the keyboard as she filled the kettle.

'I had two more parents come in to see me this morning, and they're obviously all talking about it amongst themselves.'

Sara, Damien. Good, the last thing on his mind was her book group.

She was walking back towards the sitting room when he called after her. 'What were you reading this month?'

She stood in the hallway, her hand stretched out towards the banisters, her fingers running along the painted grain of the wood. 'It was the novel by that historian, you know – the one who's got her own series about the Tudors?'

'Any good?'

'Yes, not bad.'

It was fine, none of this was a lie.

'What did the others think?'

'Some of them liked it. It was well written. But you know us, any excuse for a glass of wine.'

'Mmmm.' He was clearly no longer listening.

She waited for a second in the hallway, holding her breath, before going into the sitting room and throwing herself onto the sofa.

Little lies, that was all. Silly little lies that didn't matter.

She pointed the remote at the television, flicking idly

through channels mostly showing police dramas or property programmes.

Joe must be back home by now, turning a key in the lock and walking into one of those sophisticated apartments. He probably wouldn't collapse in front of the television like her, though: he seemed like a hard worker, driven. He was more likely to spend the rest of his evening ploughing through research papers or reading the latest medical journals.

A text pinged into her phone, and Monica's name appeared on the screen. Katie tapped to open it:

Where were you tonight, lightweight? We missed you. Everything OK? xx

She typed a reply, cursing under her breath as predictive text changed half the words into something unintelligible. Eventually, she checked it through and pressed send:

Wasn't feeling great. Sorry, forgot to let you know. Free for a drink soon? Xx

More little lies. But no one would know. Monica would never find out she'd been at the library, when she was meant to be drinking wine and discussing books.

Pete wandered in and sat on the sofa beside her, picking up the remote and changing the channel without asking.

'What?' he said, when Katie turned to glare at him. 'I want to see the news headlines.'

She crossed her arms and sighed loudly. Pete ignored her.

What would Joe be doing, right at this moment? She imagined herself sitting opposite him at the table in his smart, tidy apartment, his laptop open, a glass of wine at his elbow. She would look on as his brow creased with concentration, watching him scribble notes about whatever he was reading. Thinking about him putting down his pen and looking up at her, she caught her breath.

With a shock she realised why she was feeling so odd. This combination of excitement and anticipation, a long-forgotten fluttering in the depths of her stomach: it was desire. Every fibre in her body was longing for a man, craving him, gasping as she imagined him touching her. It was as if something deep inside her was on fire. She hadn't felt like this in a very long time.

6

Alan and Brenda arrived dead on midday. They were always on time, wherever they went, whatever they did. Opening the front door, Katie stretched her face into a wide smile, which felt insincere to her but never seemed to offend them.

'Lovely to see you! Come in, let me take your coats,' she said, holding out her hand for the matching beige Marks & Spencer macs. 'Is it raining?'

'No dear, not yet. But it will.' Her mother-in-law's voice was ripe with gloom. 'It hasn't rained for a few days now, but you can't be too careful.'

'Not quite true,' said her husband. 'We had a shower on Friday – it didn't last long, but it was precipitation.' Having given Katie his raincoat, he handed over an umbrella. 'Best to be prepared, that's what I say.' He leant forward and gave her a wet kiss, and she waited until he'd walked down the hallway before wiping her cheek with her sleeve.

She called up the stairs to the girls, then went through to the kitchen. Pete was getting glasses out of the cupboard, the clinking signalling that neither of them could contemplate going much further without a gin and tonic to steady their nerves.

Against Katie's better judgement, Sunday lunch with the in-laws had become a fixture. In the early years she'd fought against it, knowing that, if they got into a routine, they'd find it hard to disentangle themselves.

'If they start to expect it,' she'd said to Pete. 'They'll be here every week.'

She'd been right. She couldn't remember precisely when, but at some stage the infrequent invitations were dispensed with and replaced with a regular Sunday lunch to which Alan and Brenda were never actually invited, they just turned up.

Gin always eased the pain. Knocking back the first one before the ice had a chance to melt, she would furtively refill her glass while back in the kitchen on the pretext of checking the progress of whichever part of an animal she was roasting. As the drink slid through her body, she would feel the tautness across her shoulders soften, the tension in her head fall away. Buoyed up, she would return to the sitting room, feeling mellow towards her in-laws and able to face what lay ahead.

Today, Alan and Brenda had clearly been bickering before they arrived. Standing in the middle of the room, hands in pockets, Alan held forth about the weather, the latest Conservative MP to cheat on his wife, and the inflated garage bill he'd recently paid.

Meanwhile Brenda stared through the window into the garden, tight-lipped, sighing, waiting for someone to ask what was wrong. When nobody did, she could eventually bear it no longer.

'The thing your father won't acknowledge,' she said, interrupting Alan's monologue about the wheel balance on his Ford Mondeo. 'Is that we are neither of us as young as we used to be, and we need to think about how long we can manage those stairs.'

Katie sighed: it was the house conversation. Again. 'No more viewings then?' she asked.

'Not a peep. Not even a call from that wretched agent,' Brenda sounded petulant. 'It's appalling. Anyone can see what a bargain the house is and how much work we've done. That kitchen was top of the range when we put it in.'

This topic came up regularly. When it did, Katie and Pete would sometimes catch each other's eye before one of them pointed out that the top-of-the-range kitchen had been installed in 1990, more than thirty years ago. Today, neither of them bothered.

'I'm sure it will be perfect for someone,' Katie said. 'It's just a case of waiting for the right person to come along.'

Brenda sighed theatrically as she collapsed onto the sofa. 'You're as bad as Alan,' she said. 'I don't want to wait around for something to happen. We need to speed things up, get that agent doing his job properly. My legs aren't what they were, and those stairs aren't getting any less steep.'

Alan had lowered himself into the armchair in the corner. 'It's a bad time of year to sell property,' he said. 'The market's flat as a pancake. If you ask me, it's the prospect of those lefties getting in at the next election. People are terrified by what they'll end up doing to the economy, so no one is making long-term plans.'

'All we need to do is drop the price,' said Brenda, jabbing the sofa with her finger. 'Then we'd sell it in hours. It worked for the Gillespies.'

'But we're not in a hurry, so why should we drop the price?' countered Alan.

'We are in a hurry! *I'm* in a hurry!'

Katie couldn't stand it any longer. 'Just going to check on the veggies,' she said.

Neither of the girls had emerged from their bedrooms, so she yelled up the stairs again before going into the kitchen to top up her gin. The bronzed chicken sizzled energetically when she opened the oven door, pointing out that it was doing quite well on its own, thank you, and didn't need to be monitored. She loved the smells and sounds of Sunday lunch in progress: the rich meaty aroma rushing out of the oven, the crackling of hot oil roasting the potatoes to perfection, the gurgling of water bubbling up around chopped carrots and broccoli, the gentle splatting of gravy bubbling in a pan. It was a work of art in the making, a coming together of so many different tastes and textures.

It was just a pity they had to share it with Alan and Brenda.

At the dining table, Suky sulked, having been told to put down her mobile, and Anna went through the list of expensive items she wanted for Christmas.

'It's only November,' said Suky.

'So what?' retorted Anna. 'I'm just being helpful by telling everyone what I want now, so they've got time to save up for it. There's a flashing cube speaker that would go with an iPad Mini, when I get one of those.'

'How are you feeling, dear?' asked Brenda, turning to Katie as they neared the end of the main course. 'In yourself?'

Katie's chest tightened. 'Fine,' she nodded. 'I'm fine, thanks.'

'Because it's early days still, isn't it?' said Brenda.

'Yes, but I really am okay.'

'You're bound to be up and down,' Brenda ploughed on. 'That's the thing about grief, it never goes away, it just mellows over time.'

Katie wanted to scream. 'More wine, Alan?' she asked, filling his glass before waiting for an answer.

'I can still hardly believe it,' said Brenda, shaking her head. 'It seems like only yesterday your poor mother was sitting here around this table with us...'

Katie's throat was tight and her eyes were prickling. She

often felt low nowadays, on the verge of tears: reminded of her mother by fleeting glimpses of a stranger in the supermarket who had the same hairstyle, or hearing her favourite piece of music used as the soundtrack on a TV programme. She knew this was to be expected, but she didn't need Brenda to bring it all up again. Her mother-in-law meant well, but had the sensitivity of a bull elephant.

The incident in the surgery hadn't helped either; watching Mrs Burns tumble to the ground beside her. Katie didn't want to be reminded of her own mother's fall, because, as well as making her depressed, it made her angry.

As if she could read her mind, Brenda ploughed on. 'Have you thought any more about getting the police involved?'

'Mum, it's not something the police would deal with,' said Pete.

'Well, you know what I mean. Getting someone to investigate what happened?' Brenda was peering down at her roast potatoes and vigorously sawing at them as if they were personally responsible for causing the climate crisis. 'They shouldn't be allowed to get away with it.'

'Mum!' Pete was glaring at her. 'Give it a rest.'

'She was in such poor health,' said Brenda, shaking her head. 'Those people at the hospice had a duty of care towards her.'

'How's Camilla?' Katie asked, desperate to change the subject.

'Oh, as busy as ever. She's done amazing things with that downstairs loo,' Brenda was off again, easily distracted. 'You know it was blue and silver before? Well now the walls are peach, with dark red floor tiles. It's so stylish. You know what she's like, everything she does, looks like it has come out of a magazine.'

Katie nodded and smiled. *Bully for clever old Camilla.* 'She is wonderful,' she said, knocking back the rest of her wine before starting to stack the plates.

She was sure Alan and Brenda would have loved Camilla even if she hadn't had wealthy parents and a double-barrelled surname – she was a Preston-Jones when Phil met her. But her genetics, parentage and natural flair for interior design put her at the top of the daughter-in-law ladder. Which wasn't much of an achievement, since there were only two of them. Katie and her sister-in-law suffered each other's company during infrequent family get-togethers at Easter or Christmas, or to celebrate a big birthday, but had nothing in common – aside from having married a pair of brothers – and neither could see the point in pretending otherwise.

Brenda was oblivious to this and spent a lot of time talking about Camilla, who apparently worked very hard – although she didn't actually go out to work. Her children were immaculately turned out and more polite than Katie's girls – as was pointed out regularly. Phil and Camilla's home – a five-bedroom new-build, with white alabaster columns on either side of the front door – was the ultimate in sophistication and Camilla drove an expensive four-wheel drive and wore well-cut clothes that looked great on her. Katie suspected that she stayed a size ten by starving herself, or by sticking her finger down her throat and throwing up in the beautifully decorated downstairs loo.

Katie sometimes wondered if Alan and Brenda talked about her and Pete when they visited Phil and Camilla, but was sure they didn't. Although they wouldn't get much of a chance because the formerly double-barrelled daughter-in-law hardly ever invited them over, despite living just five miles away.

'Have you seen much of Phil?' Brenda asked.

Pete shook his head. 'Our paths don't cross. Haven't seen him in ages.'

'He's a busy man,' said Brenda.

'Very busy,' agreed Alan.

'All those important clients need careful handling. He works long hours.'

'Pete's been working long hours recently, haven't you, love?' said Katie, picking up the empty vegetable dishes. 'He's on the computer most evenings, marking or dealing with admin. Teachers put in so much extra time and effort, but get no recognition.'

Pete glanced up at her, half smiling, appreciating the support. 'You just do what you have to do,' he said.

Katie went into the kitchen, closed the door and mimed a scream behind it. She admired Pete's restraint. As she stood at the sink, running hot water over the encrusted oven trays, she looked out into the back garden, the lawn dotted with curled brown leaves that had spilled from the apple tree. Did Joe Harvey have to put up with in-laws every Sunday? If so, it would mean he was married. This possibility hadn't occurred to her, but of course he might have someone in his life. Gloom hit her, like a stone crashing against the pit of her stomach.

Why couldn't she get this man out of her mind? It was crazy. She knew nothing about him – apart from what he did for a living and the fact that the mere thought of him increased her heart rate – but he was in her head constantly. She kept hearing the deep resonance of his voice as he spoke about sensible eating and weight loss, remembering how relaxed he'd looked as he chatted, how his skin crinkled when he smiled, the way his gaze had bored into her as he raised that eyebrow.

Over the last few days, she had thought about Joe when she was typing something on the computer at work, running the hoover across the carpets or loading washing into the machine. She had thought about him when she was sitting beside Pete on the sofa in the evenings, watching a documentary about the traffic police or people trying to declutter houses. And while she thought about him, she imagined the two of them together: conversations they might have, restaurants they might eat in. It was always just the two of them: Katie and Joe, Joe and Katie.

Standing in front of the kitchen sink now, she closed her eyes and imagined Joe's face moving towards hers, his mouth gently brushing against her forehead, then her cheek – lingering millimetres away from her eagerly-parted lips. His hand snaked around her waist, moving across her belly and down towards her thighs. The sensation was so intense, so real, that she breathed in sharply, anticipating the feel of his fingers running across the zip of her jeans.

The door crashed open as Pete came through, carrying empty wine glasses. 'Kettle on?' he asked, going over to lift it up without waiting for an answer. 'I think we're all ready for a cup of tea.'

7

'Yours,' Katie said, throwing an invoice across the desk to Fraser. 'Bin,' she announced to no one in particular, tossing a promotional brochure onto the floor beside her desk. 'You must be kidding,' she muttered, skimming over a job application from a man with a forklift truck licence. 'You don't want to work here – save yourself, before it's too late.'

Opening the post didn't take long; most communication for Triple A Hire came via email, so the morning's Royal Mail delivery rarely yielded anything of interest. But it was a suitably mindless way for Katie to start the day and get her brain into gear.

Fraser was as taciturn as ever this morning. When he got in, he'd reluctantly asked how she was, but obviously wasn't interested in the answer. Now he was putting together the VAT return, his work peppered with sighs and the occasional exclamation of disbelief as he shuffled invoices and receipts around on his desk. His mobile phone crowed like a cockerel when it received a text, which was often.

Her own phone sat on the desk in front of her, as

obstinately quiet as Fraser's was ostentatiously noisy. Every now and then she picked it up to check she hadn't left it on silent. But the truth was that hardly anybody – other than Monica and the girls – sent her texts; it was probably just as well because she'd never really got the hang of this new phone, and thanks to predictive texting she often only realised after the event that she'd sent a message that made no sense. A few weeks ago, a neighbour had invited her to a charity coffee morning, and it was only when she was on the point of going along, looking at her texts to check the time, that Katie saw she'd replied:

Would loathe that, thanks for arseing me.

She sighed now, as rain whipped against the window. Beads of water clung to the glass before blending together and running down in jagged lines, pooling on the wooden sill around curls of flaking paint. She stared down to where the lorries and vans were parked along the fence, watching the drivers going in and out of the Portakabin. One was making a furtive phone call and someone else was stubbing out a cigarette by the recycling bins.

Idly aware of the clock ticking above her head, she would often waste minutes at a time watching the comings and goings in the yard, wondering whose sons, husbands and lovers these men were, what lives they returned to when they shrugged off their high-vis jackets and drove out of the gates at the end of each day.

Another wave of rain lashed against the window. She sat back in her chair, the frame squeaking on its wheels in protest. It was still only eleven o'clock, but she reached into her bag and pulled the sandwich from her lunchbox.

The phone rang. 'Katie, have you got the invoice for Deakins?'

Her mouth full of ham, cheese and granary bread, she

hurried to swallow. 'Got it here, Duncan. Do you want a printout?'

'No, email it to me, would you? They're querying something on the delivery.'

She pulled her keyboard towards her and tapped in a reference. The cursor flickered down the screen, tracking through documents until the relevant invoice opened in front of her. She pressed send and heard the whoosh as it disappeared into the ether, instantly materialising on another computer screen ten feet away. One of these days Duncan might walk out of his office and speak to her in person when he wanted something. She hoped he'd give some warning – it would be a shock to see him make use of his legs.

By 12.45pm she couldn't bear it any longer. 'I'm going to bank these cheques,' she said to Fraser, grabbing the bulky business paying-in book and pushing it into her bag. 'Want anything while I'm out?'

Fraser pushed his chair away from the desk and sighed heavily. 'A new car?' He rocked back, stretching his arms above his head. 'Or possibly a holiday? I could do with a week in the sun somewhere…'

She smiled tightly as she pulled on her coat: he was such a moron. A cockerel crowed, and he pulled his phone towards him, chuckling at the message as she walked out of the door. Katie guessed he was already planning his weekend nightlife. When they started working together, she'd been too polite to show indifference to Fraser's social plans, with the result that, every Monday morning, he talked her through what he'd done at the weekend – in graphic detail. After one particularly outrageous night, when he'd got so drunk that he stripped off in Bristol city centre and got arrested for public indecency, she hadn't been able to stop herself saying: 'That's awful, how could you behave like that?'

Fraser had flushed to the roots of his bleached hair and gone on the defensive. He accused her of being uptight and middle-aged, she snapped back that he was wasting valuable police time and resources, and that was the end of their Monday morning catch-ups – much to Katie's relief.

There was no queue in the bank and in less than five minutes she was back out on the pavement again. She pulled up the hood of her coat and wandered along the high street, stopping to look at the display in a charity shop window, then scanning the photos outside the estate agent's – intrigued by the million-pound properties she'd never be able to afford. One private house was so vast, it looked like an institution. It made her think of the impressive front entrance at the hospice, the flight of stairs curling upwards from the main reception area.

If only Brenda hadn't kept banging on about all that yesterday; Katie had been trying to stop herself thinking about her mother's fall, and recently she'd managed it quite well. But the conversation around the lunch table had brought everything back far too sharply. Pete kept telling her there was no point in taking things further: her mother was dead, nothing could change that. But maybe her mother-in-law was right – at the very least, Katie ought to try to find out more.

She dragged her eyes away from the mansion in the estate agent's window. Next door was the bakery, and she went in and bought a chocolate muffin she wasn't hungry enough to need. Stepping out again, she stopped abruptly; on the opposite side of the road was a large grey sign: *Pelham Green Medical Practice*. A young mother was walking towards the entrance to the surgery, pushing a pram. As she got to the door, someone came out and turned to hold it open.

Oh God, it was him.

Despite the fact that he'd been on her mind almost constantly, it was a shock to see the real Joe again. He was holding a black bag – a cross between an old-fashioned satchel and a leather briefcase. Katie watched as the pram got stuck in the doorway, and heard the mother thank him as he helped move the wheel. After she disappeared inside the surgery, he carried on holding the door. For a second, she wondered why, then another woman came outside. Joe Harvey popped open an umbrella and held it over her. Wearing high heels that made her taller than him, she was slim and pretty and was carrying a similar bag; as they walked together around the side of the building towards the car park, her blonde hair flowed across her back like silk.

Katie was too far away to catch what they were saying, but could hear them laughing. She turned and walked back down the road. Blood was rushing through her ears, as loudly as if a plane was taking off above her head. That woman had seemed very confident, but looked so young – maybe she was a trainee or doing work experience?

A long time ago, Katie had possessed that sort of confidence. When she was younger, she didn't think twice about walking into a room full of strangers and finding someone to talk to. She'd met Pete in a supermarket – he was struggling to choose between two types of washing powder and she stood beside him, suggested Ariel would keep his boxers whiter than white, and wasn't surprised when he offered to buy her a beer.

When had that self-assurance withered away? Maybe it was an age thing. Recently she'd felt acutely aware that life was passing her by. Even before her mother died, mortality had started to unnerve her; not just death itself, but the years spent waiting for it to happen. The gradual decline into weakness and exhaustion, with senility lurking around the corner and incontinence a mere dribble away. Creaking joints, rheumy eyes, rotting teeth, knotted intestines that made you fart when you walked. Even if you took dying out of the equation, ageing was grim.

Looking in the mirror the other morning, she'd been horrified to spot a single grey hair bouncing at the front of her parting. She had pulled it out, wincing at the sting, then noticed some small brown blemishes above her eyebrow. They looked like... shit, surely they couldn't be liver spots? She'd spent the rest of the day examining herself in every mirror she passed, looking for more signs that her body was giving out on her.

As Katie walked away, she glanced back over her shoulder, but Joe and his companion had disappeared around the corner of the surgery. She knew she was over-reacting, but almost felt like she hated that woman, with her tinkling laugh and glossy hair. Partly because she couldn't imagine any man looking at her nowadays and feeling a similar sense of admiration; but mostly because that pretty, self-assured young woman was walking away beside Joe Harvey.

She marched up the high street, tossing the untouched muffin into a bin. What a waste of £2.

Back at the office, Duncan had emerged from his lair and was sitting in her chair with his feet on her desk. He had picked up a pen and was tapping it against her keyboard as he talked to Fraser.

'Excuse me,' she said brightly. 'Can I just get in here?'

He took his time to swing his legs down to the floor and hoist himself out of the chair. 'That's why you need to upgrade,' he was saying. 'It's quicker and faster and means you can run the extra programmes.'

He sauntered over to stand behind Fraser's chair and Katie swept her hand across her desk, wiping off dirt left by his shoes. Neither of them noticed. Duncan had his hands in his pockets and, as usual, was running his fingers through the coins in them as he stood looking over Fraser's shoulder. The clink, clink, clink made Katie want to scream.

'Press that option there, the one with the blue icon,' said Duncan, taking his right hand out of his pocket and pointing at Fraser's screen. 'See? That's where you need to be, that's the baby.'

Katie slammed her bag down on the floor beside her desk and both men turned to her in surprise.

'You all right, love?' asked Duncan. 'Seem a bit on edge today.'

Ignoring them, she pulled her keyboard towards her and brought up the Internet. *Dr Harvey, Pelham Green Surgery* she typed into the search box. Thousands of results instantly appeared on her screen, the first of which was the surgery's website. Under the *About Us* section were tiny photos of all the GPs who worked at Pelham Green; the pretty young woman wasn't amongst them. Katie squinted to get a better look at Joe's photo, but it wasn't very good – a posed head and shoulders shot, where his smile looked forced – nothing like the natural smile he'd given her at the library. She changed the search to *Dr Joe Harvey* and a new list of results flashed up. Now there was a Dr Joe Harvey who specialised in international criminal law in Canada, and another who ran a market research team in Hackney.

She kept picturing him walking away towards the car park. He'd been wearing a dark blue jacket over jeans, casual but with a professional edge. Pete had a similar jacket, but it didn't do much for him.

'Hey, dolly daydream!'

Katie jumped.

'If you can spare the time I'd like to hear when that access tower is coming in from Marchants,' shouted Duncan, now back in his office. 'It's booked to go out again on Monday, so chop-chop.'

Fraser sniggered.

Katie looked back down at the screen. She logged on to Facebook and typed Joe's name into the search bar. Dozens of Joe Harveys were immediately listed in front of her. This was hopeless, how was she ever going to track him down? *Come on, I know you're here somewhere.* She tapped her fingers against the keyboard as she scrolled down. There would be something; she just needed to be patient.

8

'So, breathe in… then exhale. Gently counting down – five, four, three…'

In the silent room, a dozen women lay on their backs; eyes closed, minds emptied, bodies relaxed, breathing out slowly. Into the tranquillity, Katie's stomach rumbled like a lawnmower being kick-started after a winter of inactivity.

'And once again… breathe in!' At the front of the class, the Pilates teacher, Sybil, was pretending not to notice, but Katie sensed she was raising her voice. She clenched her stomach muscles in a vain attempt to stop the noise.

'And back out again – five, four, three…'

The rumble was getting louder; everyone else must be able to hear this, it was like there was a helicopter overhead. Katie imagined a SWAT team dressed in black hanging out of an open door, arc lights streaking backwards and forwards across the roof of the village hall. She put her hand on her belly, pressing down as hard as she could to stop the rumble.

'Remember,' Sybil called. 'Your spine should be in neutral!'

Katie had been coming to Pilates for six months and hated it just as much now, as she had at the start. She still didn't understand the concept of neutrality and how it related to her posture. However, she was pretty sure her spine wasn't where it was supposed to be. Nor were her legs.

She heard the soft pad of Sybil's feet and, even with her eyes closed, knew they were coming her way. A hand grabbed her bent knees and moved them slightly to one side. 'Keep in neutral, Katie, maintain that gap between your lower back and the floor. Don't forget to engage, everyone! Engage!'

As Sybil moved away again, Katie turned her head to the side and opened one eye. Next to her, Monica was in a perfect floor position: engaged, neutralised and whatever else she needed to be. In her tight leotard, her stomach was hollowed out; what little midriff flab there was, had sunk out of sight towards the floor.

Katie looked back down at her own stomach, covered in one of Pete's old T-shirts: even when she lay flat on her back, there was still a lumpy layer that refused to disappear. Thank God for motherhood: it was much easier to blame her figure on two long-ago pregnancies, than on a current excessive intake of wine and crisps.

After the class, they filed out into the chilly November evening.

'How's life in the exciting world of industrial tool hire?' asked Monica, doing up her coat.

'Thrilling, as ever,' said Katie. 'All good with you?'

'Not bad. Busy. I wish Sybil wouldn't make us do those leg lifts at the end, I don't think my body was designed to work that way.'

'Mon, can I run something past you?' Katie stopped beside her car, twisting the keys around her finger.

Monica tipped her head to one side. 'Go on.'

'That business with the hospice. I've tried really hard to forget about it – I know you and Pete said there was no point pursuing it. But I can't get it out of my mind...' She paused. It was harder than she'd expected, to put these muddled, guilty thoughts into words. 'Brenda mentioned it again at the weekend...'

'Oh God, bloody Brenda!'

'I know, but she might be right. Maybe I ought to go back to them and put in an official complaint? It probably won't change anything, but it might make them tighten up their procedures...'

Monica put her hand on Katie's arm. 'It's not that we thought there was no point in you taking this further, we were just worried it would upset you even more.'

'I know. And you're probably right. But trying to forget about it isn't working either.'

'If you want to clear the air, fine. But you need to be realistic about what it might achieve,' Monica said. 'They slammed down the shutters after your mum died, so it's not going to be any different now. I doubt they'll ever admit liability.'

'That's what Pete says. But they had a duty of care, Mon, and they let Mum down. The more I think about it, the more I feel I need to pursue it – for her sake.'

Monica pulled her into a hug. 'Then in that case, go and see them. But don't expect too much. Want me to come with you?'

Katie was touched. 'No, but thanks for offering. I'll be fine, honestly.'

'Okay, well, let me know how it goes.'

Driving home, Katie's stomach muscles were already beginning to throb after Sybil's workout, but she felt strangely energised. The conversation with Monica had left her feeling more positive: she would ring the hospice and ask for an appointment to see the director. Mon was right: the woman wasn't going to say anything, other than that they'd done nothing wrong. But Katie owed it to her mother; this was unfinished business.

She was driving through town instead of using the ring road. It was a slightly longer route, and she wasn't sure why she'd gone that way, until she passed the looming outline of Pelham Green Surgery on the left, the letters on the grey sign barely visible under the glow of a nearby streetlight.

Her online trawling had brought up a few more facts about Joe Harvey. His profile on the surgery website said he'd trained in Manchester, and she'd found more details about his qualifications and his first job, at a surgery in Stockport. She hadn't been able to find a Facebook profile but eventually found him on Twitter. She'd been pleased with herself: Suky had set her up with a Twitter account, but she hardly ever used it, so was impressed when she managed to track down @HarveyJoedoc. He was clearly careful with his social media: there were a few recent posts about working conditions within the NHS and some retweeted memes about government policy, but nothing vaguely personal. In that sort of job, you probably had to watch what you shared.

But in a world where so much information was in the public domain, it was surprising and frustrating not to be able to find out anything else about him. What she did now know was that there were plenty of medical practitioners called Joe Harvey across the world, and she'd wasted time looking up the backgrounds of an orthopaedic surgeon in Deerfield Beach, Florida and a paediatric specialist in Toronto. She even found a Dr Joe in Cape Town, who dealt with psychiatric disorders and another one in Berlin who was an expert on the impact of antibiotics on the central nervous system.

Katie slowed down and craned her neck to look at the building. There were no lights on at this time of night. Joe would be at home, possibly cooking himself something to eat in that stylish kitchen in the canal-side apartment. Did he work out? He was well built, possibly a rugby player, but he might spend winter evenings at the gym. She pictured him on a cross-trainer, his arms and legs pumping against each other, then straining to push the bar away from his chest on a weights machine. She saw sweat prickling on his shoulders, up his neck; imagined tiny muscles pulsating down the front of his chest.

The thought made her tingle.

9

Katie felt sick with nerves. She'd made the call yesterday, on the spur of the moment, giving herself no time to think about what she was doing.

'You're lucky to get an appointment so quickly,' the receptionist had told her. 'It's only because we've had a cancellation.'

Why had she done it? Pete was always telling her she was too bloody impulsive. As she walked along the canal towpath, she took deep breaths in and out, hoping it would settle her nerves. She really did feel sick, there was bile rising in her throat. What had she been thinking? There was still time to cancel. Katie stopped and pulled her phone from her pocket, her finger hovering over the screen. She could ring and say she'd been held up – or that she didn't need the appointment anymore, people must do that all the time. But if she backed out now, that would be the end of it: the end of Joe.

She shoved the mobile back into her pocket. She was being pathetic; she had to go through with it. Ahead of her were the steps at the end of the towpath and she could see the side of the building beyond them; it was too late to turn back now.

By the time she got to the surgery, sweat was prickling at the back of her neck. Dragging open the heavy door – no wonder that girl with a pram had struggled with it – she walked up to the desk. A different receptionist was sitting behind it, not the kind one in the pink cardigan who'd helped Mrs Burns. This woman didn't look up.

After several seconds, Katie cleared her throat.

The receptionist sighed and raised her eyebrows, but still didn't look away from her computer screen. 'Use the automated system.'

'I'm sorry?'

'Sign in using the automated system.'

Katie hadn't a clue what she meant. Someone tapped her shoulder; as she turned around, a man with a shock of white hair pointed to a screen at the far end of the desk.

'You have to use that!' he whispered.

'Oh!' she moved towards it, feeling stupid.

'Put in your date of birth,' prompted the old man. 'Then press female.'

With a cheerful ping the screen brought up her name and the time of her appointment. She pressed *Confirm* and moved away. 'Thanks,' she smiled at the man behind her.

'Don't worry, dear, this new-fangled stuff is tricky if you don't use it regularly,' he said, moving forward and inputting his own data with the efficiency of someone who spent most of his retirement waiting to see healthcare professionals.

She sat in the corner and picked up a magazine which was so thumbed it was almost in pieces. On a nearby chair, the white-haired man was now coughing into a handkerchief, his shoulders juddering with the effort. Looking at him, Katie pictured Mrs Burns, lying on the floor inches away from where they were sitting now. She really should have tried to find out what happened to her.

'I wonder if she broke her leg?' she'd said to Pete a few days ago.

'Probably.' He was doing some marking, not listening.

'You can't fall that hard, at her age, without causing some damage. I might ring the hospital, to ask how she is?'

'Hmmmm.'

'...Although they may not tell me anything, because I'm not family. What do you think?'

Pete had been checking something on his calculator and didn't look up.

In the end she hadn't made the call, but now, sitting back here, she felt guilty. Her mother's fall in the hospice had been less public, but just as terrifying to watch. It happened towards the end, when the cancer had eaten away at her once stocky frame, leaving her limbs spindly and her cheeks sunken. She had been trying to get to the bathroom.

'I did ring the call button, but no one came,' she later said to Katie. 'They're so busy out there.'

Unable to wait any longer, she had dragged herself from the bed, moving across the room, shuffling her feet as she gripped onto the furniture. She had probably tripped over one of her own slippers. Katie walked through the door just as her mother toppled, cracking her head on the corner of the chest of drawers. Even after all these months, Katie couldn't shake off the memory of the scarlet stains on the cream carpet. Why had no one answered that call button?

The clock on the waiting room wall ticked loudly. Katie checked her watch: it was only two minutes since she'd last looked. She nibbled at the edge of her thumbnail. Duncan had asked her to finish last month's sales figures by today, but she wasn't even halfway through and shouldn't have taken an early lunch break again – as Fraser had made clear.

'I'm popping out for a bit,' she'd said, as she pulled on her coat.

'There's a surprise,' he said sarcastically. 'I've never known you to take so much exercise, Katie. Have you got a lunchtime job on the till at Sainsbury's, or are you meeting a secret lover?'

'Don't be ridiculous.'

'Ooooh, stroppy!' he said, wiggling his fingers at her.

It was pointless reacting to Fraser, but sometimes she couldn't help herself. The other day she'd asked him not to sing along to whatever was playing through his earbuds. 'Must be the time of the month...' he had stage whispered to Duncan. 'It's hard to be nice to people when you're bleeding.' It had taken every bit of self-restraint Katie possessed to grit her teeth and look back down at her computer, when all she wanted to do was pick up the keyboard and bash it against Fraser's skull.

The silence in the waiting room was peppered by grizzling from a baby, and more coughing; every now and then a name was called out and someone got up from a chair and disappeared down the corridor.

'Mrs Katharine Johnson?'

There he was, standing just a few feet away. She caught her breath as she looked up at him.

'Mrs Katharine Johnson?'

She had to move, but it was as if she was glued to the chair. 'That's me! I'm here.'

He smiled and walked back along the corridor, Katie following him, her legs feeling as if they didn't belong to her. Inside the consulting room, he sat down at the desk by the window and swivelled his chair towards her.

'Hi, nice to see you again.'

She felt a jolt of pleasure: he knew her, they were already on familiar terms.

He gestured towards the free chair. 'Have a seat, please. What can I do for you?'

She had planned exactly what she would say, practised it in her head over and over. But now the words wouldn't come out.

All she could think about were his eyes; they were such a deep shade of blue – Cerulean maybe, or Cobalt? She racked her brains to remember the shades she'd used in art classes, so many years ago. Turquoise was too light, Prussian Blue too dark. There was an intensity to them, almost a glow.

'Mrs Johnson…?'

'Sorry!' If only her heart would stop thudding: it was so loud – surely he must be able to hear it? 'It's just… I haven't been feeling great recently.' Idiot – if she was fit and healthy, she wouldn't need to be here. But once she'd started speaking, it was easier. She'd been dreading this moment, while at the same time desperately longing for it. But as she began to lie, one untruth built on another.

'There's nothing I can really put my finger on,' she heard herself saying. 'I'm tired all the time, and not sleeping well.'

'Any particular pain?'

'Nothing specific, but my muscles ache. I get headaches, and I feel there's a tension sometimes – here.' She put her hand just under her left breast. Beneath her fingers, her heart thumped.

'Right, let's have a quick look at you.' Picking up a silver flashlight from the desk, he wheeled his chair towards her.

'Do I need to take anything off?' her voice sounded squeaky.

'No, you're fine as you are. Let's check your eyes first – look straight ahead while I shine this light into them. Try not to blink.'

She could smell him: a hint of that woody aftershave, combined with a deodorant that was familiar. His minty breath. He was so close she could see the faint wrinkles spreading out across his forehead, the pattern made by freckles on the surface of his skin, tiny pinpricks of sweat on the brow above his eyelid. Her head felt like it might explode.

He pushed his chair away again and reached for a

stethoscope. He was wearing a brown belt, and as he leant back his shirt pulled tautly against his stomach. She caught her breath and looked up to see him wheeling towards her again.

'I'm just going to have a listen to your chest. Breathe in and out normally.'

He had no idea how impossible that was, at this precise moment. His hand was on her blouse, below her breast, pressing the disc against her chest through the material.

'I can take this off,' she moved her hand up towards the buttons.

'No need, that's fine.'

Then the moment was over, and he had wheeled away towards the desk and pulled his computer keyboard towards him. Her hands were trembling in her lap and her skin felt strange where he'd touched it: tingling and hot, as if the blood underneath it was on fire.

He started tapping something onto the keyboard, his fingers flying across it. 'So, no pain anywhere?' he asked.

'No,' she said, wishing it wasn't the case.

'Eating properly?'

'Yes.'

'How many units of alcohol do you drink a week?'

'Not many,' she lied. 'The odd glass of wine.'

He turned back to face her. 'Any problems at home? Stress at work?'

'No, not really. Nothing unusual.'

He smiled, and she imagined pushing herself towards him, losing herself in that smile, diving into those eyes. 'I'm sure there's nothing seriously wrong,' he was saying. 'Your heart rate is raised, but not abnormally so. It's something we just need to keep an eye on.'

There was genuine concern on his face. She nodded and smiled: he was so kind. She knew he wasn't just saying those things, he really meant them: he understood what she was feeling, what she needed.

She realised he was waiting for her to answer a question. 'Sorry,' she said. 'I was... can you say that again?'

'Of course,' he smiled. 'I know it's a lot to get your head round. You may find that you go through different stages – you'll be fine for a while, then for apparently no reason you'll feel tired and emotional...'

Katie watched his lips as they moved. He'd stopped typing and now glanced down at his pad as he was speaking, making notes. Was that shorthand? It looked like it, but surely wasn't – hardly anyone used that nowadays.

'So, let's see how it goes for the next few weeks,' he was saying. 'Try not to drink too much, take plenty of exercise – even if it's just walking. Swimming is great, works all the muscles without putting too much pressure on the joints.'

She nodded. She ought to be asking more questions, but since she hadn't listened properly to anything he'd said, she had no idea what to ask.

'Don't worry,' he smiled again, the warmth spreading across his face. 'Many women are shocked when they realise this is happening to them – even though they know it's going to affect them at some stage, it's never welcome!'

What the hell was he talking about?

He closed his notepad, rolling the biro between his fingers. 'So, how does that sound?'

She tried to look as if she knew what was going on. 'Great. Thank you so much. I really appreciate the time you've taken to see me. It has been so helpful.'

'Come back in a few weeks' time and let me know how you're getting on,' he said, standing up and opening the door. At the end of the corridor, she could see a woman sobbing on a chair in the waiting room, and behind a closed door to the right a phone was ringing, just as plaintively.

'And remember, there's nothing to be worried about,' he said. 'Menopausal symptoms vary hugely in intensity, but if you don't feel you can cope, we can look at prescribing HRT.'

She walked to the waiting room, turning for one last look at him. But he'd already disappeared back into his room. It was only when she was standing on the grass verge outside the surgery that she realised what he'd said.

The menopause? She was only forty-three. How could he think she was old enough to be going through the bloody menopause? Part of her was offended, but it was also quite funny. She laughed out loud as she started walking away. It was her own fault for not going in there with a better plan. She should have invented painful gallstones or a jittery appendix, maybe a bruised spleen. There were plenty of problems that would have been more dramatic and required his hands-on attention.

But, despite that, she *had* been on the receiving end of those hands, and she'd certainly had his full attention. She still had the scent of him in her nostrils and could feel the touch of his fingers on her blouse – just thinking about that made her light-headed. There was something else too; the expression on his face as he listened to her and examined her, the way he stared at her, his eyes meeting hers so directly. He wouldn't look like that at every patient, would he?

She almost didn't dare believe it. But there *had* been something between them, and he was aware of it too – a frisson of excitement. Maybe he'd been thinking about her since that talk at the library? At the end of the appointment, he'd asked her to go back – he hadn't just sent her away with sympathy and a prescription. He clearly wanted to see her again. There was a chance – more than a chance – that, when she walked out of that room, he was as confused and as full of elation as she was.

Striding back towards Triple A, her body was tingling, as if an electrical current was whizzing up her neck, down her arms. She wanted to laugh or shriek – to jump in the air. Her thoughts were a muddle: her brain spinning along with the fluttering in her belly. Even though there was no one to see it, she couldn't stop herself grinning: going to the appointment had been reckless, but she'd got away with it. She'd behaved badly, but it didn't feel wrong – it felt wonderful.

10

Katie knew it had been a bad idea suggesting they go out for a birthday meal with a teenage girl who would rather be anywhere else – *with* anyone else. She smiled at the waiter, hoping to make up for the fact that Suky was deliberately ignoring him as he nipped backwards and forwards, bringing food and topping up drinks.

When she was younger, Suky had loved being brought to Valentino's. Katie remembered the top of her little blonde head poking out from behind the menu, her squeals of delight as a pizza arrived at the table, the way she took such tiny sips of her lemonade that it lasted for an hour.

In those days, the waiters had enjoyed charming her and Suky had relished being treated like royalty. Now she was slumped at the table looking as miserable as if the waiter had suggested he drill into her root canal.

'I don't care about going out,' she'd said yesterday. 'You could just give me the money instead of paying for a meal.'

'Stop being so selfish,' Katie said. 'Will it kill you to come out with your family and be pleasant for a couple of hours?'

The answer was clearly, yes. Tonight's meal had been

excruciating. Suky glowered and refused to make small talk, while Anna whined: the food was taking too long to arrive, then her cola wasn't fizzy enough, her pasta sauce too spicy.

Pete wasn't doing anything to help: he'd been in a bad mood since getting back from school. 'Do we really need to go out?' he'd asked. 'I've got prep to do for tomorrow. Anyway, if Suky isn't fussed about going, what's the point?'

'But it's her birthday, so we need to celebrate!' Katie had said. 'Honestly, Pete, you're as bad as she is. We're going and that's that.'

She shouldn't have bothered, and to make things even worse, she felt she'd done nothing but nag. 'Sit up, Anna, stop moaning please. Suky, put down that damn phone. Anna, if you just try the mushrooms, I'm sure you'll like them. Suky, put the phone on the table now or I'll take it away from you.'

Yet again she could hear echoes of her own mother's voice, which had – thirty years ago – driven her to distraction. Her mother hadn't nagged, so much as fired off scattergun instructions. 'Don't forget your bag, Katie, and tonight you're getting the bus because I'm working. Please put those shoes away. Have you got something to tie your hair back with? Can you pop to see Mrs Baker on the way back from school to pick up some bedding she's donating to the charity shop? Make sure you hand in that form about the theatre trip.'

Katie only realised how capable her mother was when she had children of her own. She'd been one of those women who always seemed in a hurry, doing several jobs at once: if she drank a cup of tea, she did so while standing at the worktop preparing food, cleaning out a cupboard, or talking on the phone – the curly cord stretching across the kitchen. Despite this she had time and conversation for Meg, the oldest, and there were always hugs for little Toby. But Katie, stuck in the middle, often felt she was left to muddle through on her own.

'She's so organised and independent,' her mother once told

a teacher at a parents' evening. 'It's such a help that I can rely on her to sort herself out.'

Teenage Katie had been shocked to hear this; she'd never thought of herself as being a useful daughter. She wished she wasn't. She wanted to be lazy and unreliable, because then she'd have more of her mother's time and attention.

All these years later, Suky didn't want more of Katie's time and attention. She didn't want any of it.

'How was the careers talk you had this morning?'

Suky shrugged. 'Fine.'

'Did they discuss work experience in the summer?'

Another shrug. 'Not really.'

Katie sighed. Had she been as curt with her own mother? As bruising with her pithy retorts? Probably – and not just as a teenager. She'd lacked patience as her mother got older; she'd been quick to snap out an answer or dismiss a suggestion.

Yesterday she had finally plucked up the courage to contact the hospice, sneaking down into the yard to make the call when Duncan was in a meeting. The woman who answered the phone had been brusque to the point of offensive. 'What's this regarding?' she'd snapped.

'My mother, Clara Jenkins. She was with you in the hospice before she died. I want to discuss her care with the director.'

'What aspect of her care?'

'I have some concerns, which I'd like to raise.'

There was a tut at the other end of the line. 'Have you lodged an official complaint about quality of care? Because if so then I would suggest you need to speak to one of our legal team...'

'No!' said Katie. 'I haven't done anything like that. I just want to come and talk to the director. Please can you book me an appointment?'

'There is no need to shout at me,' snapped the bulldog.

'Mrs Rivers can see you on Monday, at 9am. But just for fifteen minutes, she has a very busy day.'

As she ran back up the stairs to the office, Katie wasn't sure if she felt relieved, or more worried than before. Getting in late on Monday wouldn't go down well.

The waiter was now hovering with a handful of dessert menus. They looked at the list without enthusiasm and only Anna ordered a bowl of strawberry ice cream, which she stirred with her spoon until it melted into pink goo.

Suky was on her phone again, taking miserable-looking selfies, probably to show her friends what a dreadful birthday she was having. Katie itched to snatch the phone from her daughter's hand and throw it onto the floor. She imagined it shattering into thousands of pieces, each tiny shard shrieking in pain.

But it wasn't worth it. Instead, she stared out of the window, where the streetlight threw a glow onto a section of damp pavement. She tried to pick her battles, ignoring the sulky moods and slammed doors in the hope that, when she really wanted to challenge Suky about something, it would carry more weight. She wasn't convinced this approach was working: Suky disliked everything Katie did and everything she said. She laughed at her appearance – 'Your hair is awful, Mum, you really need to get it cut properly' – sneered at her taste in clothes – 'Do you have to wear those jeans? They're really old lady' – and found her presence so embarrassing that she'd rather walk a mile home from the bus stop in the rain, than have Katie pick her up outside school.

Now, sitting in a restaurant trying to pretend that they were a happy family – although Pete's mind was elsewhere and both the girls would clearly prefer to be – she was suddenly angry. *If only you knew what's going on my life*, she thought, as Suky's phone pinged repeatedly. *You think I'm a dull, middle-aged nag. But there is so much more to me than that.*

She had walked past this restaurant the previous afternoon – when she'd followed Joe Harvey back to his house. She hadn't planned to do it, but had again been out of the office during her lunch break, this time to buy a birthday card for Suky. Her heart jolted when she saw him ahead of her on the pavement. He was on his phone and she rushed into a doorway and bent down to tie a non-existent shoelace as he went past. He had a coat slung over one arm, his bulging bag in the other, and he'd walked briskly, head up, footsteps ringing out on the pavement. She didn't think about whether or not to follow him, she just did it.

At the end of the street, Joe turned left towards the library. Just before the building itself, he went diagonally across the car park and onto a footpath, which led uphill. Katie followed at a distance, but he was still on the phone and didn't turn around. The footpath came out at the top of a cul-de-sac, where half a dozen houses with inbuilt single garages were arranged around a large turning circle; when Katie stepped out onto the pavement, she saw Joe was going towards one of the houses on the left. It had a pale blue front door, with the number 15 above the letter box. An estate agent's sign speared the section of grass in the front garden, with a Let label tacked across the bottom.

Before Katie had time to worry about whether he might turn and see her, he had put a key in the lock, opened the door and disappeared inside.

She stood for a few seconds, wondering what to do. Then, pulling up her scarf to cover her face, she walked past the houses and followed the road back down the hill. The sign at the junction said Coopers Lane.

When she arrived back at the office, sweating and short of breath, she had ignored Fraser's look of surprise and sat at her computer, typing the address into Google. She'd soon tracked down the full postcode for 15 Coopers Lane, scribbling the details on a piece of paper and shoving it into her bag. It was only as she pulled a pile of folders towards her, that she realised she'd forgotten to buy a birthday card for Suky.

Now, sitting in Valentino's, twisting her dessert spoon between her fingers and half listening to Anna talk about the shortlist of names for Mrs Scratchy's hamster babies, she felt a thrill at what she'd done yesterday. It hadn't been sensible, but it didn't feel wrong either. She hadn't set out to follow Joe – or even look for him – it had just happened. And now she knew something else about him, a little nugget of information that added to the picture of his life she was building up in her head.

The house on Coopers Lane wasn't quite what she'd been expecting: it wasn't as sophisticated as the apartments down by the canal, where she'd imagined he might live. But she was sure Joe would have decorated that little house with style. She guessed his taste would be neutral: pale carpets and furniture, nothing fancy or quirky.

His kitchen was probably minimalist – men were less likely to clutter worktops with things that didn't have a function. The cupboards would be white or cream, maybe with a granite effect work surface and easy-to-clean tiled floor. There would probably be a coffee machine on the side, Joe Harvey seemed like a man who would like proper coffee; Katie had always been a tea drinker, but she reckoned she could become the kind of woman who drank head-splittingly strong coffee from tiny white cups. Those women also had swathes of silky hair that hung down their backs like curtains, and wore large designer sunglasses, even on overcast days.

'Mum!'

'What?' she jumped as Anna raised her voice next to her.

'Well, can I go?'

'Yes, if you want, I suppose,' she hedged.

Pete stared at her. 'Is that a good idea?' he asked. 'For God's sake, Katie, you know we've discussed this before.'

'Well, we'll think about it,' she snapped, covering up her embarrassment at having no idea what she'd been asked. 'Come on let's get the bill. It's late to be still out on a school night.' She picked up her bag, waving over-zealously at the waiter lurking at the far end of the restaurant.

She could sense Pete glaring at her, but didn't meet his eye.

11

It was days since she'd sat inches from Joe in his consulting
room, but Katie couldn't stop thinking about him: the way
he'd looked, the scent of his skin. In her head, she went over
and over the few words they'd exchanged, recreating every
second of the appointment. She had to see this man again; she
was losing sleep over him. Last night she'd found herself wide
awake in the darkness, the digital display of her bedside clock
telling her it was 3.35am; she wanted him so badly, it was like a
physical ache. But the more she tried to think about something
else – anything else – the more his face and his body filled her
mind.

Now, she opened the laptop and waited for the screen to
flicker into life. This probably wasn't the right way to go about
it, but doing nothing was driving her crazy. She needed to find
a way to see him again, but it was too soon to book a follow-up
appointment. Once she'd brought up a blank document on the
screen in front of her, she sat staring at it for several minutes.
What could she say? How could she phrase it, without
sounding like a psycho?

She went to find her handbag, and dug into the side pocket

for the newspaper cutting. It was now tattered and rough around the edges. She knew the text off by heart, had read and reread it so many times, as she studied his face in the photograph and ran her finger up and down the stripes of the purple and white shirt. She laid the article on the desk beside the keyboard. Looking at his face would focus her mind on what to say.

She made several false starts, typing a few lines then pressing the back arrow to erase them.

Dear Joe, her forefingers clattered across the keys as the black letters popped up on the white page in front of her. *I hope you don't mind me getting in touch with you. I came to see you the other week at the surgery, and want to thank you for the advice you gave me…*

Was that too formal?

I saw how you looked at me when we were sitting in your consulting room together, and I think that you may feel the same way…

No, no, no! Too impulsive. There had to be a balance between making him realise she was interested in him – and coming across as creepy. She must broach it slowly: thank him for his advice, but suggest there were other reasons why they needed to see each other again. They both knew why, but she couldn't be blatant about it. She must give him an opening to make the next move.

It took her an hour to come up with something she was happy with, writing and then deleting, reading and rereading, changing the occasional word then rephrasing entire sentences.

She'd always hated letter writing. In English classes at school – in the days before computers laid out documents and checked spelling and punctuation – she'd been taught how to present a formal letter: where to put the addresses and date, when to indent, how to position sub-clauses, whether to use 'Yours sincerely' or 'Yours faithfully'. It was all very logical and held her in good stead for job applications. But although she could now put together a letter that looked neat, tidy and professional, it didn't make up for the fact that she was rubbish at expressing herself.

Meg had been the one with the talent for writing. And for art, languages, maths and for translating the results of scientific experiments into neat diagrams and clear explanations. She'd had a talent for just about everything.

Following her through school, Katie grew used to teachers saying, 'You're not like your older sister, are you?' She would stick out her chin and shrug her shoulders, determined not to seem bothered by the comparison. She wasn't stupid, her marks were above average and she did well in exams. But above average doesn't seem particularly impressive when it trots along behind exceptional.

Meg had worked hard at university, sailed into a job as a microbiologist, and was now living in the Middle East with Don, her equally intellectual husband, whom Katie and Pete had only met twice – once at his wedding to Meg and once at their own. The two women exchanged irregular emails and birthday cards but they were very different; had they not been sisters, they wouldn't have stayed in touch.

Rereading what she'd just typed, Katie wondered how Meg would have phrased it, how she would have achieved just the right balance of gratitude and friendliness. It was irrelevant really, because perfect Meg would never have got herself into something like this in the first place.

Not that this was a situation where she felt there was any element of choice: at the moment Katie couldn't think about anything else. When she'd finally fallen asleep again last night, just before dawn, she had dreamt she and Joe were on a boat, then that she was running towards him down a flight of stairs – the dream confused and irrational, but her desire to be with him overwhelming, even in sleep. He was everywhere.

She glanced at the clock: it was already 11am. She had to get on, Pete and the girls would be back by midday. He had taken them to their Saturday morning activities: Anna to a dance class – which she hated – and Suky to the charity shop, where she volunteered as part of her Duke of Edinburgh award. She hated that too and her parents often agreed they had no idea how their daughter's constant scowl promoted sales of second-hand clothing, books and knick-knacks.

Katie usually spent Saturday morning cleaning the house. But today she'd been sitting in front of the laptop for ages and the place was still a tip. She fed paper into the printer, watching the letter appear in front of her before reading it through quickly. It would have to do. This was just an opening gambit – something to arouse his interest rather than an all-out declaration of undying love. The more she replayed the scene in her head, the more convinced she was that he had felt something for her too, during that appointment at the surgery. Maybe he'd even felt the same connection when they'd talked at the library? But he was in a difficult position: his professional integrity was at stake. She had to make the first move.

She grabbed a pen. Was it enough to just sign it Katie? He would probably know several Katies. At the surgery she was registered as Katharine Johnson, so she'd better use her full first name. She scrawled a signature at the bottom. She was sure he'd know who she was but, just in case, she added Johnson in brackets. It felt silly doing that, but soon there'd be no need for clarification: she would be the only Katharine in his life.

For the next hour she ran up and down the stairs, distributing piles of discarded schoolbooks, clean washing, hairbrushes, shoes and towels to various bedrooms. Dirty plates went downstairs, keys and coats were hung up by the front door, plants watered, discarded pyjamas picked up from the floor, duvets thrown across rumpled beds.

By the time the front door crashed open and Anna shouted, 'We're back!' Katie had restored some order to the house, and was on her hands and knees in the bathroom, scraping toothpaste off the floor tiles.

The letter, in a sealed envelope, addressed and stamped, was tucked into the pocket of her coat, hanging on one of the hooks in the hall. Every time she walked past it that weekend, Katie felt a glow of excitement. She would post it first thing on Monday morning.

12

She waited on a sofa in the reception area, twisting her hands together in her lap. It was strange, being back here. Actually, it wasn't strange – it was awful. Katie had virtually lived in the hospice during the last week of her mother's life, sitting beside her bed for hours on end. She would rush away to spend some time with the girls when they got home from school, but be back here by the time the staff served up the evening meal – which her mother never ate.

Katie had become accustomed to the softly carpeted corridors and subtly lit rooms, she'd grown to know the artwork that lined the walls and now her nostrils were full of the smell of the place – the heady scent of the diffusers that sat on low tables, presumably to cover up the stronger acetone smell that Katie now associated with death and which pervaded every corridor in the building.

After her mother died, she hadn't come back here. Pete and Monica had offered to go and clear the bedroom and sort through her mother's remaining possessions, for which Katie had been grateful. Then there had been the funeral to arrange, then Probate – plenty of other jobs which kept her busy. Even when she'd decided recently that she wanted to come and talk to the director about her mother's fall, she hadn't really thought about what it would feel like to be back in this place. But sitting here in the reception, she wished she had, because it was so much harder than she could have imagined.

There was a clock on the wall, and the minute hand ticked steadily past the twelve. She tapped her fingers together in frustration: Duncan had been tight-lipped when she'd asked for time off. 'I like to think I've been very patient with you, Katie. I know the last few months have been difficult for you, but you can't just gallivant off, whenever you need to book an appointment.'

'I know, I'm really sorry – first thing Monday morning was the only time they offered me. But I need to see this woman, Duncan, it's important. I'll work through lunch when I get back.'

He had sighed and walked back into his office, slamming the door.

Fraser had smirked. 'That went well.'

'Shut up, Fraser,' she said, more sharply than she'd intended. 'You could at least try to be supportive?'

He looked at her in surprise. It had clearly never occurred to him that he and Katie were anything other than adversaries in the fight for survival and supremacy in the front office at Triple A.

'Mrs Johnson?'

The hospice director, Jane Rivers, was the sort of woman who looked like she'd emerged from the womb already wearing a beautifully fitted suit and smart shoes. She glided effortlessly along the corridor in front of Katie, who tried to straighten her skirt as she followed, pushing a strand of hair behind her ear and rubbing at her eyelids in case her mascara had smudged since she left the house.

'How can I help?'

'It's about my mother, Clara Jenkins.' Over the weekend, Katie had been rehearsing what she'd say at this meeting, trying to anticipate the response she'd get. 'She was here for the last couple of weeks of her life, after she was transferred from the Royal Infirmary.'

Jane Rivers nodded, her hands clasped in front of her on the wide desk.

'She died quite suddenly.'

Another nod.

Katie faltered; wishing the woman would say something. There was nothing more off-putting than talking to someone who wouldn't talk back: it immediately put you on the defensive. 'The thing is,' she said. 'She fell towards the end, and I've always wondered whether that – the fall I mean – contributed to her death.'

Jane Rivers had tilted her head to one side and stopped nodding.

'So, I want to find out what happened here that day, because I feel that not enough was done to keep my mother safe.' There, she'd said it. The smile was frozen on Jane Rivers' fuchsia-tinted lips. The silence stretched between them and, for once, Katie resisted the urge to fill it. She had said her bit, now let Mrs Rivers come back with something.

'Well,' the woman said, after a long pause. 'That is clearly a serious allegation, Mrs Johnson. As I'm sure you are aware.'

Katie didn't say anything.

'But we take this sort of thing very seriously at St Bernard's, and obviously we will do our best to reassure you that the care your mother received while she was here, was only ever of the highest standard.'

Katie's pulse was racing and she realised she was holding her breath.

'While we don't want to involve our legal team at this stage,

I must warn you that, with this sort of unfounded allegation, we may be forced to put matters onto a more formal basis.'

Katie knew the director was trying to scare her. She didn't look away. 'I just need to find out what happened before my mother died,' she said, surprised at how calm she sounded. 'I'm not making unfounded allegations, I'm just asking you to look into what went on. I know she had a fall on that Wednesday morning – I walked in and saw it happening. My mother told me she had repeatedly rung for help. But no one came.'

'As you'll understand, Mrs Johnson, this is a busy unit.' The woman's voice was now clipped, her eyes hard and unblinking. 'We respond to requests for help as soon as we can, but it is not always possible for our staff to be at a patient's bedside in a matter of seconds.'

'It was more than seconds!' said Katie, her voice rising. 'She said she'd waited a long time.'

'Do you have an accurate record of how long she had waited?'

'No, of course I don't! She didn't make a note of it. She was ill, she needed to get to the toilet.' She swallowed hard; she would not cry in front of this woman. 'All I know is that, for whatever reason, none of the nurses or carers arrived, so she tried to get herself to the bathroom. But she shouldn't have been doing that on her own.'

Mrs Rivers forced her lips into a thin, insincere smile. 'It is understandable that you're concerned, Mrs Johnson, and obviously this is a difficult time for you. I can assure you our standards of care here at St Bernard's are extremely high, and I have no doubt our staff did everything they could in the circumstances. However, I will look into this matter and talk to those who were on duty that day.'

Katie knew she was trying to fob her off.

'Once I've done that, I will get in touch and let you know my findings. Although I can assure you this is not an instance in which blame can be apportioned. Our hardworking employees are dedicated carers, whose work is purely dictated by the interests of our patients. An accusation like this will be upsetting for all concerned.'

Katie immediately felt guilty, which she knew was the intention. 'I'm not questioning the skills of your staff, Mrs Rivers. They're lovely people, and this isn't personal.' She picked up her handbag and stood up. 'Thank you for seeing me. I'll look forward to hearing from you.' She left the door open as she marched back along the corridor.

The receptionist was on the phone as she walked past. 'We require payment in advance,' she was saying. 'There is a waiting list for beds at St Bernard's and we need to ensure you can afford to bring your father to join us.'

When she got back into her car and pulled the door shut, Katie realised she was shaking. She grasped the steering wheel tightly to stop her fingers trembling. She half expected tears to come, now she was out of that place, but to her surprise she felt buoyant, almost exhilarated. That had been bloody hard, but she'd managed it. She fumbled with the key, glancing at the clock as she reversed the car out of the space. Maybe she could slip back into the office without Duncan noticing? But actually, that didn't matter. This was important.

Accelerating down the drive, she felt brave, proud of herself. She would insist the hospice carried out a proper investigation and re-evaluated their systems. It was too late to bring her mother back, but she could make sure nothing similar happened to anyone else in their care. At the very least she might get an apology from St Bernard's, and it would be great if they admitted responsibility and promised to ensure improvements were made.

But by the time she got back to the office, her elation had

disappeared. Now she just felt low again, and a little embarrassed. Nothing was going to change, and she was no campaigning champion. She was just a grieving, middle-aged woman who was pleased with herself because she hadn't let an over-officious healthcare professional walk all over her.

13

Fraser had a hangover. When Katie walked into the office, she found him slumped on the desk, his head resting on his folded arms. Beside him was a glass of water, still frothing with tablets that had turned the liquid pink.

'What was the celebration?' she asked.

'Friend's 25th on Saturday,' he whispered. 'Massive party at Di Angelo's. Dancing, vodka shots.'

'But, it's now Monday? That's one hell of a hangover, Fraser.'

He groaned. 'I want to die.'

That sounded like a plan. She opened and shut the drawers of her desk as loudly as possible while hunting for a stapler. The vibration rattled across to Fraser's desk, where he moaned and lifted his head. He glared at her. 'Keep the noise down. You have no idea how awful I feel.'

She smiled across at him. 'Oh dear, poor you. Can I have those comparison figures for the last two quarters by mid-morning? I need to get everything typed up today. Come on, Fraser, doing some work will make you feel better, chop-chop.'

'Cow,' he muttered, and she turned away to hide her smile,

knowing he'd get his revenge when he was feeling human again.

Her phone beeped, and she felt a jolt of anticipation as she reached for it – although it was probably only Suky, demanding she come into school to deliver lunch money or a forgotten PE kit.

It was Monica; a work crisis. She read the message, sighed and laboriously started to text back, cursing herself when she hit the wrong buttons.

'A decent phone is wasted on you,' said Fraser. 'I'm amazed you even manage to turn that thing on in the mornings.'

Katie decided it was easier to call.

'I can't talk,' hissed Monica. 'I'm just about to go into a client meeting. Why didn't you text? Can you come out tonight? I'm having a bloody awful day and I need wine. The George – 6.30?'

'Well, tonight's not great…' started Katie.

'Please, just a quick one? Got to rush, it's busy here. See you later.' There was a click and the background noise of Monica's office disappeared behind a wall of empty space.

'Oh, okay,' Katie carried on. 'I'll be there, but I need to sort the girls out. Order a bottle but don't start without me. We can't have a session this time though, I must be back by midnight.' She could sense Fraser's eyes sliding towards her. 'Yes, I know I said that last week!' She laughed and pretended to examine the fingernails on her left hand. 'It was brilliant, what an evening. I didn't know you could sing like that! I ripped my tights when we fell off that table. Okay, looking forward to it, see you later.'

She hit the 'end call' button with a flourish and put it back on the desk. Out of the corner of her eye she could see Fraser turning back to his computer screen. *Hah, stick that in your party pipe and smoke it.*

Would Pete be at home later? He wasn't generally busy on

Mondays, but if he was out, she'd ask Suky to look after Anna for a couple of hours. She usually agreed to babysit if there was money involved, albeit with much sighing and rolling of eyes.

On the way home, Katie drove to the supermarket to pick up a couple of ready meals for the girls to heat up. The glass doors swished apart and, as she picked up a basket and turned to go into the store, she found herself staring at Joe. He was walking towards her, a bag of shopping in one hand. In less than a second, she registered his face, his smile, the way his fringe flopped across his eyes – and the woman he was holding close to him as they came towards the doors. She was pretty. Young and pretty.

Katie turned back to the pile of baskets, her heart thumping, her gut churning. Bending over, she picked up a second basket and stood with her back to the entrance, as people passed by.

'Excuse me,' said a man in a checked cap. 'Are you going to take both of those, or put one back?'

She looked behind her and saw the couple had gone through the door and were walking away, across the car park towards the road. Joe still had his arm across the girl's shoulders and now she was laughing, her face turned to him, as pretty sideways on as it had been from the front.

He clearly hadn't seen her. Katie breathed out in relief, realising her shoulders had been hunched inside her coat. She turned to the old man and thrust both the baskets at him. 'Here, they're all yours,' she said, and headed towards her car. Once safely inside she slammed the door and sat for a few seconds, her hands shaking on the steering wheel.

He has a girlfriend; or maybe a wife. It felt like someone had kicked her in the stomach. She'd only come across this man a few weeks ago, but he had become an all-consuming part of her life. She had thought about him, spoken to him, followed him. She had breathed in his scent and felt his fingers on her body. She knew the type of clothes he liked to wear, the sound of his laugh, the way he subconsciously ran his hand through his fringe to push it back from his face. She had imagined herself moving closer to that gentle, smiling face, touching his lips with her fingers, running her hand through his hair; kissing him deeply, more deeply than she had ever kissed another man. He was hers.

Except that he wasn't.

She *had* wondered if there might be someone in his life. But when the possibility had flitted through her mind, she hadn't let it linger there. Now it wasn't just a possibility, it was a fact. She stared through the windscreen, not seeing what was in front of her. Her temples were thumping and she was exhausted, as if all the blood had drained from her body. She felt as if she'd thrown herself off the edge of a cliff and was plummeting through the air. She tried to make her brain focus on what she needed to do next: starting the engine and driving out of the supermarket car park. But all she could think about was that pretty young woman, the tinkling sound of her laugh as she walked away.

Katie suddenly realised her cheeks were wet and the view through the windscreen had become blurry. She'd been planning for a future. It was madness, complete bloody madness, of course it was – her future was with Pete and the girls. Yet, when she thought about Joe – which was most of the time – she'd been thinking about the two of them together. She'd imagined how their lives would begin to cross over; they would meet properly, he'd get to know her better, enjoy being with her. They would call each other more frequently, then – and in her head this bit didn't take long – they would come to realise they couldn't bear being apart. She'd imagined herself being invited to that house on Coopers Lane, knocking on the door and her heart swelling when he opened it and gave her one of his smiles. It would start slowly with the letter, giving him the push he needed, offering him a way to make contact with her, then they would go for a drink, followed by a meal...

'Shit!' she said out loud. 'The letter...'

14

Two hours later, she was sitting at a table in The George. Monica was late, as always, and Katie had already drunk half a glass of wine on an empty stomach, enough to give her a warm feeling but also to worsen the thudding headache she'd had since she got home from work. Coming in empty-handed from the supermarket, she'd thrown some bacon into a pan and told the girls they were having sandwiches for tea.

'That's rubbish. I want chips!' yelled Anna from the sitting room, where she was lying across the sofa watching *Friends*.

'Sorry, but I'm going out,' Katie had said. 'It's sandwiches or nothing.'

'Nothing then, I hate you!'

Pete had got back just as she was putting slices of burnt bacon onto bread.

'Monica is having a meltdown, so I'm going to meet her for a quick drink. You don't mind, do you? I won't be long.'

'Monica? What do you mean, meltdown?' He looked pale, the bags under his eyes more pronounced than usual. She saw him staring at the worktop.

'Sorry about tea,' she said. 'I meant to stop off and get something else.'

'Great,' he said, throwing his coat across the chair. 'Bloody brilliant. It's been a really shit day and all I'm having for tea is a bacon sandwich.'

'I know, I'm really sorry. I ran out of time.'

'Why are you always so disorganised, Katie?' he said, walking out of the kitchen. 'Feeding a family of four isn't rocket science.'

She prickled with irritation. *You do it then!* she wanted to yell after him. *You juggle family life with a job. You do the shopping and the cooking and the clearing up. You take some responsibility for keeping this family on track!*

But she didn't say a word. Anyway, he was right: she'd failed to provide a decent meal for her family, because she was going to the pub with her best friend. It wasn't exactly selfless.

'Can you try to get Anna to do some homework?' she called after him. 'I think she's got a spelling test tomorrow.'

'I have got marking to do, you know,' he said, walking into the office. 'I haven't got time to be running up and downstairs, checking on the girls all evening.'

'It won't be all evening, Pete, I'll only be out for an hour or so.'

But he'd already slammed the door.

Now, nursing her wine in the pub, she was full of guilt. What was the matter with her? She should be at home, dealing with the girls while Pete got on with his work. She should have said no when Monica called – or texted back to say she couldn't make it after all. She'd been having so much fun at Fraser's expense, she hadn't really thought about any of this.

'Sorry, sorry!' said Monica breathlessly, bursting through the door and unwinding her scarf as she fell onto the empty chair on the other side of the table. 'Had to call my mum before I came out and she yammered on, something about the council coming to tear down the hedge in her front garden. I told her no one can cut down her hedge unless she's asked them to. But she's convinced they're going to do it then bill her for it, and she's getting herself in a state. Honestly, she drives me mad. Shoot me if I ever get to that stage...' She stopped suddenly, her coat half off her shoulders. 'Oh shit, sorry, Katie, that was so insensitive of me.'

Katie smiled at her. 'It's fine, honestly.'

Monica was shaking her head. 'Didn't mean to be so thoughtless. Another wine in there?'

Katie shook her head. 'No, I'll just have this. I can't stay for long.'

'I know, sorry. Hang on, I'll be right back.' Dumping her coat and scarf over the chair, Monica went to the bar, leaning her elbows on it as she spoke to the barman, saying something that made him laugh. Katie envied the ease with which she talked to strangers. Monica strode into a room with confidence, not worrying what anyone else thought about her, gushing warmth and friendliness. The older they both became, the more graceless Katie felt beside her.

They'd met as first year students at university, when Monica smuggled a bottle of wine into an English lecture and told Katie they were going to play a drinking game. Every time the lecturer said the word 'love', Katie had to have a furtive slug of wine. When he said 'death', Monica did the same. It was Shakespeare: *Romeo and Juliet* – the session was littered with references to both words. Afterwards they staggered out into the sunshine, screaming with laughter. Overwhelmed by her first weeks away from home, Katie had latched on to this bright, sassy girl; funny and irreverent, Monica made her laugh until her ribs ached.

After university Monica's star had continued to shine, and she rose through the ranks at an advertising agency before starting her own business. Katie never resented her success –

she loved her too much for that – but sometimes she felt left behind. How different might her own life have been, if she hadn't met Pete and turned her back on a career in favour of babies and intermittent domestic bliss?

'Here you go, have this anyway, I know you want it,' said Monica, returning with two large glasses of white wine. 'Sorry to drag you out, but I've had a bloody crap day, and I really need to get it off my chest.'

Katie listened and made the right noises for the next ten minutes, watching Monica's lips form words but not taking them in. She couldn't stop thinking about the little house in Coopers Lane; imagining a red van driving up to the top of the turning circle the next morning and stopping as the postman hopped out to put letters through the doors. The handwritten envelope that she'd posted first thing this morning would thud onto the carpet and sit there for hours before Joe came back from work, bending down to pick up the jumble of letters.

Except that it wasn't him she was now picturing coming through the door, but the pretty girl with the auburn hair, who would kneel to gather up the post, turning over the white envelope and seeing the unfamiliar handwriting on the other side.

'Mon, I've got to tell you something,' she blurted out. 'I think I've been a bit stupid. Well, I know I have. But I'm not sure what to do about it.'

Interrupted mid-sentence, Monica looked at her in surprise.

'There's someone I met recently, who I don't know very well yet. In fact, I don't know him at all.' Katie saw the shock on her friend's face and carried on quickly. 'But I've been thinking about him a lot, and – I've written him a letter. It's not a crazy love letter or anything. But it's a note I sent to his house, and I was hoping it might lead to other things. But now I've discovered he's got a girlfriend – or maybe even a wife, I'm not sure. But what happens if she gets the letter? And even if she doesn't see it, what's he going to think when he reads it?'

Monica's mouth had fallen open.

'Say something, Mon, please,' Katie pleaded. 'I know it all sounds a bit weird, but it isn't really – or it didn't feel like it at the time.'

'Bloody hell!' Monica sat back in her chair and folded her arms. 'I never would have thought you had it in you. But who is he? And where did you meet him? I can't believe he didn't tell you about his wife! That is just so typical, leaving you to find out when things had already got started. Men always…'

'But nothing has started, that's just it,' interrupted Katie. 'Nothing has happened between the two of us, except that I've sat in his office and we've talked about my health.'

Monica's brow creased. 'Your health. Why would you talk about that?'

'It was the only way I could get to see him! But that doesn't matter. What's worrying me is this stupid letter. As I said, it isn't really too personal, but I guess I was hoping he'd read it and we'd meet up and it would lead to something. But now I wish I'd sent it to him at work, because at least then it wouldn't be seen by his wife or girlfriend or whoever the hell she is. I posted it this morning, with a first-class stamp. It's on its way to him right now.'

Monica looked confused. 'But if nothing has happened, what's the big deal?'

'Because I want something to happen!' said Katie. The couple at the next table stopped talking and looked over at them. 'I desperately want something to happen.' She lowered her voice and leant across the table. 'He's gorgeous and I can't stop thinking about him, but it never occurred to me he'd be with someone. Now I have to get that letter back and make sure she doesn't find out something is going on.'

'Which it isn't,' said Monica.

'No, of course it isn't.'

'But you wish it would?'

'Yes! Well, I think so. To be honest I don't know what I think anymore. I feel like a bloody idiot; the whole thing is ridiculous. It's like I've got a teenage crush on someone. But I'm too old to have crushes, and I wish I'd never written the letter – even though it took ages, and actually I think it's quite good. I just shouldn't have posted it.'

'So where does Pete fit into all this?' asked Monica.

'He doesn't. He's just Pete, you know. There's nothing wrong between us. Well, no more than the usual stuff every couple goes through – we get on each other's nerves sometimes, we bicker. But this thing with Joe is… I don't know how to explain really, it's just separate.' She paused briefly. 'It feels like this isn't happening to me. It's like I have two lives, and Joe is part of my other life – the one without all the ties and the responsibilities.'

They sat in silence for a few seconds.

'I'm not sure what you want me to say,' said Monica eventually. 'If nothing has happened between you, and there isn't anything too personal in the letter, can't you just leave it? He'll probably think you're weird and wonder why you wrote it. But it won't wreck his marriage or anything.'

'I'm not worried about his marriage,' said Katie. 'But I don't want him thinking I'm crazy. I'm just embarrassed about it all. I should have taken things more slowly. I just… I want to rewind the clock, so I could stop myself putting the envelope in that postbox.'

'Well, sadly that's the one thing you can't do,' pointed out Monica, knocking back the last of her wine. 'The only way you can get hold of that letter, is to take it back from the postman before he puts it through their door.'

15

'Sorry, Duncan, but I won't be in today.' Katie made her voice quaver. 'I think I've picked up a bug from the girls. Really sorry, I'm sure it will only be a twenty-four-hour thing.' She was getting good at these little lies. As she ended the call, she didn't feel guilty, but knew she ought to. It was a relief she'd been able to leave a voicemail, she didn't fancy making excuses to Duncan in person.

'Pete, can you drop Anna at school for me? I'm not feeling great.'

He sighed and pushed his chair back from the kitchen table. 'You do realise that's going to make me late?'

'What about my netball match? Who's going to pick me up after that?' demanded Suky, balancing a mirror against her schoolbag on the worktop, applying the eyeliner that her tutor would ask her to remove in less than an hour's time.

'I'm sure I'll be fine by then,' Katie said, half expecting gratitude but not surprised there was just the usual sigh.

Once they'd all left the house she got dressed, buttered a piece of toast to take with her, and went to the car. It was only when she reached the outskirts of town that she realised she was too early: the roads were still busy with commuters and parents on the school run. Why hadn't she thought this through properly? She parked the car at the bottom of Coopers Lane just before 9 o'clock, and sat for a minute worrying that Joe might drive down the hill past her, before deciding it was more likely he would walk to work, using the footpath along which she'd followed him before. Now she just had to wait.

She tried to listen to a debate on Radio 4 about fracking, but her mind soon drifted away from the earnest scientists. When she changed the station, 'Rudolph the Red Nosed Reindeer' blasted into the car. Katie turned down the volume: she was fed up with Christmas songs already and there were still weeks to go. There had been a message on the answerphone at the weekend from Brenda, asking about their plans. Katie hadn't called her back yet, but could predict exactly how things would pan out. As always, they would invite Alan and Brenda to spend Christmas Day with them. And, as always, the invitation would be politely received with the proviso: 'Of course we don't know what Phil and Camilla are doing yet'. Then, with a couple of weeks to go, Brenda would announce with great generosity: 'We think we *will* come to you this year, dear. We always have such a jolly time with you at Christmas.'

What would be left unsaid was that no invitation had been forthcoming from the big house on the hill, and it would be obvious to Katie that her sister-in-law had – yet again – managed to hold out against Brenda's persistent hints. When Christmas came, Phil, Camilla and their charming children would squeeze in a cup of tea with the grandparents. Presents would be exchanged swiftly and efficiently, then the younger brother would slip away with his glamorous wife and perfect children to enjoy their Christmas, uninterrupted by his irritating family.

Katie felt sorry for Brenda, who didn't acknowledge the snub but felt it keenly. But despite that, for days afterwards they would hear how marvellous Camilla's presents had been, and how much Brenda loved her cashmere scarf or silver photo frame. Katie's own gift wouldn't measure up, however much time and effort had been spent on it, and Christmas dinner would be an uncomfortable combination of bad tempered girls, judgemental grandparents and flustered chefs – she and Pete invariably got on each other's nerves when under pressure in the kitchen.

Joy and goodwill to all men, she thought. *Why do we put ourselves through this rigmarole?*

The radio programme changed again, cars drove up and down the hill, residents walked their dogs. It was just after 10.30am when a Royal Mail van pulled up on the pavement beyond her. A young lad – wearing shorts despite the chill – hopped out with an armful of letters and marched down the path of the first house on the left.

Katie sat forward in her seat; she'd almost forgotten why she was waiting here. What should she do now? There were more than twenty houses in the cul-de-sac, and the postman wasn't going to reach Joe's yet. Sure enough, he put letters and parcels through the three nearest doors, before getting into the van and driving further up, parking again and repeating the process.

Should she stop the postman now, before he got there? If he was doing a few houses at a time, he might not have the right letters, so maybe she ought to drive up to the turning circle at the top? There was no sign of life in any of the houses but, to be on the safe side, she didn't pull up in front of number 15, parking on the other side, near the footpath. In her rear-view mirror she watched the van make two more short hops up the road, finally coming to a halt behind her. It had to be now. Opening the door, she stepped into the road.

'Hi!' she said brightly, as the lad got out of the van, his arms full of envelopes. Close up he wasn't as young as she'd thought, possibly early thirties, with a tattooed dragon slithering into the collar of his red Royal Mail fleece. 'I wondered if you had any post for number 15?'

He looked at her, brow creased. 'Well, yes…'

'It's just that I need to get something back, which I've posted there by mistake. I'm sure it will be in that pile because I put a first-class stamp on it yesterday.'

He suddenly understood what she meant. 'Sorry, love, no can do. All deliveries have to be made to the specified address. I can't take something out and give it to you.'

'But it's mine,' explained Katie. 'I wrote it. But I didn't mean to send it because it's not quite finished. So, if you can just give it back, I'll take it away and finish it properly, then I'll post it again.'

'Nope. Sorry.' The man turned and walked up the path towards number 13.

Katie was stunned; she hadn't expected him to say no. 'This is crazy,' she said, as he came back down the path. 'It's my letter! Surely, I can have it back if I want? I mean, I paid for the delivery, so if I don't want it delivered, then that's up to me.'

He started walking up the next path, posted a handful of letters through the door and came back towards her. 'It's the rules I'm afraid. Nothing to do with me. Legally I am obliged to deliver this mail. If I don't, then I'm not doing my job and they could sack me. Why don't you ask the people who live here to give your letter back?'

He started walking up the path towards the pale blue front door of number 15. Katie trotted after him, panic rising in her throat. 'Please let me have it! I won't tell anyone you didn't deliver it. Anyway, you did sort of deliver it – to the outside of the house.'

Feeling sick, she watched as he pushed some envelopes through the letter box. There was a thud as they landed on the floor below the door. He turned around and grinned. 'Sorry, more than my job's worth.'

She stood on the path, staring helplessly at the letter box. The envelope was feet away, but there was nothing she could do to get it back. Behind her, the engine noise from the van changed, as the postman put it into gear and drove further along to deliver to the last few houses in Coopers Lane.

Katie got back into her car and drove down towards the main road, blood pounding in her ears. She turned right and headed into town, not concentrating on where she was going. All she could think about was the pretty girl with auburn hair, who would let herself in through that pale blue door in a few hours' time, and pick up the letters from the mat.

Turning into the car park by the library she found a space and sat staring through the windscreen at the hedge in front of her. She had to get that letter back. The whole thing now seemed insane; what had she been thinking? Why had it ever seemed like a good idea to write to him at home? At the very least he'd want to know where she'd got his address – then she'd have to admit she'd followed him.

You stupid woman. What a bloody mess.

She looked across the car park and saw the opening to the footpath that went up to Coopers Lane. Grabbing her bag, she got out of the car and walked over to it. In less than a minute, slightly out of breath, she came out in the cul-de-sac at the top and marched across to number 15. If anyone was at a window watching, she had to look like she knew what she was doing. There was a tall wooden gate to one side and, without hesitating, she opened it and went through, shutting it behind her. Her heart was pounding, and sweat was breaking out on her forehead.

The rear garden was smaller than she'd expected, with a

central patch of unmown grass surrounded by flowerbeds bursting with overgrown shrubs. Next to the house was a patio, with a wooden table and chairs, so badly weathered they looked on the point of collapse. Joe and his pretty girlfriend clearly hadn't spent much time outdoors since they moved here.

Katie went up to the back door, tried the handle – locked – and peered through the glass pane at the top. The kitchen was small as well, with hardly any room between the chairs and the worktop running down the side. A newspaper was folded on the table, and a pair of men's gloves sat beside it; Joe must have left in a hurry and forgotten them.

A crack at her feet made Katie jump. A large tabby emerged through a cat flap at the bottom of the door and wound itself around her ankles. Katie stroked it absently as she knelt and peered through the cat flap. Straight ahead, at the other end of the house, was the front door, with a handful of envelopes scattered on the floor below.

Sticking her hand through the cat flap, Katie reached up towards the door handle. Her arm was at the wrong angle, so she pushed the curious cat aside and lay down on the patio, forcing her shoulder against the door to get her arm higher. Her fingers found the handle, then the lock below. But it was empty.

Damn, where would they have put the key? She pulled out her arm and stood up again, brushing leaves and dirt from her jeans. The cat was looking at her.

'Good job you can't tell tales,' Katie said.

She moved to the left and cupped her hands to the glass of the kitchen window. Below her was the sink, crockery stacked inside it: mugs, bowls, plates – clearly not just from this morning's breakfast. To the right, she could see a section of work surface beyond the draining board, and in the middle of it, was a silver key. It had to be for the back door – it was the obvious place to leave it. She lay down on the ground again, putting her arm back through the cat flap. But there was no way she was going to reach the work surface.

'This is ridiculous!' she said to the cat, as she sat beside it on the damp ground. She'd have to give up and leave the letter. What was the worst that could happen? Joe would think she was strange, no doubt about that. But it was the fact that she'd sent it here at all that worried her now, the madness of following him home, then addressing a letter to him that had come through his own front door rather than landing on his desk at work. The girlfriend could report her for harassment, get the police involved. There was a lump in her throat and she could feel tears prickling at the edges of her eyes. None of this should have happened; she'd been so bloody stupid.

Pulling her phone out of her bag, she dialled a number.

'What is it?' said Monica. 'I'm really up against it this morning and it's hard to talk. Can't you just text me?'

'I'm sorry, I wanted to tell you that I can't get the letter,' Katie whispered – not sure if she was keeping her voice low to stop Monica raising hers, or because she had marched uninvited into someone's back garden in broad daylight and was sitting on their patio. 'The postman wouldn't give it to me, and he's put it through the door, so it's now inside the house and I can't get it.'

'God, what a nightmare.'

'I know. I can't believe this is happening. What am I going to do?'

'Look, hun, I feel for you, I really do,' Monica sounded distracted. 'But if you want to get it back, you'll have to wait for him to come home from work and ask for it. Either that, or break the bloody door down. Sorry, but I've got to go, I'm getting stared at by Godzilla, you know how nosy she is. Good job we don't work from home, otherwise she'd be going through my underwear drawer.'

The phone clicked and Monica's number disappeared from the screen.

Katie took deep breaths, trying to calm a racing heart, which didn't want to be calmed. Monica was right, those were her only options. But she had no intention of waiting for Joe and asking for the letter; she had to get it back herself.

Beside the fence was a pile of bricks. She pushed herself to her feet, went over and picked one up. The back door was new with an aluminium frame, and the glass panel at the top was double-glazed. However, the kitchen window was older: a wooden frame with normal glass in it. Not letting herself think about what she was doing, Katie took off her coat and wrapped the brick in it – she remembered seeing someone do this on television, to smother the sound. Taking a deep breath, she held the wrapped brick with both hands and swung it behind her head, before bringing it forward with as much force as she could.

The brick connected with the centre of the windowpane and there was a crump as the glass shattered, followed by a high-pitched tinkling as pieces showered the dirty bowls and plates in the sink. The hole wasn't large enough for Katie to put her arm through, so she pulled out a couple of shards that were hanging off the side of the frame, placing them carefully on the worktop.

Even with the coat around the brick, the crash had been loud. She looked around; what if a neighbour had heard the noise? But there was no movement from the houses on either side, no windows were thrown open, no dogs started barking. She reached through the broken glass, picked up the key and brought it out, her hand shaking so much it took her three attempts to slot it into the lock. Eventually it turned and the handle opened.

Katie moved through the kitchen and ran down the hall towards the front door. Stooping and picking up the letters, she flicked through them and gasped in relief as she found her own neat handwriting on the front of one. She dropped the others back onto the floor and folded her letter in half, sticking it in the pocket of her jeans. Turning back towards the kitchen, she couldn't resist stopping and looking through a half-open door to the right. A sitting room: neat and tidy, with a pair of matching cream sofas and a gas-effect fire beneath a wooden mantelpiece. The television in the corner was relatively small by modern standards – their own monster at home was twice the size.

Suddenly, the doorbell rang – three cascading chimes echoing down the hall.

'Jesus!' She ran back towards the kitchen. The back door was still open, and she rushed through it, stopping on the other side to pick up her bag and pull her coat off the brick she'd left lying on the ground.

The bell rang again and, as she turned, she could see the outline of a head through the opaque glass at the top of the front door.

'Hello?' a voice called faintly. 'Anyone in?'

To her horror, she heard a key being put into the lock. Walking back along the side of the house, she opened the gate quietly and stuck her head around the corner, in time to see someone disappearing through the front door.

Katie ran. Her heart hammering against her chest, her breath bursting from her mouth, she raced across the road. Clutching her bag and coat to her chest, she nearly tripped several times as she stumbled down the footpath. The library loomed up on her right. At the bottom, she glanced back over her shoulder, expecting to see someone thundering down after her. The path was empty.

She slowed to a brisk walk, panting, each breath searing in her chest. Fumbling to open the car door, she collapsed inside, shaking. As the seconds passed, her breathing slowed. Had she got away with it? She could see the entrance to the footpath; no one had come out. Even if someone did appear now, she was safely in her car, out of sight.

When she finally threw her bag on the passenger seat and put the keys in the ignition, she realised there was a yellow piece of paper in a plastic wrapper, flapping underneath her windscreen wiper. She'd got a bloody parking ticket.

16

M onica called just as Katie was pulling into the drive at
home. 'Sorry I couldn't talk earlier. Are you still there?
What's going on?'

Katie knew she was blushing and was glad her friend
couldn't see her face. 'It was awful, Mon. I've never been so
terrified.'

'What happened?'

For a second Katie considered lying. The more she thought
about what she'd done earlier, the more appalled she felt. But
this was Monica. She had never lied to Monica in her life and
now didn't feel like the time to start.

'I broke in.'

'Bloody hell. Seriously?'

'I smashed a kitchen window and unlocked the door.'

'You're kidding! I never thought you'd actually do it?'

'How else was I going to get the letter back?' said Katie
defensively. 'I know it's bad – I feel sick remembering it now.
But that letter was too personal, too direct. I shouldn't have
written it – I really don't know what I was thinking. I was just
desperate to get it back.'

'But smashing your way into someone's house…'

'Yes, yes – it was crazy and stupid…'

'And illegal.'

'Well, obviously illegal. I know that – I don't need you to tell me.'

Neither of them said anything for a few seconds; Katie could hear a clicking on the other end of the phone – it sounded as if Monica was tapping her pen against the desk.

Katie felt awful. Immediately after driving out of the car park, she'd been on a high – as if drunk: buzzing with a mixture of relief at having got away and elation at having retrieved the letter. On the drive home, while the adrenalin gradually worked its way through her system, she'd almost enjoyed the flashbacks playing out in her mind: the brick bundled inside her coat, the shards of glass in the kitchen sink, the pile of mail on the doormat at the end of the hallway. What she'd done had been reckless and scary – yet also bizarrely exhilarating. But now she was explaining the whole thing to someone else, it sounded indefensible.

Eventually Monica spoke again. 'At least you didn't get caught. I guess that's the main thing. Thank God. Honestly, Katie, this could all have gone so horribly wrong! So, what about the man of the moment – are you going to try and see him again?'

'I don't know. Yes. No, it's not like that, I told you. There's nothing going on.'

'But you'd like there to be something?'

'Well, yes. I mean, no. Not *something* like you're meaning it. Oh, I don't know, Mon. I don't really want to talk about it, to be honest. Especially now I know he's with that girl. He's spoken for, and I've got to be realistic and get over it.'

There was another pause. 'And you're spoken for too. You're married to Pete. Are you sure things are okay between the two of you?'

'Yes fine.' Katie hesitated. 'This is all just… me.'

17

K atie woke with a start, opening her eyes in the darkness and registering the sound of Pete snoring gently, inches away from her in the bed. She had no idea what time it was, but as the memory of what she'd done yesterday came flooding back, she knew she wouldn't be able to sleep again. How could she have been so stupid? Of course she'd been desperate to get the letter back, but smashing someone's window? God knows what Joe must have thought when he got back and saw the broken glass. Even if the neighbour had called to warn him, it would have been a shock to see the damage and realise someone had been inside his home.

She could still feel the weight of the brick wrapped inside her coat, hear the glass shattering around her hand. Monica was right, she'd been lucky not to get caught, but it was an appalling thing to have done.

Hours later, as she got ready for work and put boxes of cereal on the table for the girls' breakfast, remorse was beginning to give way to disappointment. The terror she'd felt in Coopers Lane was jostled out of her mind by thoughts of the man who would have had to sweep up shards of broken glass and go online to find someone to repair the window.

It was a relief Joe hadn't read the letter, but she still wanted him to know she was there; she was desperate to see him again, or just to hear his voice. But how could she make that happen? It was too soon to go back to the surgery – she'd have nothing new to discuss with him. She couldn't even arrange to coincidentally bump into him somewhere, because in order to find out where he was supposed to be, she'd have to follow him from home or work. So far, doing that had caused nothing but trouble.

When she walked into the office, an hour later, Duncan appeared in the doorway and asked how she was feeling.

'Fine thanks,' she replied, without thinking. The confusion on his face reminded her she was supposed to have been ill the day before. 'Awful cramps yesterday though,' she said, as she turned on her computer. 'Haven't had anything like that for ages…'

A pile of folders was sitting on the desk, but she couldn't concentrate on them. Instead, she googled her usual list of obsessions: Dr Joe Harvey; Joe Harvey medical advice; Joe Harvey 15 Coopers Lane. She wasn't sure why she kept looking him up like this, because she never unearthed anything new.

In the afternoon, while Fraser was out of the office at a training seminar, she decided to try a different tack, and logged on to a website listing details of people who'd recently bought properties in the local area. She didn't find any information about 15 Coopers Lane, so looked on the Electoral Register to see if she could find out who lived at numbers 14 and 16. It was likely that whoever had been at the front door was a neighbour who'd heard the glass breaking. Then she remembered the *Let* sign outside the house – Joe and that girl were only renting the place, so even this search wouldn't lead her anywhere.

She closed down the browser and sat back in her chair. The whole thing was hopeless, she was wasting time looking for information about this bloody man. What was the point doing background checks on him, when all she wanted was to see him, touch him, hold him, kiss him. She closed her eyes and imagined Joe standing over her, bending forward to put his lips on hers, his hand running down her neck and inside her blouse, cupping her breast, the weight of his body on top of her, pushing her back into the chair as his tongue crept into her mouth.

The telephone trilled on her desk and she leapt up.

'Have you got those sales figures for me, love?' asked Duncan, phoning from ten feet away. 'Quick as you can, there's a good girl.'

18

'Not bloody "Jingle Bells" again!' Katie said. 'Aren't you fed up with all this?'

With a fortnight to go until Christmas, the shops were full of tinsel, baubles and plastic holly. Everywhere she went, she heard sleigh bells ringing and the hits of Christmas Past blasting out through tinny speakers. The girl on the checkout in Sainsbury's, who was wearing a pair of velvet reindeer antlers, looked confused.

'I mean, having to wear those things,' said Katie, pointing at the girl's head. 'Isn't it driving you mad?'

'But we're getting into the Christmas spirit!'

'Bugger the Christmas spirit,' Katie muttered under her breath. She knew she was being a miserable cow, but didn't care. She'd slept fitfully again last night and had woken at 3am sticky with sweat and feeling as if someone had shot her body through with a flame thrower. She'd flung off the duvet and staggered out of bed, going to the window and throwing it open to get some air on her skin.

'What are you *doing?*' Pete had called. 'It's fucking freezing out there!'

He was right, and the sweat had already been starting to cool on her body, making her shiver, despite the fact that she was still burning up like a furnace. She'd fallen back into bed, wondering if she was coming down with something.

Thankfully she had felt all right this morning – albeit knackered and grumpy as hell. Now, she moodily crammed half a dozen items of shopping into a plastic bag as the girl put them through the checkout. They were running low on coffee in the office, and there hadn't been biscuits in the tin all week. There was no reason why she should be the one to get supplies, but in the last three years she hadn't seen Fraser or Duncan buy a single teabag. Both knew that, if they waited long enough, she'd eventually give in and restock what Duncan grandly referred to as 'the refreshment corner'.

'It is the season of goodwill after all,' the girl said, handing Katie her change. 'Most customers really like it.'

'Well, I don't,' said Katie, ignoring the checkout assistant's wounded look as she turned and marched towards the exit.

By the time she got to the car, she was feeling so guilty, she almost turned round and went back in to apologise. Poor girl: it wasn't her fault.

After getting into the car, Katie dropped her head onto the steering wheel. She was being totally unreasonable and hated herself for it, but knew her bad temper wasn't just due to tiredness and an overload of festive merriment. She'd been in a foul mood since her escape from Joe's garden, two days ago: she had shouted at the girls, ignored Pete and snapped at Fraser.

Yesterday she'd forgotten to fill out the paperwork for an order at work, and was forced to lie to Duncan and insist his original email hadn't come through. Last night she'd locked herself out of online banking when she forgot the password, and this morning had realised – too late – that they hadn't sent

Alan a birthday card. She was losing the plot and life was starting to feel out of control.

Katie knew the business with Joe was mostly to blame, and she was angry with herself for letting it take over her life. But on top of all the other crap, was grief: she still missed her mother, every single day. She missed her smile, and the physical warmth as she grasped Katie's hands between her own. She missed her sense of humour and the way she gently teased Anna when she was throwing a tantrum. She missed just knowing that her mother was there somewhere. She was amazed at how sad she still felt, all these weeks after losing her and, with Christmas looming, everything seemed so much worse.

Clara had loved Christmas; when Katie was a child, festivities started weeks beforehand and the house had been full of sounds and smells that brought back sharp memories when she came across them years later: the sappy scent of pine from logs stacked beside the fire, oranges pricked with cloves, the metallic tang of a spray that covered everything in synthetic snow. Even as an old lady, Clara's eyes had sparkled with excitement as she helped decorate the tree and for weeks she compiled lists, in her neat curly handwriting, of ideas for presents.

Katie still couldn't quite believe that, this year, there would be an empty chair at the lunch table. She didn't want to be maudlin, but it was so hard to snap out of it: there was a lump in the pit of her stomach, and a sense that everything was pressing down on her. To make things worse, she hadn't heard a word from the hospice. She had called once, but the rottweiler of a receptionist told her Mrs Rivers was extremely busy and would contact her in due course. Katie suspected her name was on an unofficial blacklist.

Then, with no warning at all, she had burst into tears in the kitchen the other night, while serving up supper.

'Poor Mummy,' Anna had said, as she loaded butter onto her mashed potato. 'I think you need a holiday.'

During the first few weeks after his mother-in-law's death, Pete had been supportive, but now it felt like he'd run out of sympathy. 'You need to pull yourself together,' he'd said, as Katie blew her nose at the supper table. 'Life goes on. Our lives *all* have to go on. This isn't just about you, Katie, you've got the rest of us to think about.'

He was right, but sometimes she missed her mother so much it felt like someone had carved out a hole in the pit of her stomach.

19

It had started to rain again by the time she left work, a persistent drizzle that wormed its way down the collar of her coat and left her chilled in the short time it took to walk across the car park. She started the engine and turned up the heating, even though it wouldn't throw out any warmth for a while.

As she drove along the main road, she saw the sign on the right for Coopers Lane. Just the sight of it sent adrenalin pumping around her body again. Joe must have had the kitchen window repaired by now. He and that girl would have discussed the break-in endlessly. Who did it? What were they after?

She flicked on her indicator and swung the car to the right and seconds later was driving round the turning circle at the top of Coopers Lane. She pulled over and peered across at number 15. She shouldn't be here, but no one would know she had anything to do with the break-in. It was mid-afternoon and the pavements were empty; there was still no sign of life behind any of the windows.

Mind you, she'd thought that before, then that neighbour

had appeared out of nowhere at the sound of breaking glass. Her pulse quickened as she looked at the gate beside the house. The *Let* sign had gone from the front lawn, but otherwise everything looked just as it had done two mornings ago, when she watched the postman put her letter through the front door.

She glanced at the clock on the dashboard: if she sat here much longer, she was going to be late picking up Anna. Back at the bottom of the hill, traffic was queuing in front of her on the main road, and Katie tapped her fingers on the steering wheel as she inched forward. She could already picture the scowl on her younger daughter's face if she was kept waiting outside the school gates: the way she would stomp up to the car and pull open the door, bursting with resentment.

A car slowed down and she accelerated into the gap, cutting across into the other lane. Suddenly, there was a thump and she was jolted forward, the seat belt digging into her shoulder. For a second, she didn't understand what had happened: there was a white car at an angle in front of her. Where had it come from?

'Bloody hell!' She undid the belt and opened the door. Her smashed headlight and bumper on the passenger side were embedded in the front wing of a white Fiat.

'What the hell were you doing?' she asked the woman who was getting out.

'I thought that man was letting me in?'

'He was letting me out!'

'I didn't see you turning…'

'Look what you've done to my car, this is going to cost a fortune!' Katie was shouting now. 'What were you thinking?' She turned away from the damage and looked at the other driver, finding herself face to face with the pretty young woman with auburn hair; the one who'd come out of the supermarket with Joe's arm around her, laughing at whatever he'd been saying. In the space of a second, she realised the woman had been turning into Coopers Lane – where she probably lived in the house Katie had recently broken into.

'It's you!' she said before she could stop herself. 'I mean, it's you… you who should have stopped. It's your fault, all of this is your fault…'

The woman looked distraught: her eyes wide, her mouth open. 'I'm sorry but I didn't see you move forward. I was signalling to turn in. That other car had stopped. I thought that was why, to let me in…'

'No!' yelled Katie. 'He'd stopped to let me out! I'm in a hurry, I'm late picking up my daughter and I've been queuing to get through here, so why would anyone let you cut in, when it isn't your right of way?'

'All right, love, calm down,' said a man's voice behind her. 'There's not much damage done and no one's hurt, so let's be reasonable about this.'

'I will not calm down!' There was a vein throbbing in Katie's neck. She walked around to the other side of her car and inspected the damage from a different angle; it was even worse. When she turned back, the young woman looked about to cry. 'People like you shouldn't be on the road,' Katie shouted. 'You've just cost me hundreds of pounds – which I'm sure I won't be able to get on insurance, because you can never claim anything on insurance – and my husband will be furious!'

The man now came up and stood facing Katie. A car stuck on their side of the road was sounding its horn, while drivers on the other side were slowing down to see what had happened.

'Look this isn't worth getting worked up about,' said the man, putting out a placating hand.

'Not for you, it's not your car!' Katie shouted. She paused for breath and saw the woman's cheeks were wet with tears. 'Oh, that's right, start crying to get some sympathy, make out like you're the victim!' She swatted away the man's hand and stepped towards the other car. 'How would you like it if I did something stupid to your car? Something that would cost you money and ruin your day? Because that's what you've done to me, you've damaged my car and cost me a fortune and you've made me late and my daughter will be standing on her own outside school, probably in tears too.'

She stepped up to the Fiat and grabbed the rear windscreen wiper, pulling it towards her with more force than she'd intended. There was a sharp crack and she realised the wiper had come off; that she was holding it in her hand.

The man and the young woman both stared at her. He looked shocked, she looked bewildered – and a little scared.

Shit, thought Katie. *Shit, shit, shit.*

20

The school secretary was sympathetic when Katie got through to her on the phone. 'Don't worry,' she said. 'We'll keep Anna here until you arrive.'

The policeman was less amiable. 'It is a criminal offence to wilfully damage a vehicle, madam. Whatever the circumstances of the accident itself – and that's for your insurers to decide – the fact that you caused deliberate damage to that lady's vehicle after the event is the issue that needs to be dealt with. It's up to her whether or not to press charges, but I must warn you it's a possibility.'

Katie felt physically sick. She stood on the pavement, wrapping her coat around her to keep out the drizzle. Her car had been moved to the side of the road, and a line of traffic drove past slowly: drivers craning their necks, relishing the fact that someone else had drawn the losing ticket in this afternoon's going home lottery.

'I'm so sorry,' she said. 'I got angry, because she'd cut in front of me and there was damage to my car. It was stupid and I overreacted. I just lost it.'

'That's how these incidents often start,' said the policeman, writing notes on a pad. 'But road rage is an offence punishable by law, and all road users need to remain even-tempered in the face of provocation.'

Her name was Rachel Aston; Katie had overheard it when she was speaking to the police officer. A little later they had to exchange details, in order to contact insurance companies, and she found herself with a piece of paper giving Rachel's name, phone number and address. Even though she'd suspected she lived at 15 Coopers Lane, it was a shock to see it written down.

But she was relieved to find out she wasn't married to Joe; otherwise, her name would be Harvey too. Although thinking about it, that didn't have to be the case – a lot of women kept their maiden names nowadays. Looking back, Katie sometimes wondered why she had so willingly divested herself of the name she'd been born with – Katie Jenkins had more of a ring to it than Katie Johnson. But at the time she'd been pleased to take Pete's surname, relishing their new start together and the fact that everyone would now know them as a unit.

As she stood confirming her details with the police officer, she wrapped her fingers around the piece of paper, tucked safely into her coat pocket. She couldn't believe what she'd done; she was shocked and embarrassed at how vehemently she'd reacted.

'Like I said, it will be up to Miss Aston whether she presses charges,' the policeman was saying. 'Our team will follow up with her shortly and Mr Rowland, who witnessed the incident, will be making a statement at the station.' He ripped a sheet off his notepad and slid it into the front of a plastic folder. 'Are you all right to drive home? You're lucky the bulb is still working on your headlight; it's just the glass that went, so you're not illegal.'

'Yes, I'm fine,' said Katie, her voice catching. 'Sorry.'

Driving towards Anna's school she took deep breaths, willing herself not to cry. She desperately wanted to see Pete and tell him what had happened. She pictured herself admitting how upset and scared she'd been, him putting his arms around her and holding her tight, reassuring her everything would be fine.

But she'd behaved so badly: how could she even begin to explain all this? Maybe she shouldn't say anything at all. But when he saw the car in daylight he'd notice the damage to the front, so she'd have to tell him about the crash. She could leave it at that, though. There was no point mentioning what had happened with the windscreen wiper.

She thought about Rachel letting herself into the little house in Coopers Lane, imagined her kicking off her shoes, throwing her keys onto the hall table, possibly ringing Joe to tell him what had happened. She could picture the concern on his face when he got back from work, the protective way he would hug his girlfriend, tell her how dreadful the whole thing was.

Maybe he'd persuade her not to press charges? After all, the damage to Rachel's car wasn't too great, so what was the point of going through a court case just because some crazy middle-aged woman had lost the plot and pulled off her windscreen wiper? It was a reassuring thought. He would know legal proceedings could end up being prolonged and stressful, so he'd encourage Rachel not to put herself through any more angst.

The prospect of him stepping in, made Katie feel calmer. Perhaps she should write to Rachel, apologising and explaining that this wasn't like her, that she was under a lot of pressure? She could say she was having a breakdown – which didn't actually feel so far from the truth at the moment. Or Pete could be the one having a breakdown, which was affecting the whole family.

Maybe not. No more letters.

By the time Katie arrived to collect Anna, she felt calmer;

things would sort themselves out, they always did. Her youngest daughter was sitting in the school office, scowling.

'You are the most embarrassing mother in the world,' she hissed, as they walked out of the gates. 'I had to sit in Mrs Ford's chair because they wouldn't let me wait outside on my own, and it stank. Mrs Ford has smelly armpits and her chair smells as well, and I hate you for being late.'

When they got home, Suky was lying on her stomach on the floor of her bedroom, scrolling on her phone. She didn't look up when Katie came in. 'I need my PE kit washed, and I didn't have any clean shirts this morning.'

'Oh right,' said Katie. 'Well, hello to you too. You could always put your uniform in the machine yourself?'

Suky didn't reply.

Katie leant against the doorframe. 'How was your day?'

Suky shrugged.

'Mine was pretty awful, as it happens,' Katie said. 'I had an accident – I drove into someone who pulled in front of me.' She waited for a reaction, but Suky still didn't look up. 'Lots of damage to the car,' she continued. 'Which will cost hundreds of pounds to fix, and I've probably got whiplash or something. But don't worry, I'll carry on administering to your every need. Once I've washed your PE kit I'll come back and pick up the rest of the dirty washing from your bedroom floor, shall I? Then maybe I'll make your bed and take all the mugs and glasses downstairs. Oh, and while I'm here, find your homework and I'll do that as well – save you getting into trouble at school tomorrow.'

Suky didn't take her eyes off the screen.

Katie sighed and went out of the room, catching a faint 'Whatever' when she was halfway down the stairs.

How stupid to have hoped for sympathy from Suky; that was never going to happen. But she needed to tell someone about the accident. The funny thing was, even at this age, the person she invariably longed for in times of crisis, was her mother. There was something particularly comforting about being hugged and reassured by someone who knew her faults and foibles, yet still loved her unconditionally.

She started peeling potatoes for supper and wondered what the early evening routine would be like at 15 Coopers Lane. Joe would probably do some of the cooking, he seemed like the kind of man who did his fair share around the house. She couldn't remember the last time Pete had cooked in the evening; admittedly he got home later than she did, but it sometimes felt as if he thought meals prepared themselves automatically, in the same way that the hoover ran itself up and down the stairs, the laundry basket piled its own contents into the washing machine and the dishwasher took full advantage of its self-loading setting.

By the time he got home, Katie had worked up a head of resentful steam. She heard the front door slam and made a point of not turning around when he walked into the kitchen.

'What happened to the car?' he asked wearily, as he put his bag onto the kitchen table.

'Some stupid woman drove into me. It wasn't my fault but I'll probably end up having to pay for it. But I'm fine, nothing broken – although you're obviously more worried about the car than me.' She slammed a saucepan down on the hob and walked past him to the fridge.

Now Pete was here, in front of her, she didn't feel the same desperation to tell him what had happened. She was still on the point of bursting into tears, but she also felt aggrieved and hard done by. She wanted someone to hold her tightly and comfort her, but that someone wasn't Pete.

'No need to jump down my throat,' he said. 'If I hadn't asked, you'd have said I didn't care! Why do you bloody women have to be so complicated?'

When they first started going out together – so many years

ago now that she could only remember intermittent flashes of things they'd done and places they'd been – part of the attraction had been that they seemed to fit together so well. They liked the same music, laughed at the same jokes, drank the same wine. He was even-tempered and friendly; spending time with him was fun and effortless. Even Monica, who hadn't warmed to every boyfriend Katie had introduced her to, had called him 'that lovely Pete'. And he *was* lovely: kind, thoughtful, funny, hardworking.

All these years later, she still loved him more than anyone else in her world. But it was inevitable, wasn't it, that they'd both changed over the years? They certainly weren't as close as they could be. He always seemed tired and short tempered nowadays, often distracted – but he probably thought the same about her. They bickered more than ever, and sometimes she felt they were sparking off each other, like spoilt children, each desperate to outdo the other. Surely that wasn't surprising, when they'd been together so long?

He was still standing in the middle of the kitchen, looking at her expectantly.

'Sorry, Pete,' she whispered, going across to him and burying her face in his shoulder. 'I don't know what's the matter with me.' She felt his arms fold around her and relaxed into the warmth of them. 'Just a shitty day,' she said, her voice muffled against the wool of his jumper.

21

Katie turned her head one way and then the other, looking at herself in the mirror in the downstairs loo. It was shorter than she'd intended, but a nice cut. In fact, quite possibly the best haircut she'd had in years. She felt a frisson of excitement as she studied her reflection.

'It's the new me,' she'd declared to Suky, as her daughter marched into the kitchen and threw her schoolbag onto the floor. 'What do you think?'

Suky's eyebrows moved fractionally upwards and she put her head on one side. 'Not bad,' she said grudgingly.

'Praise indeed,' said Katie cheerfully. 'I'm glad you like it. I think it makes me look younger.'

Suky was already walking out of the kitchen with a fistful of biscuits. 'I didn't *actually* say I liked it,' she said, over her shoulder.

Pete was more appreciative when he got home. 'Looks great,' he smiled. 'Suits you. Did you go somewhere new?'

'Yes, I tried that salon in Overton, the one where they offer the spa treatments.'

He looked concerned. 'God, I bet that was expensive? Katie, you know we can't afford that sort of thing.'

'No, not at all,' she'd lied. 'They had an offer on, so it didn't cost much.'

Now she came out of the loo and went back into the kitchen to start cooking. As she opened the fridge, the doorbell rang.

'I'll get it!' she sang out, picking up a tea towel from the worktop and drying her hands as she walked down the hall. She flung open the door and the smile froze on her face. Two police officers were standing outside. The man was tall and dark haired, carrying a clipboard; a slight, blonde woman stood beside him, a disconnected voice crackling from the radio clipped to her waist. Both were wearing high-vis jackets and she could see the reflective stripes of their police car, behind them on the street.

'Mrs Johnson?'

'Yes,' she said, her voice catching slightly. 'That's me.'

'We're following up on an incident you were involved in yesterday afternoon,' said the policeman. 'May we come inside?'

Katie stared at him in horror; she couldn't think what to say. She wanted to slam the door in their faces, run into the kitchen and pretend she hadn't heard the bell. Where were the girls? Where was Pete? They were all going to hear this. She realised she hadn't answered the question, but could do nothing except step aside and let them in.

The policewoman closed the door gently behind her and the three of them stood awkwardly in the hallway.

'I'm Sergeant Wilkinson, this is Sergeant Brady,' he nodded in the direction of his companion. 'The incident happened at 3.15pm. I understand you were in collision with another vehicle at the junction of Abberley Road and Coopers Lane, and that an altercation took place?'

'Yes. Well, I suppose that's what happened,' Katie cast an anxious glance at the sitting room door, behind which the television blared.

'We have statements from the other driver involved, Miss Aston, and from an independent witness,' he looked down at the clipboard in his hand. 'It appears this was an unprovoked attack and criminal damage was caused to Miss Aston's car.'

'It wasn't unprovoked – or that is, yes it was, I suppose. But she cut in front of me, which was a stupid thing to do at that junction because it's so busy and everyone has to queue for a long time to get up to the traffic lights...' Katie heard herself gabbling. 'I know I shouldn't have got so worked up, and I'm sorry.'

'Hang on a minute, Mrs Johnson,' said the policeman. 'We're here to tell you that Miss Aston has come back to us and said she does not wish to press charges. The officer dealing with the case also feels that a prosecution would not be in the public interest in this instance.'

Relief flooded through her like a wave of warm water. 'Oh, that's fantastic, thank you so much,' she said. 'I can't tell you how grateful I am.'

'In a situation like this, where the victim doesn't wish to press charges, we will either issue a caution or suggest a local resolution,' he continued. 'A caution is not a criminal conviction, but it would go on record you admitted the offence. The alternative is a community resolution, which means we ask Miss Aston what she would like to do in terms of moving forward from this incident.'

Katie's brain was trying to keep up. 'What does that mean?'

'We've spoken to Miss Aston and she has agreed to accept a resolution whereby you pay compensation for the damage to her car and send her a written apology for your behaviour at the scene,' he said. 'These are standard proposals in cases like this. If you're happy, then we won't need to take the matter any further.'

'So, you're saying I have to pay for the windscreen wiper?'

He looked down at the clipboard. 'That, and the other damage to her vehicle, I believe. Yes, it says here: bodywork repairs to driver's door and front wing.'

'That's not fair!' said Katie, before she could stop herself. 'I mean she was the one who drove in front of me, so she caused the damage, but I'll end up paying for her car to be repaired as well as mine?'

'You might be able to talk to your insurance company about that, Mrs Johnson, but we're dealing primarily with your behaviour at the scene of the crime, rather than the collision. It is that overly aggressive attitude and the damage you caused subsequently which meant the matter had to be referred to the police, otherwise it would have remained as something that could be sorted out between the two drivers and their insurers. These are the terms of the resolution we're proposing. It's up to you if you choose to accept them.'

The policewoman – who Katie now realised was very young, possibly only a few years older than Suky – was staring at her intently. Maybe this was one of her first outings on the job? She would always remember tonight's visit and the road-raging woman who said it wasn't her fault.

'I'll pay for the wiper to be replaced, of course I will, that was totally my fault. But if I accept a caution, does that mean I don't have to pay for the damage to her car? Because I'd rather do that. Seeing as how I wasn't to blame for the crash.'

The police officer looked pained. 'To be honest, Mrs Johnson, if you accept Miss Aston's offer it will save you both a lot of upset and get this sorted quickly. You just need to sign this to confirm you're happy to accept a community resolution, then the officer dealing with the incident will contact you once he's got an idea from Miss Aston of the costs involved.' He turned the board to face her, offering the use of a Biro. 'Have a read, then sign at the bottom and that will take us onto the next stage. They're usually very successful, these resolutions, save a lot of police time and money, with a better outcome for all concerned. Miss Aston doesn't want to have to face you again in a court of law over this unfortunate situation – any more than you want to find yourself there.'

Katie stared at the clipboard. 'But that means she wins!' she said. 'She gets away with driving badly and causing an accident and damaging my car – and I get all the blame. I'm sorry but this isn't fair. I'm not signing anything. Give me a caution then. What is a caution anyway? Are you going to arrest me?'

The officer sighed and turned the clipboard round again. 'No, madam. In order to accept a caution, you have to admit responsibility for your actions and we officially caution you down at the station. It will remain on your records for a predetermined period.'

'Right, then that's what I'll do. You can caution me,' announced Katie, folding her arms across her chest. 'I did get cross and I admit I broke her stupid wiper – completely by accident – but there was provocation, and I'm not the only one in the wrong, so I'm not going to pay for the rest of the damage.'

She could hear herself sounding like a spoilt child, but this whole thing was ridiculous! Rachel Aston had driven in front of her, and clearly hadn't been looking where she was going. Katie watched as the officer unclipped a piece of paper from his board, folded it up and handed it across to her. He was doing everything frustratingly slowly. The television was still booming in the sitting room, but at any moment she expected Anna to come bursting out through the door in search of something to eat.

'Okay, Mrs Johnson, if that's your decision we have to

respect it,' he said. 'Officially you need to report to the police station in town within the next forty-eight hours to receive your caution – although, because it's Friday now, it will be fine to wait until Monday morning. If you change your mind in the meantime, it's not too late to go with the resolution. Have a read of this, and do think about it.'

She reached past him to open the front door and stood back while the two of them went outside, overwhelmed with relief that they were leaving. She shut the door and peered through the glass window to one side, willing the fluorescent figures to walk more quickly to their car.

'Thank God,' she said out loud as the vehicle pulled away from the kerb and headed off into the darkness.

She turned around and saw Pete standing at the other end of the hallway. 'What's going on, Katie?'

She stared at him for a couple of seconds, wondering what to say, her guilt compounded by the bewilderment and concern on his face. 'It's nothing,' she said, as she walked past him into the kitchen. 'Just a misunderstanding.'

'What kind of misunderstanding?'

'Nothing to worry about, I'll sort it out.'

'Is it to do with that woman who drove into you?'

'Yes,' she said, throwing dishes and mugs into the sink and running the tap. 'She's now saying it was my fault and suggesting I apologise to her and pay for the damage to her car, which is ridiculous.'

'But if it's not your fault – if she drove into you – why don't you just report it to the insurance company and let them deal with it? And why are the police involved anyway? Was she hurt?'

'Nobody was hurt. Things got out of hand, that's all. I got cross with her, because she'd pushed in front of me, and she didn't seem to think she'd done anything wrong.'

'What do you mean, you got cross?'

'Pete, please just leave it,' she turned off the tap and swung round to face him. 'It's no big deal and I don't want to talk about it. Stop interrogating me.' She walked out of the kitchen, marching upstairs to their bedroom and slamming the door so hard that the shade shook on the bedside lamp. Poor Pete, he hadn't deserved that. She must go and apologise. She slumped onto the edge of the bed. What was the matter with her? She remembered grabbing the windscreen wiper on that white Fiat and winced as she heard again the snap as it came off in her hand. What had she been thinking?

She closed her eyes and took some deep breaths. There were so many things going on in her life which felt slightly – or massively – out of her control: missing her mum, waiting for a response from the hospice, not pulling her weight at work, worrying that her marriage was in crisis, trying to keep things together at home. Plus, of course, there was Joe. But despite all that, it wasn't like her to be this short tempered and emotional, over-reacting to everything, losing her rag.

Opening her eyes again, she caught sight of her hair in the mirror above the dressing table. She ran her fingers through it, combing out the fringe and smoothing it with the palm of her hand. It really did hang well at the back.

Thinking about it, her new hairstyle looked rather like Rachel Aston's.

22

The next day, Suky announced she was going to a party in a field by the canal. Katie wasn't happy about it. 'How can you have a party in the middle of nowhere?' she said. 'This sounds like a bad idea. What do you think, Pete?'

He looked up, distracted.

'About this party?'

'I'm sure it will be fine,' he said, looking back at a rugby match report.

'Thanks, Dad!' Suky kissed him on the cheek, throwing Katie a victorious grin.

'But, Pete, she's only fifteen and...'

He sighed and flicked over the page. 'Katie, stop going on. She's a sensible girl, she's allowed to have some fun. Don't be such a killjoy.'

She glared at him; why did she always end up playing Bad Cop nowadays? But this battle clearly wasn't worth fighting. 'Okay, Suky,' she said. 'But be careful, and don't drink from any open bottles. Watch who you speak to, and don't wander off with anyone you don't know...'

Suky had already walked out of the kitchen.

Four hours later, Katie was waiting for her in the car when her phone pinged:

How are you? Sorted out the car yet? x

When she'd called Monica, to tell her about the crash, she hadn't mentioned how angry she'd been, or that she'd snapped off the windscreen wiper – she also left out the visit from the police. The whole thing was so embarrassing. But what Katie did want to share, was the discovery that Rachel wasn't Mrs Harvey. That was the only good thing to have come out of the events of the last two days, and the more she thought about it, the more it cheered her.

'What was she like?' Monica had wanted to know.

'Pretty. Young too, probably late twenties – a bit younger than him I'd guess.'

'That's such a weird coincidence,' said Monica. 'You could have driven into thousands of people, but you just happened to drive into her.'

'Not really,' said Katie. 'I was coming out of the road she lives in, so that narrows it down a bit. Anyway, I didn't drive into her – if anything, it was the other way round.'

'Why were you coming out of her road?' asked Monica. 'Katie, what are you playing at?'

'Nothing! I just happened to be there. Well, I was going past... anyway, Mon, I've got to go – there's someone at the door. Speak to you later.' She had put her mobile down on the worktop, feeling miserable. She couldn't justify her behaviour – even to Monica.

Now, Suky finally slid into the passenger seat; she was wearing shorts and a crop top, a strip of naked belly exposed to the elements.

'It's December!' said Katie. 'You'll freeze!'

Even in the dark, she saw Suky roll her eyes. 'Mum, can you just start the car? You're going to make me late.'

Rattling down a lane beside the canal, they joined a convey

of cars driven by anxious parents, who – coming to a dead end – disgorged their teenage passengers in front of a five-bar gate, before turning around and heading back towards town.

'Are you sure this is the right place?' asked Katie, straining to see beyond the spread of her headlights.

'Of course – why else would everyone be stopping here? Look, there's Beth.' Suky got out and slammed the door, something in her hand clanking as she did so. As the car headlights picked her out, climbing over the gate, Katie saw she was carrying a plastic bag wrapped round something that looked suspiciously like a bottle. Suky was far too young to get served anywhere so, until half an hour ago, that bottle had undoubtedly been tucked away in their drinks cupboard in the sitting room.

'You little madam,' she said, under her breath. As she watched her daughter jumping over the gate and disappearing into the darkness, Katie realised they'd been played – again. How Suky must have laughed at her stupid, gullible parents.

Driving back through town, she saw the sign for Coopers Lane ahead on the right and, without thinking, signalled and turned into it. At this time of night, the road was quiet, although many more cars were parked in driveways than during the day. She drove slowly around the turning circle at the top then started back down the hill again, pulling into the side. She hadn't chosen the spot specifically but realised it was ideal: there were no streetlights nearby and the car was in darkness, save for the reflected flashing of white Christmas lights, draped around a tree in a garden further down. By angling her rear-view mirror, she could see the front door and sitting room window of number 15, up the hill behind her. Light shone around the edges of drawn curtains in the room in which Joe and Rachel were probably sitting right now.

She leant back against the headrest and closed her eyes. What the hell was she doing here? Back home, Pete and Anna would be watching the best that Saturday night TV could offer. They'd been caught up in the terror of *Doctor Who* when Katie and Suky left the house, Anna burying herself against Pete's shoulder, screaming that she couldn't bear to watch, but peeking at the screen through parted fingers. By the time Katie got back, something less traumatic would be on, probably involving minor celebrities learning to dance or sing. The two of them would be sitting on the sofa, a bowl of crisps balanced between them, a bottle of beer in Pete's hand, a can of lemonade in Anna's.

Katie felt a pang of something, she wasn't sure what. It almost felt like homesickness – which was crazy because she was only a few miles away. But part of her longed to be sharing the sofa with them, sipping at a glass of wine, laughing at the unkind comments of the presenters and the pitiful attempts of the B-listers to show they were creative and talented.

But she also wanted to be here. Well, not exactly here. She wanted to be thirty feet away: curled up on one of those cream sofas in the sitting room of number 15, with her feet tucked beneath her, watching the blue flames lick upwards in the gas fire. She wanted to be running her forefinger slowly, gently down the soft skin of Joe's cheek, feeling the rasp of his stubble as her finger moved towards his neck, onto his chest, slipping inside his collar.

Maybe that was what Rachel was doing now. She screwed her eyes shut to block out thoughts of the pretty girl who might be, at this minute, unbuttoning Joe's shirt, and pushing her beautiful young hands across his chest. Katie imagined her slim body moving towards Joe on the cream sofa, her bobbed auburn hair falling across his face as she knelt on top of him.

Enough! For fuck's sake, what was she doing? She started the engine and accelerated away from the kerb, heading back down the hill to the main road. Why had she come here? What had she hoped to achieve by sitting in the car and staring at their house? Misery dashed her mood like a sudden rain shower. She couldn't figure out what was going on in her own head: she loved Pete, of course she did – although things weren't great at the moment, but she *did* still love him. Yet here she was, obsessing about a man she hardly knew. In the darkness it was even easier to picture Joe's face. She just wanted to see him again – not to talk to him or even get near enough to touch him. Merely seeing him from a distance would help her get through the next few days.

Pulling out onto the main road, she relived that moment from the other day: the crunch as her car plunged into the front of the white Fiat. She would never again be able to pass this junction without remembering the afternoon on which Rachel Aston had turned, a second too soon, and their worlds had collided with such intensity.

23

Pushing open the opaque glass doors of the police station, Katie's stomach churned. She'd never been in here before, although she must have driven past hundreds of times. The waiting room had a row of chairs along one side and a square window, like a serving hatch, straight ahead. She could hear a telephone ringing, along with the clatter of fingers on keyboards; when she got to the window, she saw a room on the other side, with a handful of people sitting at desks.

A uniformed officer came to the window.

'I'm here for a caution,' she said. 'Katie Johnson.'

He looked down at a list on the desk in front of him. 'Can't find anything here. Who did you speak to?'

'Sergeant Wilkins, I think his name was, or Wilkinson?'

'Take a seat.' The officer stepped away from the window and Katie turned back to the row of plastic chairs. On the opposite wall was a poster reminding people to watch out for pickpockets, showing cartoon fingers about to pluck a mobile phone from someone's bag. *Don't play into their hands!* read the caption along the bottom. Of all the places to remind people to look after their possessions, this was possibly the one least in need of a poster.

She had rung Duncan earlier, to say she'd be late into work, ignoring the irritation in his voice. 'I'll be there by ten,' she'd promised. Now she sat nervously, knowing she would probably be later than that, and trying to quell her frustration at being kept waiting.

Eventually a security bolt was released on the door next to her and it swung outwards.

'Mrs Johnson?' a short, grey-haired officer propped open the door with one arm. 'This way please.'

She followed him down a corridor, their footsteps clicking on the linoleum floor, then up some stairs and through a door on the left. The room was windowless, with a fluorescent ceiling light flagging up stains on the brown carpet and ring marks on the desk, evidence of the countless half-drunk cups of coffee that had worn away the polish over the years. A long time ago the walls may have been white, but they were now so dirty they looked cream and in places the paint was peeling away, revealing patches of plaster underneath. The officer signalled to a chair and Katie slid into it, clutching her bag. Her irritation had scuttled away while she was walking up here. Now her hands were shaking and there was a lump in the back of her throat, making it hard to swallow.

'Right, Mrs Johnson, I understand you were involved in an incident the other day?' he looked at her over glasses that had slid down his nose.

'Yes, but it wasn't really my…' she started to explain.

'There's no need to go into the detail again,' he said, scribbling on a form on the desk. 'Sergeant Wilkinson has already discussed the incident with you and filed an official report. You are here to accept a caution, so for the purposes of this visit I need you to understand what's involved. You're not being arrested or charged with any crime, but you have admitted your guilt and refused to accept a resolution offered by the victim, so as an alternative I'm now going to issue you with a caution. It's not a criminal conviction, but it will go on your record and remain there for a period of up to five years. If you appear in a court of law in connection with any crime during that period, the caution will be taken into account as part of your previous record. Do you understand that?'

'Yes,' whispered Katie.

'Very well,' he continued, looking up at her. 'I am issuing you with a caution following an incident that took place at the junction of Abberley Road and Coopers Lane, at 3.15pm on 10th December. You have accepted that you wilfully caused criminal damage to a vehicle belonging to Miss Rachel Aston. You do not have to say anything, but anything you do say may be given in evidence should this caution become relevant in a court of law. Do you understand the reason for this caution and the fact that, now it has been issued, it will remain on your record?'

Katie nodded, then realised he was waiting for her to speak. 'Yes.' She was holding back tears, terrified by the starkness of the room.

'I'm signing the caution sheet to confirm what we've done today and you also need to sign, to show you agree and understand.' He passed the form across the table and Katie grasped the pen tightly, trying to stop her fingers trembling for long enough to write her name.

'Here's a copy for you, and obviously we have copies for our records,' he said, looking up at her and smiling. 'That's it. All done.'

She smiled, but it felt more like a grimace, because she was trying not to cry. Back outside the station, she let the tears slip down her cheeks as she walked up the road, not caring that a woman stared curiously as she went past. She reached the car and threw herself into the driver's seat, sobbing.

The whole thing was so unfair. Bloody Rachel Aston, with her pretty face and beautifully cut hair. She must feel smug and secure in her world: loved by her partner, undoubtedly comforted and supported by friends, family and work colleagues. They would have been horrified at what happened to her – the way she'd been shouted at and attacked by a stranger who drove into her car then stood in the road screaming at her. Katie could imagine how she told the story; she could see Rachel twisting her hands together, explaining to Joe how frightened she'd been, how vulnerable she'd felt. *Poor darling Rachel*, he would have said. *What an awful thing to happen.*

There was nobody to comfort her in the same way – although that was her own fault. She still hadn't told Pete about this, although it had been on her mind all weekend, and she'd nearly started the conversation several times. But the longer she left it, the harder it felt to admit what had happened. Why was she being so pig-headed? He'd be shocked at first, and probably tell her she'd been an idiot – which was true. But after that he was bound to offer sympathy and comfort. So why wasn't she letting him? It was possibly pride: not wanting to admit she'd behaved badly and was now being punished for it. But she was also scared of admitting just how far from normality this had all drifted.

She sat in the car until her tears dried up. Then she stayed for a few minutes longer, waiting for the blotchy marks to fade around her eyes. When she looked presentable again, she started the engine and drove across town to Triple A. As she turned in through the gates, it occurred to her that one reason for not involving Pete, was because it would feel as if she was letting him into this private new world of hers, sharing something she'd much rather keep to herself. He would only need to hear the basics – and he'd never know there was a connection between Rachel and Joe. But it still felt like opening a door which led into a secret room, and letting him peek over her shoulder at the treasures she had hidden in there.

They were rivals, these two men – although neither of them was aware of the other's existence.

24

Katie was wide awake at 5am, her brain buzzing with all the things she had to get done during the day ahead. Most urgent was creating something for the cake sale at Anna's school that afternoon, which she'd been too tired to think about last night.

A flyer had been sent home in the children's book bags, reminding them what fun they could have, getting creative in the kitchen while helping raise money for the school. But few of them ever baked a biscuit or whipped up a Victoria sponge. It was their mothers who, burdened by middle-class guilt and a desire to outdo each other, slaved over cupcakes and coloured icing, producing beautifully decorated treats, which would be sold for pennies to go towards new playground equipment.

Katie rolled out of bed, put on her dressing gown and padded down to the kitchen, pulling packets of flour and sugar out of the cupboard. After weighing ingredients into a bowl, she turned on the radio and sang along to Ed Sheeran; she kept getting the words wrong – thank God Suky wasn't around to laugh at her. As she ran the whisk around the edge of the bowl, catching up stray dustings of flour, Rachel Aston's face popped into her head. Would she be awake yet? Katie wondered if Rachel had heard from her insurance company – she'd had a depressing conversation with her own insurer yesterday.

'If you went into her vehicle, it suggests you were the one with the ability to brake,' the girl had explained. 'Which means it's likely this claim will involve a settlement against you.'

Katie had hung up feeling nearly as angry as when she ripped off the white Fiat's windscreen wiper.

While the sweet smell of baking cupcakes filled the house, she went to get everyone up, which was like having to raise the living dead. Most mornings, Katie ended up hoarse from yelling up the stairs to check the girls were awake.

Pete left earlier than usual; he had a meeting at school with Sara, the head, to discuss his plans for moving the Damien situation forward. Over the last few days, he'd spent hours tapping away at the computer and poring over books, scribbling notes on scraps of paper. When he was immersed in a work crisis like this, it felt as if there was no space inside his head for the rest of them. Katie moved forward to give him a kiss, but he was distracted, searching for something in his coat pocket, and went out of the door without looking back.

'Have a good day,' she called. 'Good luck!'

The local newspaper had been pushed halfway through the letter box and Suky tugged it out and slumped at the kitchen table, flicking through the pages as she ate her cereal.

'Oh, my God,' she said suddenly.

'Oh, my goodness,' corrected Katie.

'You're in the bloody paper!'

'Don't swear, Suky. What do you mean I'm in the paper?'

Her daughter was staring at her, horrified. She looked down at the page then back up again, stabbing it with her finger. 'Here. Is this you? It has to be – you said you'd crashed into somebody. I can't believe it. How could you?'

Katie went to the table and looked over Suky's shoulder. It was a short piece, just a few lines. She skimmed through them, then sat down heavily on a chair. 'Bloody hell.'

'Is it true?'

'Well sort of. There was an accident, but it wasn't my fault and I have no idea how they got hold of this. It's outrageous. Shouldn't they have asked me before printing something?' She could feel her face flushing under Suky's glare and looked back down at the article, re-reading the six lines of print. 'I mean this bit here – "Mrs Johnson threatened Miss Aston and damaged her car, attacking her with a windscreen wiper" – that is not how it happened, because I didn't mean to damage her stupid car. I certainly didn't attack her! And that headline – "Road Rage Woman attacks Innocent Driver" – it's ridiculous!'

Suky was leaning back in her chair, arms folded across her chest. 'I can't believe you've done this,' she said, shaking her head. 'What's the matter with you? That poor woman. Why did you threaten her?'

'I didn't!' said Katie. 'This is all a load of rubbish. She drove into me – well, I sort of drove into her – and we both got out and I may have shouted a bit, but that's all. Apart from breaking her wiper, but I didn't mean to do that, I was just showing her how easily things can get broken if you're not careful…' She trailed off. Her daughter had got up and left the kitchen. Katie ran after her. 'Suky, I'm trying to explain. Please don't walk out while I'm talking to you.'

The girl was halfway up the stairs. 'You've got a screw loose,' she hissed at Katie through the banisters. 'You're mad and I can't believe you're my mother – I want to die of embarrassment!' She stamped up to the landing.

'Oh great, so this is all about you?' Katie shouted up after her. 'Never mind how I'm feeling – you're just worried about what your friends will think? Well too bad, Suky. Let them think what they want!'

'They'll think my mother is insane!' yelled Suky. 'I can't bear being in this house with you. As soon as I'm sixteen, I'm going to leave home.'

Katie walked into the kitchen and noisily collected dirty bowls, glasses and cutlery from the kitchen table before slamming them on the worktop. Why had she yelled at Suky? It wasn't going to help. But how typical that her daughter would believe some rubbish made up by a journalist, rather than her own mother's account of what had happened. She picked up the paper and was about to throw it in the recycling bin outside the back door when she paused. Ripping out the page containing the news item, she folded it up and put it into the side pocket of her handbag, where it slipped neatly beside the well-thumbed article about Joe Harvey.

Anna came into the kitchen. 'Suky says you're mad and you've nearly killed a woman,' she said. 'Can I have a Penguin in my lunchbox today because it's almost the end of term?'

25

Katie didn't always find time to look through the local paper, but it seemed as if she was the only person in the entire county who didn't read it from cover to cover. When she got to the office, Fraser was almost hopping up and down with glee.

'Good morning, Road Rage Woman!' he said, as she walked through the door. 'Did you manage to drive here without getting into a punch-up along the way? Maybe when the lights turned red too quickly, or someone stepped onto a zebra crossing in front of you?'

'Fuck off, Fraser,' said Katie, walking to her desk.

'Temper, temper!' he said. 'I always knew you were highly strung, but I never had you down for a violent woman. I must remember to park my car as far away from yours as possible. Is it just windscreen wipers you pull off, or are you tempted by wing mirrors and door handles as well?'

'Just fuck right off,' she said, turning on her computer and sitting down heavily in her chair. She wanted to cry, but wouldn't give him the satisfaction.

Within ten minutes her mobile had rung three times. The

first two calls were from Brenda, and she pushed the button to reject them. The third was an unknown mobile number and she answered it without thinking.

'Katie, was that you in the paper today? I thought, there can't be that many Katie Johnsons, so I was pretty sure it was you. But then I said to myself, would she really get herself involved in something like that?' It was Fiona: chair of the school PTA and mother of Anna's friend Daisy. 'Henry was a victim of road rage once and it shook him up for weeks afterwards. There was this awful man who started shouting and swearing at him, and he had the girls in the car too, which made it even worse. I said to him afterwards, you should have been the bigger man, Henry, you should have just walked away. But he couldn't actually move because the man had him pinned to the side of the car and was jabbing him in the stomach.'

'Listen, Fiona, I can't talk right now...'

'I'm sure you must have been provoked, because I can't imagine you being unpleasant to a stranger. I know how stressful life is, we working mums have so many demands on our time – it's like we're on a big hamster wheel that's spinning round and we're constantly trying to get off...'

'Got to go, Fiona, bye!' Katie threw the phone back onto the desk. That was stupid, she should have been more contrite and explained the paper had got the story wrong. But right at this moment she couldn't be bothered. Fraser was sitting at his desk smirking, then started humming to himself. He saw her glaring across at him. 'What's the matter? Great song that, by Catatonia. It's called "Road Rage".'

There was silence for a second and then he started humming again. 'Da da da da da da nah nah nah... That one's called "Kung Fu Fighting" – know it, Katie?' Shortly afterwards he moved onto the theme from *Rocky*.

It was a long day.

Duncan was at a trade fair in Birmingham, so Katie left ten minutes early. Fraser would tell him, but she didn't care. For once she was slightly early for school. Having found a parking space, she wandered back towards the gates, hugging her coat around her and looking out for a friendly face.

There weren't any. Two of the mothers from Anna's class were standing nearby, heads together in animated chatter, but as they saw her approaching, they glared and turned their backs.

Oh God, the article. Katie stood beside the railings. None of the other parents were meeting her eye. A small group stood by the noticeboard, and she saw one woman look over, see her, then turn back to the others. One by one they turned and stared, their faces displaying a mixture of curiosity and animosity. Maybe she was being paranoid? They could be talking about anything. But she knew they were talking about her. Christine, whose son was also in Anna's year, looked at her and shook her head – whether in disbelief or disapproval Katie wasn't sure – before turning her back.

Even if just a couple of parents had read the item in the local paper, it was obvious all of them would soon know about it. Katie had naively thought she'd be able to put her side of the story if someone brought it up, explain the misunderstanding and the fact that she was the innocent victim of a careless driver. She would shake her head at the laziness of the journalist, who'd misrepresented the facts. She had even imagined herself getting sympathy for it all: she was another victim of press intrusion. *Poor you*, the school gate mothers would chorus; *what an awful thing to have to put up with.*

But if they were going to be chorusing anything, it wasn't sympathy. And it would be accompanied by whispering, finger pointing and accusatory glares.

Katie didn't want to stay standing beside the gates on her own, but couldn't think what else to do. She wondered if she should brazen it out, go up to one of the groups and introduce the subject herself. But there was a prickling behind her eyes, and she didn't think she could carry it off without bursting into tears. So, she stood, hands plunged into the pockets of her coat, staring through the railings at the deserted playground. When the bell finally rang, Katie realised she was holding her breath, and had to take several gulps of air before she could breathe normally again.

Anna was never among the first out – she invariably had to find a lost lunchbox or a missing glove, or just stand chatting to a friend in the cloakroom. Today was no exception and by the time she wandered across the playground, dragging her bag along the ground behind her, Katie felt as if she had been stared at and discussed by every adult outside school, and that her violent and unprovoked behaviour may as well have been announced by loudspeaker.

When they got into the car she burst into tears, fumbling to put the key in the ignition as she wiped her eyes with the back of her free hand.

Anna turned and stared from the passenger seat. 'What's the matter?'

'Nothing, don't worry,' Katie tried to smile. 'I'm not feeling very well.' She started the engine and pulled out into the road.

'I think you need a hug, Mummy,' said Anna, pulling her lunchbox from her bag and taking out a satsuma, pulling off bits of the peel and dropping them onto the floor of the car. 'Maybe Daddy will give you one later. I don't think Suky will, because she thinks you're mad. I'll give you one in a bit, but I've got to eat this first.'

$\sim$

As they walked through the front door the landline was ringing, and Katie eventually found a handset wedged down the back of the sofa.

'Hello?'

'Ah, Katie, there you are!' Brenda sounded plaintive. 'I have been trying to call you all day. Did you get my messages?'

'No, I've been at work.'

'I've left several. Is this you in the paper? The one who attacked that woman in broad daylight? We saw it this morning and thought it couldn't be you, Alan was sure you would have mentioned it, but I said you'd hardly go around admitting to people that you'd been in a fight.'

'Yes Brenda, it was me,' said Katie wearily, collapsing onto the sofa. 'But the paper got it wrong, that isn't what happened, I didn't…'

'I knew it!' said Brenda.

'Hang on. As I was saying, the paper got it wrong, I didn't attack her, she drove into me, and then her windscreen wiper got broken, but it was her fault for not driving carefully…'

'You did break the wiper!' exclaimed Brenda. 'What on earth possessed you? You can get treatment you know, for this sort of thing – has anyone suggested anger management?'

Katie sighed and moved the phone away from her ear. Even holding it on her lap she could still hear Brenda's voice, reedy and shrill, rattling through the speaker. She lifted the handset back up. 'Sorry, Brenda, I have to go. I know it sounds awful, but it really wasn't such a big deal and I have no idea how it got into the paper. Please don't give me a hard time about it, I'm feeling bad enough as it is. I'll call you soon.'

She ended the call and threw the phone down on the sofa beside her. Thank goodness her own mother wasn't around to hear about all this. Clara would have been so disappointed in the daughter who'd lost her rag and damaged someone else's car. Through the sitting room window, she watched her elderly neighbours wander slowly past on their way back from the shops. They stopped outside the gate and looked up at the house, faces tilted towards each other, discussing something with animation. Then they shook their heads and shuffled on towards their own gate.

Katie buried her face in her hands. Jesus, how had she got into this mess? She was a social pariah.

26

'I'm going to be late home,' said Pete. 'Sara has asked me to talk to the governors about Damien. The little bugger kicked me in morning registration and I had to drag him out of the classroom. The meeting starts at seven so I'll grab a sandwich and catch up with some work here.'

'Oh, but can't you come home first to…?'

'Got to go, Katie. Hectic day here.'

He ended the call and Katie put her mobile back down on the kitchen table. She'd been gearing herself up to tell Pete about the newspaper article when he got back this afternoon. It would mean he'd find out about Rachel Aston's bloody windscreen wiper, but he was going to hear about that from someone anyway, and she'd rather it came from her. The more she'd thought about the conversation, the more she persuaded herself that it would be fine: he'd listen, give her a hug and reassure her everything would be all right. They'd been bad tempered with each other recently, mutually irritated by everything the other did or said. But it was just a phase, and they'd work through it. Pete was a kind man; she was lucky to have him.

But now Sara had ruined everything and he wouldn't be back for hours. Her black mood overshadowed her again like a cloud. The last time she'd bumped into Sara, had been at the school fete, back in July. 'Nice to see you, Katie,' she'd said, arms crossed, smile perfunctory. 'Everything all right with the family?'

Katie had smiled back, aware Sara couldn't remember the girls' names. She'd joined the school a year earlier, a forceful head teacher, younger than most of her staff and full of grit after several years at an inner-city primary. Katie found her terrifying. They'd stood chatting for a minute, before Sara got called away and Katie breathed a sigh of relief.

'Bloody Sara,' she muttered now, knowing it was too early, but pouring herself a glass of wine. She sat in front of the television, unable to concentrate on the game shows that seemed to be on every channel. Sod it, she couldn't just sit here. She knocked back the rest of the wine and tossed the remote onto the sofa.

'Suky, I'm going out!' she called up the stairs.

No reply.

'I won't be long – can you keep an eye on Anna for me?'

Silence.

'I don't need her to keep an eye on me,' shouted Anna, from her bedroom. 'I can keep an eye on myself.'

There was still a lot of traffic on the roads, so it took half an hour to get there, but when Katie parked on the side of the road it was still earlier than when she'd stopped in exactly this spot last Saturday night. She sat back in her seat and pulled out her phone, pretending to look at it whenever someone walked past.

A middle-aged woman came into view, walking briskly up the opposite pavement and, a few steps behind her, to Katie's horror, was Rachel Aston, a handbag over one shoulder and a bag of shopping in each hand. Sliding down, Katie leant towards the passenger seat, pretending to look for something. Why had she not expected this? She suddenly realised Rachel might recognise the car, but the young woman passed by with her eyes fixed on the pavement in front of her.

Sitting up again, Katie watched her in the rear-view mirror, as the top of Rachel's head moved along the path and stopped outside number 15. She couldn't tell whether she'd knocked or whether Joe had seen her arrive, but the door opened, throwing a shaft of yellow light into the darkness, and she caught a glimpse of the side of his face and his hair as he stepped back to let her in. She strained to see more, but two seconds later the door shut again.

She stayed for another twenty minutes, unsure why she was still sitting there, but not wanting to be anywhere else. Rachel must have been walking because her car was in for repair. Katie had received an email notification that an insurance claim had been made against her. She printed it out, but reading it made her so angry, she crumpled up the piece of paper and threw it in the bin.

The temperature had dropped and Katie's feet and fingers were freezing. She'd just decided to head home, when a beam of light flashed in the mirror, and she saw Joe and Rachel coming out of their front door. Her heart pounding, she turned to watch them cross the road towards the footpath down to the library.

She got out of the car and walked up the hill. She was wearing her work shoes, with heels that clicked noisily; why hadn't she put on something more sensible?

By the time she got to the top, they'd disappeared; she ran across to the entrance to the footpath and was just in time to see them near the bottom, approaching the streetlight in the car park. Joe had his arm flung around Rachel's shoulder and their heads were tilted towards each other. They went through the car park towards town. Katie followed, as quickly as she dared, keeping behind the parked cars.

As they went along the high street, they stopped to look in the window of an art gallery, and Katie moved back into a doorway, blood pounding across her temples, her mouth dry: she must look so suspicious.

At the end of the road, they turned the corner and, as she ran to catch up, her heel caught on the edge of the pavement and the shoe twisted off her foot, sending a stab of pain through her ankle. 'Damn,' she said, bending to retrieve the shoe from the gutter. 'Bloody thing.'

When she reached the corner, they were nowhere to be seen. There were a couple of restaurants further along the street, and a big pub at the far end; she could look through the windows, but what was the point? Even if she found out where they were, all she could do was hang around outside then follow them home again. Dispirited and cold, she hobbled up to Coopers Lane, her ankle throbbing.

When she got home, Pete's car was in the drive. Coming through the front door, she could hear his voice in the kitchen, the familiar rumble as he spoke, followed by a laugh. She thought someone else might be there, but when she opened the door, he was on the phone. As he turned around and saw her, his eyes widened slightly. 'Anyway, let's discuss it tomorrow,' he said. 'See you then.'

'Who was that?' she asked, going to fill the kettle.

'Who was what?'

'On the phone, just now!'

'Oh, Sara. Yup, just debriefing.'

'How did it go?'

'Grim,' he replied. 'They're worried about adhering to our anti-bullying policies. But I'm not going to be forced to do things I don't feel are right. I'm following procedure but I also need to think about Damien. Sara is worried about the other parents.'

Katie wasn't interested in Damien. She didn't want to think about the impact the little bugger was having on Hope Primary School. 'Oh dear,' she said, opening the cupboard and looking at the empty crisp and biscuit wrappers the girls had thrust back onto the shelves, after eating the contents.

'Where've you been this evening?'

'Just out with Monica,' said Katie. 'She wanted a chat, problems with work, usual stuff. We just had a glass of wine and a bowl of pasta.'

Pete was looking at her strangely. It flitted through her mind that he might not believe her, but she smiled at him as she took a couple of mugs out of the cupboard. He had no reason to think she was lying.

27

The overhead lights went off and a ripple of anticipation ran around the school hall. The music began, quietly at first then gathering pace as it increased in volume. It was awful. Either the piano was out of tune or the boy hammering away on it wasn't hitting the right keys. Possibly both. Two girls with violins were sawing bows in unison, but didn't seem to be playing the same piece. At least all three of them were drowning out the girl on the trumpet.

In the semi-darkness, dozens of children dressed as sheep began to file into the hall, tripping over their own feet, pushing each other forward in their excitement. Then came a gaggle of elves, clapped loudly by the proud parents who'd made their tinsel headdresses.

Anna was one of the three Wise Men but came on too early, which meant she had to fill time by adopting a succession of thoughtful poses while a scene change took place behind her. She then delivered her lines so loudly that the set wobbled. Katie and Pete both gave her a thumbs-up as she exited stage right. She grinned and waved, knocking over an elf.

Afterwards they stood outside in the playground, smiling

and exchanging pleasantries with other parents, most of them already comparing the videos they'd taken on their iPhones. Mrs Hall, Anna's teacher, strode past. 'Your daughter was marvellous!' she bellowed. 'Anna, good girl! That was fantastic projection. We'll see you on stage at the National in years to come!'

Anna frowned. 'The National what? Anyway, we all went wrong, loads of times. Lily forgot her lines completely and Harry kept farting in the donkey costume – did you hear him? I could smell it where I was standing, it was disgusting.'

Having staged more than his fair share of primary school nativity plays, Pete knew how much effort had gone into the production, and how much store parents would set by it. 'Helen, what a talented son you have!' he congratulated one mother.

'Mr Lewis!' He tapped the Reception teacher on the arm. 'An excellent production, well done.'

Coming from anyone else, the words might have sounded patronising. But Pete clearly meant them, and Katie could see how his praise was appreciated by those receiving it. She watched as the other parents swarmed around him, the men shaking his hand, the women leaning in towards him, some planting a kiss on his cheek. Was it her imagination, or were many of them not making the same effort to acknowledge her? There were certainly people here this evening who hadn't greeted her as warmly as they might have done a few days ago.

To Katie's relief, Pete hadn't mentioned the road rage, so he clearly hadn't come across a copy of the local paper. She'd begged the girls not to tell him about it. 'Dad's having a bad time at work at the moment, and doesn't need any extra stress,' she said to Suky. 'So please don't mention this.'

'Aren't you going to tell him about the crash?' she'd asked.

'I have. I told him when it happened.'

'Yes, but you didn't tell him about the road rage bit, did you? You didn't tell him you'd damaged that woman's car?'

'I will tell him. Just not at the moment.'

Suky clearly hadn't believed her but, so far, she'd kept quiet. Katie had half expected Pete to pick up a copy of the paper at school, and she knew she couldn't keep it from him for long. Even if no one else thought to pass on the details, Brenda was bound to see it as her duty. For the last few days Katie had made sure she got to the landline first whenever it rang.

Now here she and Pete were, standing side by side, laughing as the music teacher told them about a fraught dress rehearsal involving a missing violin and a group of crying elves. To all intents and purposes, she hoped they seemed like a normal, happy family – smiling, chatting and keeping up appearances. But it all felt like a sham: her teenage daughter hated her, her husband had his mind on everything except home, she was falling to pieces whenever she was reminded about her dead mother, and – worse than any and all of that – even standing here in the school playground, with her hand on Anna's shoulder, she couldn't stop thinking about another woman's lover.

They were home by 7pm and, as Katie pushed a whining Anna towards the stairs to get ready for bed, she turned to Pete. 'I've got to pop back to work and finish off some paperwork for Duncan. Do you mind? I'll only be an hour or so.'

'He's never asked you to do that before?' Pete was surprised.

'No, I think there's a bit of a crisis,' she said. 'Anna, have a shower, then straight into bed, do you hear me?'

Twenty minutes later, she arrived at her usual parking spot on Coopers Lane, turned off the engine and sat, watching people drift back up the hill towards their homes. Why had she lied to Pete again? There was no point coming back here, but she didn't want to be anywhere else.

There was no sign of Rachel this evening, and no lights were on at number 15. They might both be working late, or maybe they'd gone out straight from work? The thought depressed her: she imagined them meeting in a bar, throwing coats over the back of their chairs: one bottle of wine, two glasses.

She saw herself sitting opposite him, not Rachel. Those blue eyes staring intently into hers, his hand reaching across the table to grasp her own, the little crow's feet running across his cheeks as he laughed at a joke she'd made. It would be so wonderful to be out together, to sit across a table from each other and behave like a normal couple. They would talk about their day, and he'd listen as she relayed Fraser's latest outrageous comments, and tell her what a saint she was to put up with him. He'd discuss what was happening at the surgery – without breaking rules about patient confidentiality of course. But there were bound to be awkward colleagues, problems with the administration system, patients who were regulars in the waiting room despite having little wrong with them.

'You're a good listener,' she imagined him saying. 'I can tell you anything.'

A knock on the window made her jump and shriek.

'Who are you? What are you up to?'

She fumbled for the switch to lower the window but it wouldn't work without the engine on, so she found the handle and opened the door instead. 'Sorry?'

'I said what are you up to, sitting here like this?'

An elderly woman was peering at her through the darkness, her face illuminated by the light from inside the car, casting shadows up her forehead.

'I'm not doing anything,' said Katie. 'I'm just waiting for someone.'

'I've seen you before. This is a private road you know, there's no reason for you to be sitting here in your car every evening. I'm going to call the police; we don't like strangers spying on us. What are you up to?'

Katie felt sick. 'I'm not up to anything,' she said. 'There's no law against me being here. I'm not doing any harm, I'm just waiting.'

'You could be planning to murder us in our beds – or burgle us! Working out what time we all get home, seeing whose house is empty.'

'I'm not!' said Katie, realising that was exactly what she appeared to be doing. 'Look I'm leaving now, okay? There's no need to call anyone or make a fuss – it's a free country.'

'I've written down your registration number,' said the woman. 'You'd better not come back here again.'

Katie had been fumbling for the keys, and her fingers suddenly skimmed over them in the well beside the gear stick. 'Okay, I'm leaving, keep your hair on,' she said angrily. 'This is ridiculous, you don't own the road.' She put the key in the ignition, started the engine and slammed the door shut and pulled away. In the mirror she saw the woman standing in the road, staring after her.

As she headed back out of town, a police car streaked past in the opposite direction, its flashing light creating blue streaks on a nearby bus shelter. Her pulse raced at the sight. She took a deep breath; it was fine, the police car was on its way to an emergency, not heading at high speed to Coopers Lane – even if that woman had dialled 999, saying there was a murderer sitting outside her house in a Renault Clio.

28

___

'I still haven't found those shoes for Suky,' said Katie. 'And I've no idea what to get for your dad.' After two hours of Christmas shopping in the rain, they were tired, soaked and fed up. The list Katie had made earlier that morning was now smudged and illegible, but even if she'd been able to read it, she knew she could only have ticked off a few of the items.

Sitting in a chair by the steamed-up window in Costa, she stared out at the puddles on the pavement, moodily stirring the contents of her mug. They both drank their coffee strong and white, nothing fancy. But the girl behind the counter, wearing her branded baseball cap at an angle, had talked them into trying the festive specials. Now Pete was sitting in front of a frothing toffee pecan latte with whipped cream, while Katie's drink tasted like sugared milk, although it was supposed to contain crushed almonds and cinnamon.

'I don't know why we always leave Christmas shopping until the last minute, and end up panicking like this,' she said. 'It's so busy you have to queue for ages and everything is overpriced. I bet they even increase car park charges in

December.' She knew she was being grumpy and hated herself for it.

Pete was staring gloomily into his mug of festive caffeine and didn't reply.

Yesterday – the last day of term – he'd been summoned to another meeting with Sara and Geoff, the chair of governors. It hadn't gone well. 'They're under pressure from the parents to do something,' he'd said, when he got back. 'I know Sara will suspend Damien next term, if his behaviour doesn't improve.'

Katie had wanted to be sympathetic, but her mind was on other things, going over the fight they'd had the previous evening.

'I've had a letter from St Bernard's,' she'd said, holding out a piece of paper.

'Who?' Pete glanced up.

'The hospice!'

'Oh right, yes. What do they say?'

'Nothing, that's what they say. Absolutely nothing. Mrs Rivers has investigated my concerns and is reassured that her staff acted appropriately.'

Pete had been leaning down, pulling a packet of cheese out of the fridge. He shrugged. 'Well, that's that then.'

'How can they have "acted appropriately" when they weren't where they should have been? Their neglect led to Mum's fall, and I know the fall contributed to her death.'

'Katie, you can't prove that...'

'Even if I can't prove it, medically, I know it's true. I was with her for the last few days. She went downhill so quickly. This letter is fobbing me off. Mrs Rivers is trying to cover it up. She's hoping I'll go away and forget about it.'

Pete had sighed, taken the letter and skim-read it. 'She's using very neutral language,' he pointed out. 'She hasn't used the word complaint anywhere, or allegation. Nothing like that.

It's all very low-key. They're not trying to get one over on you, Katie; they're just responding to what you said. You're being paranoid.'

Furious he didn't understand why she was so upset, Katie had stormed out of the kitchen. Later that evening, both tired and stressed, they had argued loudly and angrily. It had started with the usual domestic bickering – Katie complaining about the mess in the hall, Pete accusing her of nagging – and had escalated into a full-blown row about the fact that neither of them felt the other was pulling their weight. They had both said things they knew they would regret afterwards.

'What's the matter with you?' he'd snapped. 'It's like living with a stranger at the moment. You're bad tempered and critical and all you do is shout at the girls.'

'Well, you're not a little ray of sunshine yourself,' she retorted. 'I'm fed up with hearing about Damien McCrory and what's happening at school. There are other things that matter more in our lives, Pete!'

'That's rich coming from you! Sometimes I think you're using Clara's death as an excuse, Katie. But you need to pull yourself together and get over it. Elderly parents get ill and die, that's what happens. It's a bloody fact of life. You're not the only person to have ever lost a mother. To be honest, I'm fed up with coming back to your miserable face every night, I've got enough on my plate without worrying about what I've done wrong this time.'

They had gone to bed still not speaking, and at breakfast this morning Anna had looked from one to the other with interest. 'Are you sure you're not getting a divorce now?' she asked, into the silence.

'No of course not,' Katie said.

'You can if you want,' said Anna. 'It's okay, I don't mind. On *Newsround* they said you can get divorced online.'

The planned shopping trip – now desperately overdue with

only a few days left until Christmas – had gone ahead anyway, although they sat in silence during the drive there. They were speaking again now, but it felt awkward. Their eyes didn't meet properly as they sat across from each other with their coffees.

'We could get your dad a bottle of whisky,' she said, pushing a wad of receipts into her purse. 'Though I'm pretty sure we did that last year. Or maybe a book? I need to keep looking for those shoes Suky wants, and I ought to get something for the Hendersons and Mrs Dreyfus.'

Pete's phone pinged and, looking down, they both saw Monica's name appear on the screen.

'Why is Mon texting you?' asked Katie.

Pete sat back in his chair. 'If you have to know, it's about your Christmas present,' he said, picking up the phone and clearing the screen. 'She's been asking me about something she wants to buy you.'

Katie immediately felt bad. 'Oh, I see, sorry. I just thought…'

'What did you think, Katie? Honestly, I wish you'd stop jumping down my throat about every little thing.'

They sat in silence for a few seconds before Pete announced he needed to buy a present for his friend Andy. The café was packed, and as soon as they got up from the table, another couple pushed forward and grabbed the chairs.

Katie wandered in and out of shops, irritated by the themed music, the slow-moving crowds and her own lack of inspiration. She wished she could buy a Christmas present for Joe – something so special that no one else would think to get it for him. It would have to be a gift that would last, nothing cheap or flippant. She would sit opposite him as he unwrapped it, watching his face, waiting for his reaction – anticipating that moment when he'd look up at her, his eyes full of love and appreciation.

She caught sight of herself in a mirror and was pleased at

what she saw. She had been back to the expensive salon in Overton to have highlights, and the colour suited her. She was also trying a new eye shadow.

'I'm looking dowdy,' she'd said to Monica. 'I think women get to my age and let themselves go, they stop caring or making any effort.'

'Mid-life crisis,' said Monica. 'You're hurtling towards fifty and can't face what's happening.'

'I'm nowhere near fifty! Anyway, what's wrong with wanting to take care of myself? And why is it fine for you to get your hair done and wear short skirts and lipstick, but not for me to do the same? That's double standards.'

Monica had laughed. 'Lighten up, Katie, you're taking life very seriously suddenly. For all I care you can strip naked, hang baubles from your nipples and dance in the square outside the town hall. Just make sure the baubles don't clash with your fancy eye shadow.'

The conversation had left Katie feeling deflated. How could Monica understand what it felt like to be a dumpy, middle-aged mother of two self-centred girls? Many men had drifted in and out of Monica's life over the years, but none had secured themselves a permanent place there. Now in her early forties, with no children and no understanding of the restrictions of family life, she was selfish in the unintentional way some childless people can be. How could clever, successful Monica – whose years of uninterrupted sleep had left her skin glowing and unwrinkled – understand Katie's sense of panic that life was passing her by and no one was giving her a second glance?

Standing in a queue in Boots, Katie kicked her wire basket along the floor in front of her and wondered if she was just tired. She still tossed and turned for what seemed like hours most nights, dragging the duvet irritably towards her when Pete seemed to have more than his share, watching the luminous numbers change on the digital alarm clock, waiting for dawn to creep below the curtains. There had also been a few more occasions when it felt as if her body was being consumed by fire – mostly at night, but once when she was sitting in the office. 'What's the matter with you?' Fraser had asked. 'You've got bright red and you're sweating!'

'I'm fine!' she'd said, pushing her chair back from the desk and pulling off her jumper. 'It's just warm in here. Do you mind if I open a window?'

'Yes, I do mind!' said Fraser.

Duncan had wandered out of his office, his hands jingling the change in his pockets. 'Bit of a hot flush?' he asked. 'Sue burns up like a bloody bonfire.'

Katie had glared at them both and turned back to her computer, ignoring the trickle of sweat dripping down her forehead into her left eye. She supposed – even though she didn't want to admit it even to herself – that this was a hot flush, but she was damned if she was going to get into a conversation about hormones with these two.

The queue in Boots moved slowly forward and she kicked the wire basket a few more inches along the floor. It wasn't just how she was feeling physically, though. The pressure of lying to Pete was also getting her down. She wasn't sure why she'd felt drawn back to the house in Coopers Lane, or what she'd been hoping to achieve by her nocturnal visits. She certainly hadn't enjoyed sitting on her own in the car, the cold night air seeping into her bones, the minutes passing so slowly that each one felt like an hour. But being able to park near Joe's home, and sit in the dark knowing he was just feet away, had been reassuring. Although she couldn't physically be with him, she could be close to him, and that had almost been enough.

But now she didn't dare go back. It was unlikely that woman had taken down her number plate – or called the police. Even if she had, they had more important things to deal with. But if she'd been trying to frighten Katie, it had worked: she'd been on edge since it happened. Angry too, because there could be no more evenings spent in Coopers Lane. Now that had been taken away from her, she would have to find another way to satisfy her craving.

29

'So,' he said brightly. 'How have things been going?'

Katie smiled and leant forward in the chair. 'Not bad. But I've still got loads of aches and pains, and I'm not sleeping well.'

She had wondered how to play this. She didn't want to sound as if she was feeling better – then there would be no point making further appointments with him. But on the other hand, she didn't want to look or sound too ill. She had spent a long time on her make-up when she left work, balancing a small mirror on the dashboard and reapplying eyeliner and mascara that had faded since this morning, and adding lipstick – which she only usually wore when she and Pete went out.

'I get breathless, every now and then, and I'm exhausted most of the time.' That bit was true. By early evening she felt wiped out, even though she'd done nothing more energetic than sit at a desk and drive a car.

Joe leant across and picked up her hand, the shock of his touch causing her heart to flip. 'Let's just check your pulse again.' He put two fingers against the underside of her wrist, holding them there while he looked at the second hand on his watch.

She suspected everything would be racing – although what she was mostly feeling at this moment was relief. Just minutes ago, when she was sitting in the waiting room, Katie had realised there was a chance Joe might put two and two together.

He and Rachel would have talked about the accident; even if he hadn't read the report in the paper, his girlfriend might have mentioned the name of the crazy woman who had driven into her car, then separated it from its rear wiper. She froze in her chair in the waiting room, holding her breath. Why hadn't she thought of this before? Maybe she ought to get up and leave? But she couldn't make her legs move. The prospect of seeing Joe again had been the only thing keeping her going over the last few days; she had been longing for this second appointment, excited by the prospect of being in the surgery, just feet away from him. But she was suddenly shocked at the risk she was taking. What would she say if he came right out and asked if she was the woman who'd assaulted his girlfriend?

She had grabbed her bag, willing herself to get up and leave. But then he was calling her name: 'Katharine Johnson?'

She'd stood up slowly, hardly able to breathe with fear. But, as she began to walk towards him, she knew it was all right. He was smiling, and held out an arm to shepherd her along the corridor. He didn't know. Thank God, he had no idea. The name was different, she suddenly realised. She had been Katie in the newspaper story; Katie was the name she'd given the police and written down on the piece of paper she handed to Rachel. But here, at the Pelham Green Medical Practice, she was Katharine – because that was the name on her health records – so he hadn't made the connection.

Sitting beside him now, in his consulting room, she tried to keep her hand from shaking as he took her pulse.

'Let's do your blood pressure while we're at it,' he said, wrapping a length of material around the top of her arm and connecting it to a machine that silently filled the cuff with air to the point where she felt her arm might burst, before it slowly began to deflate and digital readings registered on the screen.

Katie found herself studying the skin on his forearms and the backs of his hands. He was still slightly tanned, even though it was December. Maybe he'd been away for a late holiday with Rachel – who probably looked sensational in a bikini. Katie's buoyant mood began to evaporate: she didn't want to think about Rachel; she wouldn't allow that woman to worm her way into this moment.

'Right, your BP is slightly high and your heart rate is still raised too,' he began to type on the computer keyboard. As his fingers drummed against the keys, she imagined them running up and down her body; the mere thought of his soft touch sending her weak with desire.

'...else going on in your life?'

'Sorry?' She snapped her attention back to him. 'I didn't quite...'

'I just wondered whether there was anything else going on, at the moment. Anything that might have been causing you undue stress?' He had turned his chair towards her. 'Are things okay at home?'

She nodded. 'Everything's fine.' Then suddenly the words were coming out of her mouth before she even knew she was saying them. 'I lost my mother.'

His expression changed immediately, his head was tilted slightly to one side, his eyes narrowing slightly, his eyebrows pulled down in concentration. 'Oh, I'm sorry to hear that. Was it unexpected?'

She tried to speak, but suddenly realised she couldn't. There was a lump in her throat and her eyes were filling with tears. 'She... no, she had cancer. But it wasn't... that is, I didn't think she was going to die.' The words sounded so stupid and she could feel herself blushing. 'Not that soon,' she added, in a whisper.

Suddenly, he was rolling his chair forward and passing her a box of tissues. She tried to smile, but her mouth was trembling and it turned into a scowl. 'Sorry,' she said, shaking her head angrily as she pulled a tissue from the box.

'Mrs Johnson, you've got nothing to apologise for,' he said. 'You've suffered a bereavement, and that's always a shock – even when you've had time to adjust to the fact that a loved one is seriously ill.'

She nodded, swiping at her eyes with the tissue.

'We all deal with these things in different ways,' he was saying. 'And this has been an awful time for you. But sometimes we try too hard to keep going and be brave for the sake of everyone else around us. The temptation is to carry on and be superhuman! But you need to let yourself grieve properly for your mother – you're allowed to do that. It's perfectly understandable if you're having trouble coming to terms with what happened.'

He reached forward and rested his hand on her forearm, giving it a gentle squeeze. Katie caught her breath as she stared down at it; through the sleeve of her shirt, the gentle pressure of his fingers was warm and her arm tingled beneath his touch. Then the moment was over, and his hand was drawing away again as he turned back to his computer.

'I don't think your symptoms are anything to worry about,' he was saying, starting to tap at the keyboard. 'I think it's highly likely that the way you're feeling is a result of the stress of what you've been going through recently – possibly accentuated by peri-menopausal changes. But because of the raised heart rate and blood pressure, I'd like to take some bloods. It's probably unnecessary, but I want to make sure we check you out thoroughly, if you're happy with that?'

She nodded. 'Yes, of course.'

'Roll up your sleeve, whichever arm you want.'

She fumbled with the button on the sleeve of her shirt and pushed it up, exposing flesh that looked pale beside his healthy forearm.

At the back of the desk, Joe's mobile phone started to flash. It was on silent, but they both saw the screen light up with a photograph and incoming call symbol. He glanced at it, then looked back at the computer. For several more seconds, Rachel's pretty face smiled out of the phone as her call went unanswered, then Katie's shoulders dropped with relief when the screen went blank. Why was she phoning Joe at work? She must know he couldn't take personal calls when he was with patients.

He had produced a couple of plastic tubes and a syringe, and wrapped a thick elastic strap around her upper arm, tapping the exposed skin below it with his finger. 'Need to find a vein,' he smiled. 'Just relax.'

It was impossible: relaxing wasn't an option. Blood was racing round her body at such speed that she almost expected the syringe to fly out of his hand once he began to draw it back and the dark liquid flooded into the tube.

'I'm afraid we won't get the results for a while now, maybe not until the start of January,' he was saying. 'They usually take three or four days, but the lab won't be processing any more routine samples until after Christmas, and even that won't be a full working week. But I'm sure everything will be fine. In the meantime, take it easy, try to eat sensibly – it's always good to cut down on sugar – and get as much sleep as you can. Most of all, try not to worry.' He stood up and walked towards the door, turning the handle and opening it for her. 'Go easy on yourself,' he said, smiling. 'Have a lovely Christmas.'

Walking down the corridor, Katie felt as light as air. Just sitting opposite him for those few minutes had left her ecstatic, her entire body buzzing. She couldn't stop thinking about the way a tiny muscle twitched next to his left eye when he smiled, and one eyebrow raised itself fractionally higher than the other when he talked; the expression on his face as he leant forward and stretched out his hand to touch her. Joe Harvey hadn't just been doing his job in there, those few minutes had been about more than that. She hadn't got any of this wrong – he felt something for her too.

As she walked into the waiting room, a small child leapt in front of her, yelling and brandishing a plastic sword. She shrieked and stepped against the reception desk, her elbow catching a vase. It tipped backwards, throwing water and flowers over the receptionist, her computer and the desk.

'For God's sake!' the woman leapt up and began to dab at her skirt.

'I'm so sorry!' said Katie.

Realising that the computer was more important than her clothing, the receptionist grabbed the keyboard and held it up as water streamed onto the floor.

'I really am sorry,' said Katie, leaning over and standing the vase upright. 'What can I do to help?'

'You've done quite enough,' snapped the woman.

As Katie turned around, she realised every pair of eyes in the waiting room was focused on her, apart from those belonging to the mother of the child holding the plastic sword, which were firmly fixed on the magazine in her lap.

'It would help if you kept your son under control!' Katie said, stepping forward, her face burning with humiliation.

The woman looked up.

'Did you see what he did?' asked Katie.

The woman shrugged. 'Wasn't his fault,' she said. 'You knocked it over.'

'Yes, but only because he scared me!'

The woman shrugged again and looked back down at her

magazine and the little boy stuck out his tongue at Katie. She glared at him, wishing she could grab his plastic sword and snap it in two.

Back outside, she stomped towards the road: yet again she'd got the blame for something that wasn't her fault. What was wrong with everyone at the moment? But it didn't matter; none of it mattered. She'd done what she came here to do, which was see Joe. He'd been so kind, so caring. She couldn't help smiling to herself as she pictured his face again, leaning forward as he placed his hand gently on her arm, the memory of him washing away irritation about plastic swords and water damage.

She felt strangely powerful: while he'd been with her in that consulting room, Joe had ignored Rachel, turned his back on her pretty, smiling face as it flashed out from his phone screen. She really wasn't imagining any of this; he was aware of a connection between them too. He'd definitely felt comfortable and relaxed with her, it wasn't just his GP's bedside manner. Had he been thinking about her, since the last appointment?

A van slowed as it drove by; Katie heard a whistle and saw the driver turn his head as he passed. Her cheeks glowing, her self-esteem soaring, she flicked her hair back over her shoulders and sucked in her stomach, her heels clicking along the pavement.

This really was a great haircut.

30

When she got into work on Christmas Eve, Katie was surprised to find a card on her desk, from Fraser.

'Thanks, that's kind,' she said. 'I haven't got you one I'm afraid; we're not doing Christmas cards this year, cutting back and all that.'

'Don't worry,' he said, stirring his mug of tea with a spoon. 'I didn't buy it specially for you, I had some left over from last year.'

'Right. Well thanks anyway.'

Duncan came ambling out of his office, jingling his change in his pockets as usual. 'All ready for the onslaught, Katie?' he asked. 'Got the bird prepped and the presents wrapped?'

'Just about. Pete and the girls are off to pick up the turkey this morning. How about you?'

'Yep. All in hand.'

Although she'd worked at Triple A for three years, she hadn't learnt much about Duncan's private life. He rarely spoke about his mousy wife, Sue – apart from sharing stories of her hormonal struggles – but had mentioned they lived on the new estate out towards Dunmore. He had two grown-up sons and had been in the same line of business all his life; he drove a BMW 5 Series estate, played golf, and he and Sue holidayed in Mallorca every summer. That, in a nutshell, was Duncan. Occasionally she tried to steer the conversation, ask how he'd spent his weekend, but he was never forthcoming.

In some ways that was a good thing: Fraser's openness about every aspect of his social, sexual and personal life – whether she was interested or even listening – was lively enough for all of them, not to mention exhausting.

Soon after they started working together, the three of them had gone out for a meal at Christmas – their office party, they joked. But a few weeks later Fraser and Katie fell out and the atmosphere became strained. A festive lunch had never been suggested again. Instead, Duncan acknowledged the imminent arrival of Christmas by handing them each an envelope containing a crisp, chemical-smelling £50 note, and – with relief – they dispensed with the pretence of shared bonhomie.

There was hardly anything to do in the office this morning, apart from a small amount of paperwork that couldn't wait until after the holiday. Just before midday, Duncan announced he was leaving shortly, so unless they wanted to spend Christmas locked within Triple A's four walls, they should make themselves scarce. Fraser whooped and shut down his computer, leaping across the room to drag his coat and scarf off the hook by the door.

'Adios, people, have a good one,' he said. 'May Father Christmas bring you everything you've asked for. Did you remember to put a sense of humour on your list this year, Katie?'

As she got into the car her phone rang.

'Katie dear, are you out and about – can you do me a favour?'

Her heart sank. 'Actually, Brenda, I'm just on the way home.'

'You couldn't pop into a chemist, could you? We're nearly out of paracetamol and I'd quite like some cough mixture in case this tickle gets any worse. But Alan is out playing golf and I can't get hold of him. It would be such a help.'

Unable to face going into town at lunchtime on Christmas Eve, Katie took the bypass and headed to the shopping centre towards Overton. There was a Boots at the far end and, after queuing to buy Brenda's medicinal supplies, she came back outside and stopped to look at the window display in the clothes shop next door. She didn't need anything new to wear, and definitely couldn't afford it. But what the hell – there was no harm taking a look.

She flicked through some shirts on a rail to the left, then some dresses further along. A soft green cardigan caught her eye – smart enough for work, so she'd get plenty of wear out of it. She glanced at her watch: it wasn't even 1pm yet. Unsure about Duncan's definition of a half day, she'd told Pete she might not be back until mid-afternoon, so had plenty of time.

The fitting room was at the back of the store, and she stood patiently while a woman in front of her sorted through armfuls of clothes, after being told she could only take in six items.

'Sorry about the wait, can I help?'

They stared at each other, both shocked into silence.

The first thing Katie noticed was that Rachel seemed shorter. She must have been wearing heels before. She was no longer smiling and now looked pale – and worried.

'Just the cardigan?' Rachel tucked her hair behind her ear in a gesture that looked automatic rather than necessary, and reached for a red tag with '1' printed on it. 'Down there on the right.'

Katie took the tag and nodded her thanks, walking through the carpeted space. Finding an empty cubicle, she pulled the curtain across after her, leaning against the wall and clutching the cardigan. Her heart was thumping and, looking sideways in the mirror, she saw her cheeks were pink.

Katie was shocked at coming face to face with Rachel Aston, but almost as surprised by the fact that she worked here. She'd been wondering what the girl did for a living. The newspaper had said she worked in a shop, but Katie had expected something different: managerial at least, possibly an area sales rep or someone who ran training courses? But now here she was, standing in a fitting room, putting crumpled dresses back on hangers and handing out plastic tags.

She's a shop girl. Just an ordinary shop girl.

Katie hung the green cardigan on a hook and took off her coat. She'd been convinced Rachel would be smarter than her, well-educated with enhanced career prospects; a young woman who was going somewhere in the world. Why else would Joe be with her? Katie had presumed he was the sort of man who'd be attracted to a girl who could match him in terms of conversation, wit and knowledge; he was bright and she was sure he had a great sense of humour, so he'd want the same in a partner. Of course, the fact that she worked in a shop, didn't mean she wasn't all of those things, but seeing her here was somehow a huge relief.

Katie pushed her arms into the cardigan and adjusted the neckline to make it hang properly. It looked good: lovely colour. Maybe theirs wasn't a match made in heaven then? They might not have been together long? She turned around and peered over her shoulder to see how the cardigan looked from the back. It really suited her.

But they *did* live together, so it wasn't just a casual relationship. Although nowadays young people looked on that as less of a commitment – Fraser had moved in with two girlfriends during the time Katie had worked alongside him. And on both occasions moved out again fairly quickly. Anyway, however long Joe and Rachel had been together, it didn't mean it was serious. She thought about the pair of them coming out of the supermarket then, a week or so later, walking down into town, Joe's arm around Rachel's shoulder. She batted the images away, remembering instead how, during her second appointment at the surgery, he'd glanced at the ringing phone, but had ignored it and turned all his attention back to her.

He was going out with a girl who worked in a clothes shop. Not just any clothes shop, granted, a well-respected chain where Katie had shopped regularly over the years. But nonetheless Rachel spent her days standing around in an artificially lit box on an industrial estate, making conversation with women who were trying to squeeze their cellulite into expensive outfits which didn't fit or suit them.

'Not bad,' she said out loud, turning around again to see the front view. The cardigan was £40: more than she should be spending, particularly at this time of year. But she could hide it for a couple of days so Pete didn't see, then hint that Monica had bought it for her as a Christmas present.

She put on her own clothes again and grabbed the cardigan and pulled back the curtain. At the entrance to the fitting rooms, Rachel's place had been taken by a willowy blonde, who held out her hand.

'That's okay, I'll have this one,' said Katie, handing over the plastic tag. 'Um, the girl who was here just now...'

'Rachel? Gone on a break,' said the girl. 'Was she meant to be getting something for you?'

'No, that's fine,' said Katie, moving out onto the shop floor again. She took a circuitous route to the tills, but there was no sign of her. Handing the cardigan to the girl behind the counter, she dug out her purse. 'This is such a lovely colour,' she said, tapping her card against the machine. 'I think it suits me!'

The assistant was barely out of her teens, petite, with hair piled high on top of her head. She smiled insincerely, showing plenty of teeth behind lips plastered in crimson. She clearly didn't care whether or not Katie looked good in the green cardigan.

Clutching the bag to her chest, she walked towards the exit. The fact that she'd found Rachel here today was a sign. Their meeting was meant to happen. She now just had to work out what she did with this new-found knowledge.

31

She woke early the next morning and, as was often the case nowadays, was instantly alert, her mind churning over the events of the day before, with Joe at the forefront of it all. It was 5.50am – an irritating no man's land of early morning: too soon to get up, but too late to go back to sleep. Pete turned over beside her and his arm bumped against her elbow. She lay still until she heard his breathing even out again, and knew he was fully asleep.

They hadn't made love for a long time, several weeks. In fact, now she came to think about it, months, long before her mother died. She felt guilty, because she knew she hadn't encouraged closeness between them. But right now, she didn't yearn to feel the touch of his skin against hers, the heat of his breath on her face, his dry lips on her own. She loved him, but the thought of him didn't excite her.

When she closed her eyes, she saw Joe; it was his soft warm breath she wanted to feel against her cheek, the brush of his smooth lips pushing forcefully against hers. She imagined his hands running over her body, one around the back of her neck, scooping up her hair as he pulled her head towards his.

She was now fully awake, with no chance of going back to sleep. She slipped silently out of bed, throwing her dressing gown over her shoulders. It was cold downstairs so she pressed the button to advance the heating and filled up the kettle, flicking on the radio and hearing the chimes of Big Ben.

'It is the 25th of December. Here are the news headlines,' purred the announcer. Katie wondered if she'd drawn the short straw and been ordered to work on Christmas Day, or whether she'd chosen that shift. If the pay was good, it was probably worth it: she'd be back with her family before mid-morning.

She picked up an empty orange juice carton from the worktop and took it out to the recycling box in the utility room. The turkey had been soaking there overnight in a large bucket, to which they'd added fruit juice, stock, herbs and spices. The naked flesh on its rump looked like the goose-bumped skin of an old woman.

Announcing he was taking over in the kitchen for Christmas lunch, Pete had pinned a piece of paper to the wall with timings, temperatures and tips he'd gleaned from newspaper cuttings and television programmes. Katie was delighted to let him have control of the catering.

She made a cup of tea and sat at the table flicking through the Christmas edition of the *Radio Times*, its pages peppered with fluorescent pink and yellow rings, where Anna had marked the shows and films she wanted to watch. She would never manage it – sometimes there were rings around programmes going out at the same time on three different channels.

The hands on the clock were creeping towards 6.30am. Joe wouldn't be awake yet: he and Rachel were probably lying side by side, maybe spooning, his arm flung carelessly around her waist. Katie wished she'd been able to slip upstairs when she was inside 15 Coopers Lane, to take a look at their bedroom.

She just wanted to know whose taste had prevailed; if it was Rachel, she suspected the curtains would be flounced and frilly, with matching cushions on the bed and the colour scheme would be pink or peach. How hideous: poor Joe.

With no chores to do and nobody to talk to, she wandered into the sitting room to put on the television. She glanced towards the fireplace and saw three stockings lined up along the hearthstone; all red with white trim, they were packed with items that pushed the original sock shapes almost beyond recognition. From the open tops peeped the edges of boxes and plastic packaging, a glimpse of gold coins in one, the top of a candy cane in another.

'Oh fuck,' she said.

There had only been two stockings on the hearthstone the night before, after she and Pete had finished stuffing them with the bits and pieces they'd bought for the girls. The third had appeared overnight, every bit as laden as the others, carefully placed alongside them so none of its contents spilled out.

She moved across the room and knelt down, picking up the third stocking and looking inside it. On the top was a tube of expensive hand cream, beneath it a large slab of chocolate, laden with nuts and raisins and wrapped in a red ribbon. Tucked down one side was a paperback and a little further down was a pair of fluffy socks – the kind you wore instead of slippers – then a pretty make-up bag followed by a Chocolate Orange. A boxed ink pen came next, then some bath salts and a bottle of nail varnish. Right at the bottom, tucked into the foot, was a bag of chocolate coins.

She sat on the floor, holding the empty stocking in her hands and feeling sick.

Every Christmas she and Pete put together a pile of goodies for each other, carefully packed into a stocking that would mysteriously appear overnight on Christmas Eve, beside those they'd done together for the girls. They would separately sneak back into the sitting room before bed, pretending to go down for a glass of water or to check the doors were locked, and four stockings would be lined up ready for the morning, when the girls burst from their beds and tumbled downstairs to see what bounty Father Christmas had shoved down the chimney.

But this year she hadn't done a stocking for Pete. She hadn't even thought about it. She'd done no planning and no secret shopping. Even while buying bits and pieces for the girls, it hadn't occurred to her that she had bought nothing for him. He hadn't featured in her thoughts.

Her mouth was dry and her head had started to thump. What on earth was wrong with her? This was insane: how could she have been so preoccupied that she forgot to put together a stocking for Pete? She wondered frantically if there was anything she could muster at the last minute: there was a jar of chutney in the cupboard that she'd bought to have with cheese over Christmas, and a box of fudge she'd thought she might give to Alan. There was also a new pocket-sized AA map book upstairs, which she'd been sent when she renewed her car insurance; she could possibly put that in.

'Mummy! What are you doing?'

She jumped and knocked her knee on the corner of the hearthstone.

'You've opened your stocking already, that's not allowed!' shrieked Anna. 'You're meant to wait for all of us on Christmas Day! Why did you start without us!'

Upstairs Katie heard a thud as Pete's feet hit the bedroom floor. There was little chance anyone could have slept through Anna's rant.

She looked down and saw the empty stocking hanging from her hands; the collection of carefully chosen gifts spread out around her on the carpet, presents picked with care, specifically with her in mind. She wanted to cry but no tears came, just an overwhelming feeling of nausea.

32

Brenda and Alan arrived at midday, straight from the Christmas Day church service, which they attended every year. Neither of them believed in God – 'We don't actually *do* religion,' said Brenda – but they felt it was their right to be entertained by this festive fixture. This year it had been a disappointment. Sipping at their gin and tonics, they criticised the vicar's sermon, the choir's lack of harmony and the appalling behaviour of the younger members of the congregation.

'In my day, children had to sit and listen quietly. It was a sign of respect,' said Alan. 'I blame the parents. If Peter or Philip messed around in church, I'd have given them a good smack.'

'I don't know why we bother going,' said Brenda. 'No one had turned on the heating so we sat there shivering in our coats. They didn't even have "In the Bleak Midwinter". We always sing "In the Bleak Midwinter"! Is it any wonder people are deserting the church in droves?'

Katie sat swirling the ice cubes around in her glass, watching the lights on the Christmas tree flash in a rhythm that was awkwardly out of time with the carols playing in the background.

'So, darling, what did Father Christmas bring you?' asked Brenda, turning to where Anna sat on the carpet, making bracelets from a craft kit.

'Oh, lots of stuff,' she said.

'What sort of stuff?'

'Well, pens and books and chocolate.'

'That sounds nice?'

'Yeah, it was okay. Suky got better things though, she got proper make-up and something to curl her hair. And earrings. It's so unfair that I didn't get anything like that. I'm not allowed to have pierced ears, even though everyone in my class has their ears pierced except me.'

'What, even the boys?' asked Katie.

'No of course not, don't be stupid!'

'Anna, that's not a nice way to speak to your mother,' said Alan.

'Well, she's not nice to me!' shouted Anna, flouncing out of the room.

Katie shook her head at her in-laws. 'Christmas is such a special family time,' she said.

'Oh, you're right, dear, very special,' nodded Brenda.

The day Brenda understands sarcasm, thought Katie, *my life's work will be complete.*

Pete was in the kitchen doing something with the juices of the turkey, which had now been cooking for several hours. He had also made bread sauce, chopped up piles of vegetables, par-boiled potatoes before putting them in to roast, wrapped cocktail sausages in strips of bacon and done something creative with cranberries. Katie was desperate for another gin but couldn't face going back into the kitchen.

They had skirted around each other for the last few hours, polite but distant, avoiding eye contact. Suky had spent most of the morning in her room, sharing feelings of Christmas boredom on Snapchat, and Anna had been playing in the sitting room, distracted by the disappointing contents of her stocking. The absence of the girls made the kitchen an even more awkward place: cold, despite the heat that roared out of the oven, and lonely, although there were two of them in there.

She had apologised. Several times. She'd explained that she'd been so distracted lately – also that she thought they'd agreed last year not to bother with the tradition of doing stockings for each other? That wasn't true, although the more she thought about it, the more she convinced herself they might have had that conversation twelve months ago, kneeling in front of the fire and watching the girls squeal with delight as they pulled surprises out of their own stockings. 'Let's not waste money on each other,' they might have said. 'We can go out to dinner instead in the New Year, treat ourselves to a night away?'

Except they hadn't said anything of the kind, and they both knew it.

Katie had asked if she could help in the kitchen, and Pete had said no. So now she sat with Alan and Brenda, surrounded by Christmas decorations and presents waiting to be unwrapped, listening to carols, absently counting the Christmas cards that she'd slipped over a piece of string running along the wall. She yearned to feel a warm festive glow, but it was as if a handful of stones were lodged in her gut.

Pete's Christmas lunch was a triumph: there were steaming vegetables piled into serving dishes, sizzling sausages, roasted chestnuts mixed in with the sprouts, the turkey moist and flavoursome, a gravy boat so full that thick, brown sauce dribbled over the edge when Brenda lifted it. Once they'd helped themselves to as much as they could fit onto a plate, they pulled the crackers piled in the middle of the table.

'This is good!' said Alan, his mouth full of food; a few flecks of gravy shot from his lips and landed on the table next to Suky, who wrinkled her nose in disgust.

'You've done us proud, Peter,' said Brenda. 'This is very tasty. I didn't know you had it in you!' She giggled and her paper crown slipped over her eyes.

'It is good, delicious,' agreed Katie, who had no appetite. She forced forkfuls of food into her mouth, chewing it dutifully although her gullet threatened to bring it back up again. Her head was thumping, probably because she'd furtively managed to top up her gin before they started eating.

'Is there any more of that wine?' asked Brenda, adjusting her hat. 'I know I shouldn't, I'm a bit tipsy already.'

'It's Christmas, Mum,' said Pete, topping up her glass. 'Treat yourself. Happy days and all that.'

Katie wondered if the pain in his voice was obvious to anyone except her, and hoped it wasn't.

Alan raised his glass. 'A toast!' he said. 'Absent friends.'

'Absent friends,' they echoed, Katie's stomach lurching suddenly. This time last year her mother had been at this table with them, weak, but keen to be out of bed for as long as she could manage. A week or so earlier, she had been into hospital for more tests. They hadn't been given the results by that stage, but they knew it was likely the cancer was back. Sitting between Alan and Brenda, Clara had played around with the food on her plate, eating little but covering up for it by pulling her cracker with enthusiasm, unrolling the piece of paper inside and trying to explain the joke to the girls.

'It's not very funny, Granny,' Anna had said.

'No,' her mother had laughed. 'You're right, it's not funny at all.'

'Next year I'm going to do home-made crackers and write all the jokes myself,' Anna had pronounced. Now it was next year, and she'd forgotten that plan. Katie didn't see any point in reminding her; there was so little to laugh about.

They ate until they were full, and then ate again, stuffing themselves in a way that would have seemed obscene on any other day. Even Suky, picky about food, had seconds of roast potatoes then continued to spear sausages with her fork from the large serving dish, bypassing her plate and popping them straight into her mouth. Pete carried in a Christmas pudding, a sprig of holly in the top, its surface lapped by a blue flame.

'Marvellous!' shouted Alan, his cheeks rosy. 'We could never light them like that. Must be a top-quality pudding, did you make it?'

'No, the supermarket provided this,' said Pete, setting it down on the table.

'I made all our Christmas puddings myself,' said Brenda, her voice brittle. 'There was nothing wrong with them, Alan. They would have lit perfectly well if you'd done it properly.'

'Not like this one,' Alan ploughed on. 'This is the real McCoy. Look at that thing burn! Fantastic, eh?'

'Well, it probably won't taste the same,' sniffed Brenda, as Pete scooped little brown mounds into bowls. 'Shop-bought puddings never do. I used to make mine weeks before Christmas and let the ingredients soak. It was sheer perfection on the day.'

'Oh, this is excellent!' said Alan, spraying bits of fruit across the table. 'Bloody excellent, Peter. You'll have to give your mother the recipe – she can take a leaf out of your book!' He barked a laugh and turned to beam at Suky, who looked as if he was something that had died and gone rancid.

Leaving the table covered in debris – empty plates, dirty glasses, the mismatched ends of crackers and candles burnt to a stub – they moved next door to turn on the television. Both the girls sloped away, Suky to find the phone that she'd been banned from bringing to the Christmas lunch table, Anna to play games on the laptop.

Pete's eyes were fixed on the television, but Katie knew he wasn't paying attention to it. The expression on his face was impossible to read, and he'd done a good job of pretending to enjoy himself during lunch. But he hadn't looked at her all day, and Katie suspected he'd avoid meeting her eye even if she asked him a direct question. Being a coward, she had no intention of doing that. She looked at his hand, resting on the arm of the chair, and reached out her own hand to cover it, moving her fingers over the top of his. He didn't respond.

Alan had started snoring in the armchair, his head on one shoulder, his mouth open. Brenda tutted and folded her arms across her chest, sighing deeply before being distracted by the film that was starting. 'I love *Indiana Jones*! That Harrison Ford is a handsome man. Are we going to watch this? A cup of tea would go down nicely in a bit – whenever either of you feels like making one.'

Pete didn't answer and stared straight ahead.

What would Joe and Rachel be doing now? Were they on their own at home having a quiet day? Or had they gone to visit relatives? Maybe they were away somewhere, just the two of them, staying in a chic hotel that marketed itself as perfect for romantic breaks. Katie screwed her eyes shut to block out the picture in her head; the thought of Joe and Rachel together, holding each other, exchanging gifts. It was too much to bear.

She imagined herself sitting beside Joe, his arm flung loosely around her shoulder, his fingers running softly over the skin on her forearm. He would have bought her something perfect: a piece of jewellery – silver and diamonds – or a gorgeous new coat, in just the right colour. Of course, it would be her size – he wouldn't need to ask about things like that. She saw herself unwrapping a package, him looking on with enthusiasm, waiting to see her reaction, those little laughter lines creasing at the sides of his blue eyes.

Brenda started snoring gently, almost in time with the rasping snorts that were coming from Alan. Katie sat stiffly on the sofa next to her mother-in-law, her eyes on the small figures chasing through the jungle on the television screen, her mind five miles away, in a small detached house in a cul-de-sac on the outskirts of town.

33

Monica was staying with her mother in Southend on Sea. She had driven there on Christmas Eve with gifts, wine and much reluctance. 'I'm dreading it; we'll just get cross with each other,' she'd said to Katie before she left. 'I'm a forty-something woman and she still treats me like a teenager. She'll nag me about spending too much money and not wearing sensible shoes, and if I want to go out on my own – even to buy a paper – she'll look offended and suggest I shouldn't have bothered coming if I don't want to be with her.'

Katie laughed and told her to stop complaining. 'It's only once a year,' she pointed out. It flashed through her mind that Monica was being insensitive: moaning about having to spend time with her mother, knowing this was Katie's first Christmas without hers. But there was no point taking offence – Monica wasn't deliberately cruel, just thoughtless. Anyway, Katie wasn't feeling too low about Clara. She was coping well; most of the time.

It just seemed extraordinary that so much had changed in the last year. The news that there was no point in further chemotherapy, the final few weeks in hospital and then in St

Bernard's. The funeral. Meg had flown in from the Middle East with a checklist of things that would need to be attended to. Pete and Katie had invited her to stay, but were secretly relieved when she said she'd booked into a hotel.

'Easier for all of us,' Meg had said. 'You've got the death certificate, haven't you? I've arranged an appointment with an undertaker tomorrow morning. If you can pick me up from reception at 9 o'clock, we'll get on with it.'

Katie had done as she was told and ferried Meg from one appointment to the next. Two days later, with all items on the checklist ticked off to her satisfaction, Meg flew back to the Middle East, from where she organised the order of service and finalised numbers for the wake, via a stream of efficient and clinical emails. They had expected Meg to bring Don back with her for the funeral, but she flew in alone. Toby also arrived the night before and the three siblings had an awkward dinner at Meg's hotel, connected by blood but divided by so much physical distance and emotional lack of interest in each other's lives that they struggled to maintain a conversation. None of them cried at the crematorium the next morning, although, sitting looking at the plain oak coffin, Katie felt like someone had scooped out her insides.

But that was months ago now, and Katie had moved on.

'You're lucky your mother wants to spend the holidays with you,' she'd said to Monica, as she moaned about her trip to Essex. 'She's not as bad as you make out, she's always been really sweet when I've met her.'

'You don't know her properly,' grumbled Monica. 'She's a wolf in a lambswool jumper.' Since her arrival in Essex, she'd sent a couple of texts saying how bored she was, and Katie had replied with inanities of her own. She hadn't told Monica about the stockings on Christmas morning; the bewildered expression on Pete's face and the way Suky had picked up on what had happened.

'Where's Dad's stocking then?' she'd asked, icily, as the four of them sat on the floor of the sitting room, with the girls surrounded by the goodies they'd received from Father Christmas.

Katie couldn't think what to say and didn't look at Pete. Luckily Anna had interrupted, oblivious, as always, to the atmosphere around her.

'You know I don't believe in him anymore, don't you?' she said, as she tugged open a bag of chocolate coins, spilling them onto the carpet. 'But that's okay, I know it's you and Daddy who do stockings, and I don't mind because it means next year I can just ask you for things instead of having to write stupid letters and post them up the chimney.'

Katie had looked away from her older daughter's accusing stare and got to her feet. 'Cup of tea anyone?' she said breezily, heading towards the kitchen. Later that morning she'd started to write a text to Monica, but kept deleting it after a few lines. She didn't know how to describe what had happened, and had no idea what she expected Monica to say. She wanted to tell someone why she'd forgotten to put together a stocking for Pete, and have them understand and sympathise with her. But that wasn't going to happen if she couldn't explain it to herself.

By early evening on Christmas Day, when Alan and Brenda had gone home – grumpy and hungover from their lunchtime drinking – she couldn't hold out any longer and went into the back garden and dialled Monica's number.

'Hello, you,' she said. 'Had a good day?'

There was a laugh at the other end. 'Well, it depends on your definition of good. I've cooked lots of average-tasting food, watched hours of crap telly, opened some presents that don't suit me, and had a row with my mother about whether the new *Doctor Who* will be able to save the planet. How about you?'

Katie smiled, warmed by the sound of her friend's voice.

'Fairly awful. Pete's been miserable, the girls have been spoilt brats and Alan and Brenda drove me round the bend.'

'Situation normal then?'

'Yes, pretty much.'

'You do sound low,' said Monica. 'Is it really that bad or have you just got the Christmas blues?'

'I don't know,' said Katie. 'I think it's really that bad actually...' She felt a sob catch in her throat. 'Oh, Mon, I don't know what's going on here, I'm so unhappy.' Her voice wobbled and she put her hand over her mouth to try and stop the sobs, the darkness of the garden blurring through tears.

'Sweetheart, don't cry – I wish I could be there to give you a hug. It can't be that terrible. Why is Pete miserable? And tell those girls to pull themselves together – it's Christmas after all, they can make some effort!'

Monica's sympathy made Katie cry even harder. 'I know,' she gulped. 'It's not them really. It's not Pete's fault either, it's all mine. I'm just feeling down.'

'Listen, you're tired,' Monica insisted. 'Christmas is a horrible time; it does this to everyone. I'll probably be in a police cell charged with matricide by the end of Boxing Day. But you need to keep smiling and pretending to be cheerful. When I get back, we'll squeeze in a drink, maybe Friday if you're free? We can offload and moan and make each other feel better. How does that sound?'

'Yes, it sounds good,' sniffed Katie, wiping her eyes with the palm of her hand.

'And in the meantime,' said Monica. 'Drink more wine, eat more chocolate!'

Katie gave a choked laugh. 'Wish you were here now.'

'Yeah, me too. But I'll see you Friday, right?'

'Yes, okay. I'll look forward to it.'

'Got to go, I can hear the old bat hollering for me. Take care of yourself.' Monica ended the call and the screen of

Katie's mobile went blank. She looked at it for a couple of seconds, wiping it with her finger, then turned back towards the house to go inside.

Pete was standing on the back doorstep watching her. He had his arms crossed in front of his chest and his face was drawn, the skin unnaturally pale in the darkness.

'Who is he?'

'What do you mean?'

'Who is he, Katie? Who's the bloke you're seeing? I know there's someone – it's the only thing that would explain all this.' Pete stepped out through the door and pulled it shut behind him. 'You've been moody and angry for weeks, as if you'd rather be anywhere except at home with all of us. I know you're missing Clara, but it's more than that. Look at what you've done to yourself – the haircut, the make-up, you've tarted yourself up so much, it's like you're trying to reinvent yourself. I know you've lied to me over the last few weeks, about what you've been doing and where you've been going. I know about the time when you attacked that woman in her car – although it would have been good to hear about it from you rather than other people. Now it's Christmas Day and you're standing out in the garden, talking to someone on your mobile, crying. Don't tell me nothing's going on, because I won't believe you.'

She looked at him – properly looked at him for the first time all day. She was exhausted. It flashed through her mind that she could tell the truth. *His name's Joe*, she imagined herself saying. *He lives in town and he's a doctor. He's a bit younger than you, Pete, a little taller, dark brown hair, dresses nicely, has a lovely smile.*

She imagined Pete's face falling, the incomprehension showing in his eyes: her words causing him physical pain. Then after the truth, she could carry on and tell yet another lie. *He has a girlfriend, but he's going to leave her. They're living together at the moment but she'll be moving out shortly. He wants me to move in with him; he wants us to get married. We might go away for a bit, travel for a few months. He's the most wonderful man I've ever met and we love each other, so there's nothing you can say to stop any of it happening or to make me change my mind.*

But the words stayed in her head. And Pete was still standing looking at her, arms folded.

'No one. There's no one,' she said. 'That was Monica on the phone. You can check if you like, here – hers is the number I last dialled. There's no one else.'

She went past him into the house, not looking at him. In the kitchen she opened the fridge and started pulling things out: cold turkey, a dish of congealed white sauce, a Tupperware container of leftover vegetables. Then cheese, together with some pâté, a box of breadsticks, celery, cherry tomatoes.

Pete had followed her in and stood just inside the back door. 'What are you doing?' he asked. 'No one's hungry yet, Katie. We've hardly stopped eating all day.'

'Don't tell me what to do!' she snapped, shocked by how shrieky her voice sounded. 'Why does everyone think they can tell me what to do and how to live my life? I'm a grown woman.'

'Well, isn't it time you started behaving like one then?' said Pete coldly.

He walked past her out of the kitchen, went into the office and shut the door behind him. In a fury, Katie flung out her arm and swept the food off the table onto the floor. A plate shattered and the turkey skidded across the tiles and ended up propped against the skirting board, surrounded by bits of cheese. Cherry tomatoes rolled in every direction, the last one coming to a standstill in front of the oven. As it rocked backwards and forwards, Katie remembered the apple on the floor of the surgery by Mrs Burns' foot. For a second she was back there: the crash of the tumbling body echoing in her ears.

Suky had come into the kitchen. 'Wow,' she said. 'What happened here?'

Katie bent over the kitchen table, both her hands planted on it, her breathing heavy. Her hair was falling across her face and her eyes were closed, shutting out the sight of the food spread over the floor. She was appalled at herself.

Silently, Suky reached around the back of the door for the broom and started sweeping the debris into a pile.

34

'Can you give me a lift to the shopping centre?' Suky was standing in the doorway, holding her mobile.

'What, right now?'

'Well, in half an hour.'

Katie was sitting on the edge of her bed, sorting through a mountain of clean laundry. Why were there always so many odd socks? She could swear she'd only put matching pairs into the machine.

'I suppose so. Do you want to spend your Christmas money?'

'Sort of. I also want to meet Adam.'

'Who's Adam?'

'Just this boy I know. He's going to be there this afternoon.'

Intrigued, Katie tried not to show it; Suky rarely mentioned boys. 'Okay. Anna and I may come too, and have a look at the sales.' She turned and caught Suky's scowl. 'Don't worry, we won't embarrass you in front of your mates.'

Forty minutes later they arrived at the shopping centre car park, which was as full as it had been in the run-up to

Christmas. Katie couldn't understand where people got the money to fund this ongoing spending frenzy. Suky immediately walked away from them.

'You've got two hours!' Katie called. 'After that we'll be ready to go home.'

She left Anna looking at jewellery in Claire's, telling her she'd be back in ten minutes. As she walked out of the door, she turned left, and realised where she was heading. Had this been subconsciously at the edge of her mind since Suky asked for the lift?

It was pandemonium at the front of the shop: rails were crammed with marked-down clothes, and many more were being trampled underfoot by women looking for bargains.

Katie saw Rachel immediately, standing behind the tills. She was talking to a customer, while packing clothes into a plastic bag. She moved behind a display, suddenly nervous. She pretended to flick through a rail of coats, watching what was happening at the tills.

'If it's not suitable, bring it back,' Rachel was saying. 'You've got twenty-eight days for an exchange, but I wouldn't leave it that long, we're low on stock because of the sale.'

Katie lurked behind the coats, waiting for the queue of customers to wind their way forward. As soon as Rachel's till was free, she moved out; a few steps and she was standing in front of her.

'Hello again,' she said.

Rachel glanced up and the smile froze on her face. She looked terrified.

'I'm not here to cause a scene,' said Katie. 'I just wanted to come and see you, and find out how you were. I want to apologise.'

Rachel was holding a coat hanger in her hand and had taken a step backwards.

'I can't believe how badly I behaved before, and I'm really sorry,' Katie continued. 'I was having a difficult time, what with one thing and another, and I took it out on you, which was awful. So, I wanted to say sorry and see if I could buy you lunch. Or something…' She trailed off.

Rachel now looked bewildered. Katie noticed her hair was limp and there were bags under her eyes. Maybe they'd had a bad Christmas, argued a bit. Or possibly they didn't get on with each other's families, always tricky at this time of year. On the other hand, she could just be shattered after spending hours dealing with shoppers in search of sale bargains. She should get a trim though: that haircut was growing out, and it didn't look as good when it was longer. Subconsciously Katie ran a hand through her own hair, brushing a loose strand behind her ear.

'Please say you forgive me? I know it's a surprise, seeing me like this. But I've been worrying about you and what happened, and when I realised you worked here, I thought I had a chance to come and put things right,' she smiled cautiously. 'I don't blame you if you hate me after what happened, but I'd like to make it up to you, show you I'm not some mad woman who makes a habit of driving into people and then screaming at them.'

'Look, it's fine,' said Rachel, turning to throw the hanger into a box behind her. 'Don't worry about it.'

'Let me buy you lunch,' insisted Katie. 'It's the least I can do. Please say yes. How about tomorrow? We can go over the road to Pizza Express, my treat. What time do you start your lunch break – 12.30? One o'clock? I'll book a table.'

'Well, it's not easy to…'

'Let's say one. It's all on me. Thank you so much for agreeing to come, you're such a kind person. I can't tell you how much it matters to me, being able to make this right.'

Katie stepped back and swung her bag onto her shoulder. 'Tomorrow then. I'll see you there!'

She moved away before Rachel could say anything else. As she walked back to the car, she felt exhilarated, buzzing with adrenalin. Getting in, she closed the door and sat looking through the rain-spattered windscreen at people scurrying to and from the main doors of the shopping centre.

Her mobile rang, and she fished it out of her handbag, surprised to see the office number displayed.

'Katie?'

'Hi, Duncan, how was your Christmas?'

'Where the hell are you?'

'Overton. I'm out shopping with the girls. Why?'

'You're meant to be here. In the office.'

'But we don't start back until the 28th?'

'Today is the 28th, Katie.'

'Oh shit, is it? Duncan, I'm so sorry. I've sort of lost track of the days. I mean… I thought that was tomorrow. Are you sure it's the 28th? No, of course you are, I'm not thinking straight. Bloody hell, I'm so sorry.'

After hanging up, she dropped her forehead onto the steering wheel, groaning. How could she have been so stupid? Work hadn't crossed her mind at all. That was the trouble with Christmas, normal routines went to pot. But after letting him down today, how could she ask Duncan for a long lunch break tomorrow? She would have to find a way; she wasn't going to back out now. She hadn't intended to invite Rachel for lunch, she'd just wanted to apologise. But as the words came out of her mouth, they felt appropriate. This was a way of making amends. She was so glad she'd thought of it – she felt lighter, more cheerful. For once she was doing the right thing, making up for the way she'd flown off the handle after the accident.

She would just have to come up with a good excuse for Duncan.

Katie started the car and reversed out of the parking space, realising as she did so that she couldn't go home yet, because both her daughters were still wandering around inside the shopping centre.

35

'Are you ready to order?' The waiter was standing beside the table, notepad and pen at the ready. He had a splattering of inflamed acne across both cheeks and looked about twelve years old.

'No, I'm waiting for someone,' said Katie. 'Can I get a glass of white wine though?' She put the menu on the table and twisted her fingers together. She never normally drank at lunchtime, but a small glass wouldn't do any harm. Despite her exuberance yesterday, she was nervous. She glanced at her watch: it was 1.03pm. There was no sign of Rachel, but maybe she didn't get off work until one.

Katie had never liked pizza and, picking up the menu again, couldn't get enthusiastic about anything on it. She might have something with olives, or possibly anchovies: maybe La Reine would be more interesting than Fiorentina.

Duncan had been tight-lipped when she said she'd be out for longer than usual at lunchtime.

'I've got to get the brakes checked on the car,' she lied. 'There's something wrong with them and with all the rain we've been having, I don't feel safe.'

'You'll have to make up the time,' he said testily. 'I can't have the two of you swanning in and out when you feel like it; we need continuity in here. There are those new equipment specs to go up on the website.'

'I know, I promise I'll get it done,' she said meekly. 'I can do some of the web updates at home over the weekend if you like. And I'm sorry again about yesterday, Duncan. Christmas just seemed to fly past this year.'

'Be as quick as you can today,' he'd said, walking into his office and slamming the door.

He wasn't just irritated with her; Fraser had sprained his ankle at a party over the holidays, and the lower half of his leg was swathed in a white bandage. When he got to work, he'd made a song and dance of climbing the stairs and hopping around the office, using furniture to propel himself across the room. 'I'm sure it's broken,' he'd whined, hoisting his foot onto the desk. 'The nurse at A&E said it isn't, but she hadn't got a clue. She was from Romania or somewhere and couldn't understand what I was saying. The pain is so bad, worse than anything I've ever been through, you just have no idea.'

'Can you wiggle your toes?' asked Katie. 'And bend the foot?'

Fraser did both, with reluctance and some baring of teeth.

'It's not broken,' she said, turning back to her computer. 'Best thing is to rest it and keep the foot raised until the swelling goes down. I've got ibuprofen in my bag if you want some.'

'I don't think that would be strong enough for pain like this,' he groaned. He had then spent the rest of the morning on the phone telling friends about his injury.

By 1.15pm Katie was feeling stupid. Why had she expected Rachel to turn up? She'd hoped that, by not giving her a chance to say no, the girl would feel obliged to come. She seemed like someone who didn't like letting people down. But there was no point staying any longer; she drained the last of her wine – now wishing she'd ordered a large glass – and pushed back her chair.

'Sorry to have kept you waiting,' said a voice beside her. 'There's always a rush at lunchtime and I couldn't get away.'

Rachel was wearing a bright red bolero jacket – *too flimsy for the time of year really*, thought Katie – and a black knitted beanie, from which strands of hair peeped out at either side. She had more make-up on today and looked pretty and flushed, as if she'd been running.

Katie pushed back her chair and stood up. 'Oh,' she said. 'I didn't think you were coming.'

'Sorry. As I say, it's been manic.'

'That's fine!' Katie smiled, gesturing to the chair on the other side of the table. 'Sit down, please. It's great you're here. Do you want something to drink? I've just had a glass of wine – I don't usually drink at lunchtime – but if you're having one, I might have another small one.'

'No, thanks. I'll have some sparkling water.'

Katie waved at a passing waitress, who ignored her. Turning back to Rachel, she folded her hands together on the table in front of her. 'So, this is nice.'

Rachel stared at her.

'I mean it's nice for me, that you've come. I appreciate it. I think we got off on the wrong foot last time, so it's good to have this chance to start again, you know, get to know each other properly.'

'We didn't get off on any foot,' said Rachel. 'You went ballistic.'

'Yes, I did. Sorry.' Katie knew she was blushing. 'I'm not asking you to forgive me – I don't deserve that. I just want to buy you lunch to show how bad I feel. The whole thing was upsetting for me, so it must have been even worse for you.'

'It was awful,' said Rachel. 'And then, when you refused to

agree to a resolution, we had to go through the insurance companies, which seemed very unnecessary.'

Katie twisted her fingers together. 'Look, I feel bad about that. I don't know why I didn't agree. I was still angry, but that would have been the sensible thing to do, and I *am* sorry. I got upset when the police came to the house, which was when they asked me about the resolution. You see, I hadn't told my husband about it.'

'Why not?'

'I'm not sure. We weren't getting on anyway – before that – and I thought Pete would get cross and blame me for the damage to the car. He can be a bit... difficult.'

Rachel looked concerned. 'Difficult in what way?'

'Well, he shouts a lot and gets worked up,' said Katie. As the words came out of her mouth, she couldn't believe she was saying them.

'That's awful, he sounds like a bully. But even so, he's your husband, he should have been worried about you. How did you tell him in the end?'

'I didn't,' said Katie, looking down at her hands. 'I was too scared.'

She looked up and saw Rachel's appalled expression. 'Oh, you poor thing,' she said. 'That's so sad you have to hide things from him. Did the police turn up with no warning?'

'Yes,' nodded Katie. 'They parked right outside the house and the officers were in high-vis jackets – they couldn't have been more obvious if they'd tried. Luckily, I managed to talk to them without Pete and the children hearing, but that's why I said I couldn't go for the resolution, I was terrified they were there and wanted them to go away again as soon as possible.' She sighed. 'Now of course I've ended up with a police caution because of it, and what's even worse is that you had to go to more effort to get your car fixed.'

'Well, that's not such a big deal,' Rachel said. 'It sounds like things are worse for you; at least my boyfriend was supportive about the whole thing.'

'Lucky you,' said Katie, not bothering to hide the envy in her voice. They definitely weren't married then. *Thank God for that, only a boyfriend.*

'Shall we get some food?' said Rachel, picking up the menu in front of her. 'I ought to be back in forty-five minutes.'

'Yes of course, good idea. What do you fancy?' Katie picked up her own menu and looked at it with interest, as if she hadn't already been rereading the options for fifteen minutes. 'I think I might have a Giardiniera?'

'That sounds good, I'll have one of those too,' smiled Rachel. 'I love pizza, it's my favourite food. You couldn't have picked a better place!'

'Me too!' said Katie. 'I'd live on pizza, given half a chance.' She waved at the waitress again, who continued to ignore her. But the young lad loped over with his pad and pen. 'Two Giardinieras please,' said Katie. 'And some sparkling water.'

The boy took a long time to write down their simple order, and the harder he concentrated, the more flushed his cheeks became.

'He must be new,' she said, once he'd gone. 'He doesn't look old enough to be working here!'

Rachel laughed. 'Poor boy. I had awful acne when I was a teenager. I tried everything but nothing made any difference.'

'Me too,' said Katie. 'And I can't believe I'm now buying the same stuff for my own daughter!' As soon as the words were out of her mouth, she regretted them. She hadn't wanted to give away too much about herself.

'So how old are your children? One's a teenage girl, obviously!'

'Yes, she's fifteen and her sister is nine.'

'So, you and Pete must have been married for a while then?'

'Oh, years,' said Katie, desperate to turn the conversation away from herself. 'How long have you and Joe been together?'

Rachel paused. 'How did you know his name?'

'You said it earlier, when you were talking about the car insurance,' said Katie, not missing a beat.

Rachel looked confused. 'Did I? How strange, I don't remember that. Anyway, we've been together for three years now. We moved here a few months ago, when Joe got a new job. We're renting a house, on the other side of town. It's really convenient for him, because he can walk to work, and I'd need to drive to get to the store anyway, but it doesn't take long.'

'That's good,' said Katie, watching the young girl's slim hands as they waved around while she talked.

'It was always going to be harder for me to make the move down here because I didn't have a job. And I did struggle at first, not knowing anyone. Joe was very busy at work and never seemed to be around. But things got better once I found this job, and the people I work with are great.'

The waiter arrived with a bottle of sparkling water, and Rachel started talking about her plans to work her way up to junior management.

Katie poured the water, smiling and nodding. Rachel's eyes were a deep brown and her hair looked better today, shiny and lustrous. She was very pretty, but the sort of girl who doesn't realise how lovely she is.

The pizzas arrived and they began to eat; the conversation moved on, covering work, television programmes they'd both watched, predictions of snow. Katie found herself relaxing, forgetting the reason for this strange lunch. She rarely met new people nowadays; it was fun to sit opposite a different face, hear an alternative take on life. She told Rachel some of the silly things Anna had said over Christmas, and they laughed about Fraser's drama queen antics at A&E.

'This has been great,' Rachel said, as the waiter came to

clear away their plates. 'An hour ago, I really didn't think I'd be saying that! To be honest I wasn't looking forward to today, I was a bit scared about seeing you.'

'I can understand that,' said Katie. 'But hopefully I've proved I'm a human being, not a monster! Thank you for coming – I've enjoyed it too. Maybe we can do it again? We should swap numbers.'

'I'd like that.'

A few minutes later, the waiter brought the bill and Rachel tapped her phone to check the time. 'I need to get back I'm afraid. I'll just nip to the loo.'

As she disappeared through a door at the far end of the restaurant, Katie's eyes dropped back to the table. Rachel's phone was sitting there, and the screen was still illuminated. The lock hadn't clicked back on. She slid out her hand and span the phone around. Joe smiled out at her: his lips slightly parted, his hair tousled, fringe falling across his eyes, the blue so intense it looked as if the photo had been enhanced. She caught her breath and ran her forefinger across his cheek, the cold, smooth glass beneath her skin, at odds with the warmth of the face that smiled out from it.

She pressed the button again and apps filled the screen. It wasn't the same phone as hers, but she instantly recognised the universal green phone symbol. Two more taps and she had a list of Rachel's recent calls in front of her.

There was his mobile number, right at the top.

She scrabbled in her bag, blood pounding across her temples. Her hand was shaking and she could hardly hold the pen as she scribbled the number onto a paper napkin. The phone screen went dark and she span it around again and sat back in her chair, putting the pen and napkin into her bag.

'Right, I really must go,' said Rachel, sliding back into her chair and putting her arms into the red jacket. 'We're so busy at the moment, and it's not fair to leave the others on their own.'

'Of course, I'll sort out the bill.'

'Are you sure? It's very kind of you.' Rachel pulled her hair out from the collar of the jacket. 'I've enjoyed it.'

Katie smiled back, enveloped in the warmth of the girl's laughter. 'Me too,' she said. 'It's been fun.'

36

The server had been down all morning and Fraser was furious. 'This is bloody ridiculous!' he kept saying, having repeatedly failed to log on to the internet. He jabbed at his keyboard. 'It's driving me mad!'

'Get on with something else,' said Katie, sorting through a mountain of paperwork she'd pulled out of what she optimistically called her in-tray. It wasn't so much an in-tray, as a dumping ground for everything that came into the office. Maybe she should create an out-tray for items that had been dealt with? But she'd only be doing it to make herself feel like she was achieving something. 'Why don't you get on with the accounts instead?' she asked, as Fraser span around in his chair, his head thrown back as he studied the stains on the suspended ceiling.

'They're not due until Thursday.'

'So do them now and get ahead of yourself.' She found a final demand for payment hiding amongst the papers and put it on a separate pile. 'Please stop spinning, Fraser, you're making me dizzy.'

She jumped as her mobile phone trilled on the desk in front

of her, for an instant hoping to see Joe's number displayed on the screen – although knowing that wouldn't happen.

'I'm afraid Anna isn't feeling well,' said PTA Fiona.

'Can you hold on to her for another hour or so?' whispered Katie. 'I can't leave work yet.'

'Katie, I'm sorry but I think you ought to come and get her. She's very pale.'

'I'll see if I can get hold of Pete.'

Although it was still the school holidays, he'd gone in for an emergency meeting about Damien, so she wasn't surprised when there was no reply from his phone. She stuck her head around the door of Duncan's office. 'I'm sorry, but Anna's not well. I've got to go and pick her up.'

He sat back in his chair, arms crossed in front of his chest. 'Katie, this is not good enough!'

'I know, I know. I'll come in early tomorrow morning – or I'll stay late.'

'It is totally unacceptable…'

'Duncan, I'm really sorry.' She backed away before he could say anything else, grabbing her bag from beside the desk and pulling on her coat. Why did this have to happen today?

Twenty minutes later she was on Fiona's doorstep.

'I feel sick,' said Anna.

'Oh dear, I'm sure you'll be fine,' said Katie, smiling brightly. 'Have you had your hair done, Fiona? It looks fantastic, really suits you. Daisy, did you have a lovely Christmas?'

Trying to charm Fiona was part of her new behaviour policy – one she would put into practice properly once she was back outside the school gates next week. The whispering and cold-shouldering had continued right up to the last day of term, and Katie hoped the two-week break over Christmas would have helped the mummy mafia forget about, or possibly even forgive, her indiscretion behind the wheel of a car. But she knew she'd need to work extra hard on her public image; she would be cheerful and friendly, say hello in all directions, enquire after other people's children, ask whether they'd had a good holiday, listen to idle gossip from the sidelines and dispense sympathy, dismay or admiration, depending on what was required.

It was going to be bloody hard work.

'I can't stand the inane yakking,' she'd said to Monica, in the past. 'Everything revolves around the kids or the school. The other day this woman announced they were going to start collecting used toothbrushes in the recycling box, because each one raises 4p for the school. What is the point? I'd rather throw my old toothbrush in the dustbin and give them a quid.'

'I'm with you,' Monica had said. 'There's nothing more dull than a bunch of bitchy mummies – but it's easy for me to say that, because I don't have to mix with them.'

Now Anna sat back in the car and closed her eyes. 'I'm really going to be sick.'

'Nonsense,' said Katie, starting the engine and pulling out into the traffic. 'You'll be fine. Let's just get home and...' There was a choking beside her and she turned to see her daughter vomiting into her own lap. The car was instantly filled with the stench, and Anna began to scream.

'Bloody hell!' shrieked Katie.

'Eeuuw!' screamed Anna.

'Keep it all there, don't spill it in the car!' yelled Katie, accelerating.

'It's disgusting!' sobbed Anna, tipping up her skirt so that the regurgitated contents of her stomach sloshed onto the floor and dribbled down the inside of the passenger door.

Back home, Katie helped Anna strip off her clothes and stood her under a hot shower. She dumped the stinking pile by the washing machine, and headed to the car with a bucket of water, detergent and cloths. Nearly half an hour later – despite strenuous scrubbing – the car still smelt of vomit. An open bottle of wine was sitting on the worktop and, although it was only 4pm, she poured herself a glass.

'Desperate measures,' she muttered.

The front door slammed and Suky wandered into the kitchen, laughing at something on her phone. 'Bit early to be drinking, isn't it? Why does everywhere smell of sick, it's vile.' She pulled a packet of fairy cakes from a shelf, ripped it open and walked out of the kitchen, carrying three of them.

Katie slugged back the wine and topped up her glass before going into the sitting room. Anna was on the sofa, wrapped in a blanket, wet hair hanging in shards over her shoulders.

'How are you feeling?'

'Better. Can I have something to eat?'

'Wait a while. You don't want to be sick again. Give it a couple of hours and see how your tummy feels.'

Anna didn't argue, and turned back to the cartoon figures on the television. *She must be ill*, thought Katie, *she hasn't told me how cruel I am for starving her.*

She sat down on the sofa, and Anna snuggled up to her. She couldn't remember when they'd last sat like this, but it felt good to have the warm little body wedged into the crook of her arm. They sat in companionable silence while the cartoon played out on the screen in front of them and the sky beyond the window grew dark.

Katie put her hand in the pocket of her cardigan and wrapped her fingers around the napkin she'd taken from Pizza Express. She had transferred the number to her phone, saving it as J, but she'd also kept this scrap of paper because it felt like some sort of talisman. Every time her fingers skimmed across it, a thrill shot through her body.

She heard the front door open and waited for Pete to wander into the sitting room to find them and tell her what had happened in his meeting. When he didn't, she disentangled herself from Anna, picked up her wine glass and went into the kitchen.

He'd taken off his coat and thrown it over the back of a chair, and was sitting at the table. He was pale and Katie was struck by how tired he looked. He stared at the glass in her hand and she bristled. 'Before you say anything, I've had a bad day,' she said. 'I know it's too early for a drink, but Anna was sick in the car on the way home and I spent ages clearing it up, and if I have to take time off work tomorrow to be with her, Duncan will be furious.'

He looked up, bewildered, as if unsure why she was telling him any of this. 'Damien's parents have put in an official complaint,' he said. 'He told them I hit him at the end of last term. They contacted Sara yesterday and said they were going to the police. It's a lie, I would never hit him, and she knows that. It was the day he kicked me, do you remember? He was out of control, so I grabbed him by the wrist and took him out of the classroom. I might have pulled him a bit, but I didn't hit him.' He slumped back in the chair, staring through the kitchen window but not seeing out of it. 'She's put me on an official warning, and we've spent all afternoon trying to decide how to deal with this.'

Katie stared at him. 'But she can't do that! What's wrong with her? Why isn't she backing you up and telling his parents to take a running jump?'

He shook his head. 'It's not her fault. With a complaint like this, you have to be seen to be responding. They've involved the police. Sara has called an emergency governors' meeting for next week, but she wanted to warn me and work out what we do next.'

Katie sank into the nearest chair. 'Oh, Pete, this is awful. What happens now?'

'No idea, we've never been in a situation like this before.'

He leant forward and rested his elbows on the table, dropping his head into his hands.

Katie could picture Sara's face: the sharp cheekbones, the pinched lips, the cold eyes. Whatever Pete said, she wasn't at all sure he had Sara's support.

37

As Katie got ready for work, the house was unnervingly silent. Yesterday, although he'd still been on holiday, Pete had been up early, making a cup of tea while she sorted her lunch. But this morning he didn't get out of bed. He'd worked his way through a bottle and a half of wine last night, and eventually came upstairs at about 2am, turning on the overhead light, staggering against the wardrobe and swearing when he stubbed his toe on the chair. She knew he'd be foul-tempered and hungover when he did wake up this morning, so it was best to let him sleep on.

Too lazy to make any lunch, she decided to pick up something at Sainsbury's. Although it was early, there was a great deal of activity beneath the giant orange signage: workers buying food on their way to the office, night shifters doing the same on their way home, mothers who had already been up for hours, pushing trolleys containing wailing toddlers.

As she walked in, she passed a couple of women in pale blue uniforms. One of them looked familiar, and Katie wondered if she'd seen her before at the hospital or St

Bernard's. It must have been the former, she was fairly sure the staff at the hospice had worn white uniforms.

She still hadn't done anything about the letter she'd received from Jane Rivers. The chaos of Christmas had meant everything was put on hold but, even now the festivities were over, she wasn't sure how to deal with this. She had reread it a dozen times: studying the choice of words, trying to work out whether the formal, noncommittal sentences could be interpreted in any other way.

'You've got to let this go,' Pete had said the other evening, finding her with the letter in her hands, again.

'But then they'd win,' she said.

'It's not about winning,' he said. 'You aren't in a fight with these people. You had some concerns, they've answered them.'

'But they haven't really answered them, they've just palmed me off.'

'You're getting obsessive about it,' he'd said. 'You're never going to be able to move on, Katie, unless you can put this to one side and forget about it. You should throw that letter away.'

Maybe he was right; as the days went by, she could feel her anger waning. The intensity of the emotion was still there, but the hard knot of rage inside her was shrinking bit by bit, like air silently creeping out of a balloon.

She stood in front of the supermarket chiller cabinets, stocked with a huge range of sandwich, wrap and salad options. The smell of bacon drifted down from the café on the first floor, and she moved along to look at the cakes. She probably ought to stick with a low-fat sandwich: she'd been feeling bloated recently, even before the gluttony of Christmas. As she sat in front of the computer at work yesterday, the waistband on her skirt had cut uncomfortably into her stomach and she'd run her fingers around the edge of the material to lift it over the little roll of fat that appeared when she sat down.

Dieting was hard, but she'd decided to have smaller portions at mealtimes, and cut out snacks. No more biscuits and crisps. Definitely no chocolate.

Rachel had been wearing a little black skirt with her bolero jacket – Katie noticed it when she was walking away from the table in the pizza place. It stopped above the knee and was cut beautifully, hugging her hips in all the right places. Katie wasn't sure she could carry off something like that, but it would help if she was half a stone lighter. In the meantime, she'd buy some streamlining knickers – M&S did loads of them, maybe she'd take a look at the weekend.

She picked out a chicken wrap and joined the queue at the till. Someone moved in behind her and, glancing over her shoulder, she drew in her breath. It was Joe. A week had gone by since her appointment with him: seven long days – and seven even longer nights.

Even before she found his number on Rachel's phone, she'd thought about him dozens of times every day. She was living out an entire imaginary life with him. She'd pictured them spending Christmas together, holed up in a romantic boutique hotel on the south coast, then they'd flown abroad for a city break in Europe – other women in the airport casting jealous glances as he grabbed her hand and pulled her towards him while they waited to pick up their luggage.

They had bought each other expensive presents; shared a bottle of wine in a piano bar; he had smiled as he looked across at her, laughing at her jokes, putting his arm around her shoulder and kissing her lips slowly, nibbling her ear and grinning when she protested it tickled. They had eaten tapas at a little café overlooking a square in Barcelona, strolled hand in hand at night, along crowded streets. And they had had sex; endless, rampant sex that made her buzz with desire, every bit of her body craving him, needing to have him beside her, inside her, his moist lips covering her with kisses, running down her back, along the top of her thighs, between her legs.

Now here he was. Standing two feet away from her in Sainsbury's, holding an egg mayonnaise sandwich and a bottle of orange juice.

She was shaking, aware she must be the colour of a tomato. She wanted to walk away, hide herself in a different queue: he mustn't see her like this. But she couldn't move.

'Can I take that?' The girl at the till was reaching out, and it was a couple of seconds before Katie realised what she wanted. She passed across the wrap, digging into her bag for her purse.

'Thank you.' Once she'd handed over a five-pound note, the girl took a frustratingly long time to count out the change. Another assistant opened a second till, and suddenly he had moved forward and was standing beside her.

She knew she could pretend not to see him, keep staring straight ahead as she waited for her change. But she couldn't help herself; an invisible force dragged her eyes sideways. 'Hi!' she said over-brightly. 'How are you?'

He looked at her and smiled with recognition. 'Hello! I'm fine, how are you?'

She wondered if he could hear the blood racing around her body: the noise in her own ears was deafening. 'Great, well not too bad – you know how it is!' Jesus, of course he didn't know how it was. Why did she blather like an idiot when she saw this man? 'Did you have a good Christmas?' she blurted out.

'Yes, not bad thanks. And you?'

She nodded enthusiastically.

'Great, really enjoyed it.' She couldn't think what else to say, her mind was blank. But now that he was here next to her, she was desperate to keep the conversation going. 'And you?' she finally said. 'Your Christmas I mean, was it okay?' As the words came out of her mouth, she knew she'd already asked him the same question, just seconds earlier. He must think she was a total idiot.

'Yes, I did,' he nodded. 'Seems a distant memory already! But it's always the way, when we rush back to work afterwards.'

The girl behind the till was passing over her change, and when Katie put out a shaking hand to take it, she dropped a ten pence piece on the counter. She scooped it up and quickly put the handful of coins into her pocket. 'I might need... that is, I think I might have to come and see you again though. Sometime soon. I still have some questions.'

He nodded, but she sensed she'd lost him. 'That's fine. Just call and make an appointment.' He smiled at the girl who was handing him a receipt, then briefly at her again. 'Have a good day,' he said. 'Nice to see you!'

She watched him walk away, then, when the woman behind her coughed loudly, realised she was still standing at the till, holding up the queue. Her knees were trembling along with her hands, and dizziness rocked her as she walked towards the exit. Why had she said that about needing to see him? It was as if a shutter had come down: he clearly felt uncomfortable talking about work in such a public place – which was understandable for someone in his profession. She should have kept the conversation light, maybe asked if he was getting time off at New Year. No, that would have been too personal. How the hell was she meant to handle this?

As she came out into the car park, she could see him walking towards the exit at the far end. She stopped in her tracks and stared after him. Although she'd hoped to get a different reaction – even if it was just a fleeting change of expression or a look in his eye – it wasn't surprising he'd played it cool. Even if you took the fact that he was a GP out of the equation, of course there was no way he could talk to her in public. Their relationship, whatever was happening between them, was something they needed to keep private – she should have been more careful. He had a reputation to think about, and it didn't take much for people to start talking.

Stupid woman; bloody stupid. She was furious with herself.

But by the time she got into the car, she'd calmed down. It would all be fine. He'd obviously been glad to bump into her too, but he didn't need to make it obvious. It was enough that they both knew what was going on. She heard his voice again in her head – 'Have a good day, nice to see you!'

Her body felt lighter somehow, less solid and middle-aged. She flicked her hair back over her shoulders and sucked in her stomach; going without breakfast wasn't that hard: she could probably lose a few pounds quite easily if she tried. The sun was coming out, sliding through a gap in the clouds, for what felt like the first time in weeks. As it sparkled on car windscreens and cast shadows across the dull tarmac, she thought what a difference it made; how much better life seemed when the skies were blue instead of metallic grey.

Nice to see you!

The thought of Pete, lying in bed with a thumping head, flickered by. But she put it out of her mind again and started the engine.

38

'It's having a knock-on effect on everything else,' he said, 'which is just not acceptable.'

'I know,' she said. 'But things have been tricky lately – for all sorts of reasons…'

'Katie, I don't need any more excuses.'

'You've been really understanding, Duncan, and I do appreciate it. I'm going to stay later and make up some of the time…'

'Sorry, but that's not good enough. I need people I can rely on. I don't get that from you any more, Katie.'

'But…'

'I'm going to have to let you go.'

The words slammed into her.

'I'll pay you for the next four weeks, but it's probably easier if you don't work out your notice period. I'd rather get someone else lined up to take over as soon as possible.'

There was a roaring in her ears, as if a train was thundering past the window. 'But, Duncan…'

'Sorry, Katie, the decision has been made. There's nothing more to say. If there's anything you need to hand over to

Fraser, I'd suggest you do it this morning. Then clear your desk. I've got a temp coming in after lunch, to get on top of the invoicing.'

She stared past his head, out of the window overlooking the yard. A lorry was backing in, its reversing alarm beeping persistently as it trundled towards the warehouse doors.

'I'll send on your P45 in the next day or so.'

She knew she should be saying something, arguing her case – telling him he couldn't do this. Or crying. Why wasn't she bursting into tears? She seemed to cry at the drop of a hat nowadays. But she just felt numb.

She didn't look at Fraser as she walked across to her desk, but knew he was staring at her. She sat down and began to gather together pieces of paper. The in-tray was full of letters and printouts of emails she hadn't responded to, requests for quotes and messages from suppliers. The sick pay record sheets hadn't been updated since early December, and she knew there were also outstanding invoices lost amongst the clutter. It was a mess.

Duncan was right, she hadn't been keeping on top of anything. She felt sick. How had she let things drift this badly?

'Are you okay?'

She looked across at Fraser, preparing herself for sarcastic comments. But he looked shocked. 'I had no idea he was going to do that,' he said quietly. 'I'm really sorry, Katie.'

When she got into the car, an hour later, she sat for a while, not sure what to do. She was clutching a plastic bag, into which she'd put the few personal possessions she'd had on her desk: a photo of the girls, a half-dead cactus, the mug saying *World's Best Mum*, which had been a birthday present from Anna last year. She couldn't go straight home – what would she say to Pete? She'd have to drive around for a while, find a café to sit in.

A headache was filling every inch of her skull, but she felt surprisingly calm. She was probably still in shock but, strangely, didn't feel angry. Duncan had always been flexible and understanding, especially over the last six months when she'd had to ask for so much time off work. After her mother died, he had rung her at home and told her to take as long as she needed. 'Don't come back before you're ready,' he'd said. 'You need to give yourself time to grieve. I didn't do that when my dad died, and it makes it harder in the long term.'

She'd been touched by his concern, and by the fact that he'd shared this snippet from his closely guarded private life. But that was then. Now, nearly three months after Clara's death, Katie had abused that sympathy and understanding. She had arrived at work late, left early using numerous excuses, taken overly long lunch breaks. And her mind had definitely not been on her job. It was no wonder he'd lost patience with her.

She drove into town and parked in the multi-storey; at the back of her mind was the worry that someone might recognise the car, wonder why she wasn't at work. But that was ridiculous: most people were still on holiday anyway, between Christmas and New Year. Even so, she avoided the places where she usually went with Pete or friends, and found a table in a dark corner of a café down near the canal. Wrapping her hands around a mug of coffee, she put her phone on the table, checking to see whether anyone had called or texted. As usual, there was nothing.

It was still only 11am. How was she going to fill the next few hours?

Her fingers tapped the screen and she flicked through apps without thinking about what she was doing. Her contacts list appeared in front of her, names listed alphabetically, and she scrolled down until she found it. She clicked on the number and put the phone to her ear. It rang twice; three times. Four. She was about to end the call.

'Joe Harvey?'

The sound of his voice made her heart jolt, and she breathed in sharply.

'Hello…?'

It's me, she wanted to say. *It's me, Katie. I just had to hear your voice, remind myself you're out there somewhere. I want to be near you, hold you, breathe in the scent of you. I want to feel your arms around me, and listen to your heart beating next to mine, through the shirt which smells of your body. I want to put my hand against your cheek, feel the rough stubble on your chin, slide the tips of my fingers across your lips.*

'Hello… who is this?'

The room in front of her had gone blurry, the shape of the counter and the waitress serving behind it, now indistinct. She heard the click of the call being ended, and only realised she had been holding her breath when a sob forced her to gasp and fill her lungs. She put the phone on the table and stared at it through the tears that were filling her eyes.

39

'This is very decadent of us,' said Monica, pulling her chair in towards the table and picking up the menu. 'Ladies who lunch!'

Katie smiled back. 'I thought we deserved it.' When she arranged to meet Monica here, she'd been intending to tell her what had happened at work. It was a piece of news she didn't want to share – even with her oldest friend – because it was so humiliating; she'd been the architect of her own misfortune. But as the hours went by yesterday, the pressure had built up inside her. What had happened was too important, too terrifying; she had to tell someone and, if that person couldn't yet be Pete, it must be Monica.

But sitting here now, she didn't know how to start. On several occasions she took a deep breath, prepared herself to launch into it. But then she bottled out, and the conversation went off on a different tack.

'Then of course, he got all shirty and decided that it was my fault for being late!' Monica took a sip of her water. 'You can't win with some people.'

Katie laughed. She had left the house just after 8am this

morning, as normal. Pete – hangover-free – had rolled over in bed when she got up, yawned and said he was getting up. But she'd taken him up a cup of tea and told him to enjoy his lie-in.

'Won't stay here for long,' he mumbled. 'I'm going to ring the union, see if they can suggest anything.'

As she pulled out of the drive, she'd wondered where on earth she would go. Yesterday had dragged interminably. After making two coffees last as long as possible in the café, she had driven out of town to a local viewpoint, and joined the swarms of dog walkers who were enjoying the winter sunshine. She couldn't go far – her work shoes were impractical for muddy paths – but it had felt good to be out in the fresh air.

Today she only had to pretend to be out of the house for a half day, because it was New Year's Eve. So, she'd turned towards town again and headed to the library. As she walked up the stairs, she couldn't help remembering her previous visit to this cavernous, old building; the way she'd sunk down in the chair at the back of the room, shifting from side to side to catch glimpses of Joe, going to speak to him at the end of the talk, sharing that conspiratorial smile. It seemed such a long time ago.

She was regretting calling his number yesterday. It had been good to hear his voice, but it had also been an incredibly stupid thing to do. He wouldn't have recognised the number, but there was nothing to stop him calling back to find out who had tried to get hold of him, and what would she say if he did? The thought filled her with a mixture of desire and total panic. But as the hours passed, she had gradually relaxed. He must just have thought it was a cold caller; he was far too busy to waste time returning a call from a number he didn't recognise.

She'd expected to be bored stiff at the library, but had actually enjoyed wandering around the shelves, picking out books and taking them to one of the little kiosks by the window. She flicked through a couple of novels, neither of which grabbed her, then found a book on local history, with photos of the town from a hundred years ago. The day's newspapers were piled up beside the desk, so she helped herself to a tabloid, full of gossip about the stars of the TV reality shows that governed Anna's life.

Even so, this lunch with Monica hadn't come a moment too soon.

'How is everything?' Monica was asking, as she speared the chicken in her salad with her fork. 'With you, I mean? You're looking tired.'

'I am a bit,' said Katie. 'Too many late nights over Christmas.'

'Are you okay in yourself though, not feeling too down?'

Katie folded the napkin carefully beside her plate, taking too long to iron out the creases with her palms, wondering how to answer. She suddenly felt tearful again. She wanted to be able to smile and tell Monica that everything was fine, that she was coping well. But it wasn't true.

'Katie?'

Her lower lip was wobbling, and she angrily put her hand over her mouth, looking up at Monica as her eyes filled with tears. 'Bloody awful actually.'

'Oh, sweetheart...' Monica reached across the table, grabbing Katie's free hand. 'I'm sorry, I've been wittering on about stuff, and you needed to talk. I'm not surprised you're feeling shit. This is such a difficult time of year. It's all too intense and emotional; it makes the memories harder to bear.'

Katie nodded, not trusting herself to speak.

'Is it just that you're missing your mum?' asked Monica. 'Or is it something else? It sounds like Christmas was hard work. Did you get any time to yourself?'

Katie shook her head. 'Not really.'

'I bet now everything feels like it's piling on top of you.

This isn't going to be a quick fix, Katie, you need to be kind to yourself. This was your first Christmas without her. But you've got through it! You made it out the other side, so you must be proud of yourself for that.'

They were easy words to say, harder to act on. And Katie knew she hadn't made it through Christmas very well at all. But admitting it had been a struggle, felt like such failure. She was sure Monica would never go to pieces like this, if – when – her mother died.

Anyway, it hadn't all been about her mother. The rows with Pete and her problems at work had been in the background, and overshadowing everything was her obsession with a man she hardly knew, but whose handsome face she couldn't get out of her mind.

'The other bit of bad news is that Pete has been suspended from school,' she said. 'He's very stressed about it all.'

Monica nodded, taking another sip of her water. 'Yes, he texted and told me. Not surprised he's upset, poor Pete.'

Katie looked up in surprise. 'Did he?'

'This chicken is amazing,' said Monica. 'Do you want to try some?'

Katie shook her head. She was playing around with the salmon on her own plate, unable to get enthusiastic about anything.

'What about the hospice letter?' said Monica. 'Have you decided what to do about that?'

Katie sat back in her chair, indescribably weary. 'Not really. It's frustrating they dismissed it so lightly, but Pete wants me to drop it – he says it's making me more stressed, and I'm beginning to think he's right. The longer it goes on, the more I just want to forget about the whole thing. But on the other hand, doing nothing would make me feel guilty, like I'd let mum down.'

It suddenly struck her, out of nowhere, that there was

another reason why she was scared of giving up now and backing away. Doing so would mean she'd need to acknowledge the end of this fight and the start of something else: a new existence, with a big Clara-shaped hole in it. Maybe that was what she was putting off?

An hour later, they paid the bill and wandered into the street, stepping out of the way as a pair of men ran along the pavement, sweat glistening on their foreheads, their yellow T-shirts startlingly bright on a winter's day.

As she said goodbye to Monica and turned to walk back towards the library, Katie's phone bleeped. She knew before she looked at the message, that it would be from Rachel. When she pulled out the phone, the screen was still illuminated. Beginning to read, her pulse quickened.

That would be great! CU when u come in. Rx

40

When she got back, the house was deserted. She saw Pete through the kitchen window, standing in the back garden holding a pair of shears. 'What are you doing?'

'Thought I'd cut back this hedge. I think this is the right time of year for pruning.'

Katie watched him struggle to reach the higher branches, many of which had grown out of the hedge at angles, like jets erupting from a fountain. 'Are you sure it's the right time?'

Neither of them were interested in gardening, and they ventured outside on maintenance missions only when the shrubs grew so lanky it was hard to get through to clear the mess left on the lawn by next door's cat.

'Yup, think so,' he was out of breath with the effort of holding up the shears. 'It's good to get on with it, while it's not raining.'

Walking back into the kitchen, she sighed as she looked at the domestic devastation. It was great Pete was doing something constructive outside, but why couldn't he clear up in here on his way through? The table was still covered in plates from breakfast; the dishwasher had finished its cycle but not been unloaded; there was a pile of clothes in the washing basket, waiting to go into the machine. Why was she the only one capable of thinking about any of this? She wiped surfaces, put away cereal packets and stacked clean plates, bowls and glasses into cupboards.

The phone rang and she looked at the incoming number before deciding against answering. It was Brenda. She'd probably been trying to call all afternoon, but Pete wouldn't have heard the phone from the garden – any more than he would have heard Katie throwing cutlery into the drawer, slamming cupboard doors and muttering under her breath.

Ten minutes later she was back in the car, heading to the bypass. Anna had wanted to come too. 'I'm bored! I've got nothing to do.'

'Too bad. Didn't you have any homework over the holidays?'

'I've done it.'

'All of it?'

'Well, not all of it. But it's very hard. I don't know how to do it and I need help, but you're going out and Daddy's in the garden and Suky told me to bugger off. She shouldn't be allowed to say that because it's swearing, but when I told her, she just said it again.'

Katie had expected the shopping centre to be busy, but the chaos was still frustrating and, she drove around for several minutes without finding a space. Seeing a car's reversing lights come on, she stopped and waited for it to back out but then, as she inched forward, a silver BMW glided up and manoeuvred into the space.

'Hey!' She started to wind down the window, preparing to yell at the balding man in the driver's seat. But as she did so a picture popped into her mind, of the stark room at the police station. She could see the officer writing on the form in front of him, almost hear the pen scratching across the paper. Fear washed over her. Taking a deep breath, she sat back in her seat and made an effort to lower her shoulders. If deterrence was the aim of police cautions, it was working a treat.

A blast of warm air hit her when she walked into the shopping centre, along with a burst of something from Beyoncé being played over the Tannoy – she was proud of herself for recognising it.

Rachel was behind the tills again. 'Hi!' she said, smiling as she looked up from the cash register. 'Just let me finish with this customer and I'll be with you.'

Katie stood to one side, flicking through skirts on a railing.

'Right, hello again. That was good timing, I was about to go on a break.' Today Rachel had her hair piled into a messy bun on the top of her head, with wisps straying down around her ears; it looked effortless but Katie suspected it had taken ages. Surely it wasn't possible to look that good without a lot of hard work? Rachel looked very young and as pretty as ever, in a beige jumper that complemented the brown of her eyes.

'I don't want to take up your break,' she said.

'That's fine,' said Rachel. 'I'm flattered you've asked me to help. Let's have a look round, shall we. What sort of things are you after – smart or casual? It is for work or to wear out on special occasions?'

'Both really,' said Katie. 'I'm useless at shopping so I never find things that suit me. But that green cardigan I bought here the other week was great, and you looked amazing when you came to meet me for lunch. That's why I thought you might give me some advice.'

'I'd love to!' Rachel swiped carelessly at a wisp of hair that was trailing in front of one eye. 'Come on, let's start over here.'

This girl was impossible to dislike, Katie thought, watching her walk across the store, pointing out a top here, a skirt there, running her hands down the sleeve of a cashmere jumper and smiling back at Katie. She was naturally warm, with no pretensions, seemingly unaware of her own charm. Possibly rather naïve too, in the nicest possible way.

They wandered around the shop, Rachel picking out clothes and holding them up against Katie, whose arms gradually disappeared beneath a pile of items to try on. A coat hanger clattered to the floor and a jumper slipped down after it. 'I think we've got enough to be going on with.' Rachel bent to pick them up. 'Come on, I'm due back on shortly, so I can swap with Ginny in the fitting rooms and be there when you try it all on.'

Manoeuvring into a cubicle and closing the curtain, Katie stood and looked at herself in the mirror. Arms still full of clothes, she leant forward and examined the wrinkles around her eyes, noticing another strand of grey poking through the parting on top of her head. There were times when she thought she didn't look bad for her age, but having spent twenty minutes basking in the glow of Rachel's fresh, unlined complexion, she felt even more jaded. She sighed and turned her head sideways: at least she wasn't jowly – PTA Fiona had an excess of wobbly skin beneath her chin. Katie smiled and noted her jawline tighten as she did so.

'How are you getting on?'

She backed away from the mirror and started hanging up the clothes. 'Slowly! I'll be out in a minute.' She undid the zip on her skirt, wriggling it down over her knees and kicking off her shoes, before grabbing one of the skirts Rachel had selected. It was tight, however hard she sucked in her stomach, but the material was nice and it was a great colour. She pulled on a jumper and stepped out into the narrow passageway.

'That looks great! How does it feel? I like that colour on you.'

Katie put the fingers of both hands inside the waistband of the skirt and tried to swivel it. 'It's a bit tight to be honest,' she admitted. 'But I like it.'

'I'll get someone to fetch the next size; try on something else in the meantime,' said Rachel, turning back to the door and waving at a colleague.

When Katie finally emerged from the fitting rooms, she was amazed to see it was nearly 4pm. Rachel had taken away the clothes that weren't right, but there was still a large pile: two skirts, a pair of trousers, a shirt, another cardigan and a jumper – the same beige one that had done amazing things for Rachel's eyes.

'I shouldn't be buying all this,' she said, standing outside the fitting rooms.

'Well, it's up to you, but it all suits you,' said Rachel. 'I'm not just saying that because I want you to spend your money with us – a couple of the other tops didn't work.' She looked at Katie and beamed. 'And it was fun! I like it when customers ask for my advice – it makes me feel useful.'

Katie smiled back. 'It was fun for me too,' she said. 'Rachel, you've been so kind. Let me buy you a coffee sometime to say thank you properly, or better still a glass of wine. How about next week? That would make me feel less guilty about taking up your time today.'

Rachel laughed. 'There's really no need, but go on then, a glass of wine would be great.'

'Good, I'll text you,' said Katie. 'It's been great to see you again, I've really enjoyed it.'

'Me too,' sparkled Rachel. 'Now I must get back to work.'

And after that you'll be going back to the little house you share with Joe, to carry on with your happy life, thought Katie as she walked over to the tills. *With your pretty face and your great figure and oh-so perfect hair. You'll be kissing the man I want; holding him, hugging him, making love to him. I should hate you Rachel Aston, because you've got everything I want. Why are you so bloody nice with it?*

41

By the time she got home it was dark, and the wind whipped her hair into her eyes as she got out of the car. There was more rain on the way, possibly a storm. Katie opened the boot to take out the bags of clothes, then thought better of it and slammed it shut again, locking the car as she walked towards the door.

She was horrified at how much she'd spent. When the girl on the till rang up the total, Katie felt her mouth drop open. 'Are you sure?' she'd asked.

'I'm afraid so,' the girl grinned. '£318.75 – and that's including the fifteen per cent discount from today's special offer. I deducted that automatically for you.'

Katie had fumbled for her purse and flicked through the plastic cards. Duncan had said she'd get paid for the next month, but her personal bank account was overdrawn at the moment. Back in November, she and Pete had put the deposit for next year's summer holiday onto one credit card, and they'd used the other to pay for Christmas. Anyway, the statements came to Pete so she couldn't put this bill on it without telling him, which at the moment wasn't an option.

As she flicked through her purse, the girl pushed a form across the counter. 'How about applying for our store card? It only takes a few minutes to set up. Your first payment won't be due until the start of the following month, so you've effectively got several weeks of credit.'

Katie didn't hesitate, although she'd always shied away from store cards: 'If you can't afford it, you shouldn't be thinking about buying it,' her mother used to say.

'Great idea, why not?' she said, taking the form and rooting in her bag for a pen.

By the time she left the shop, fifteen minutes later, her mood was upbeat. She had filled in the paperwork, passed the credit check, watched the girl wrap her purchases in pretty mauve tissue paper and been told her new card would arrive in the post in the next few days.

Putting her key into the front door, she decided to smuggle the clothes into the house in stages, and gradually integrate them into her wardrobe. She could say she'd bought the skirts with Brenda's Christmas cheque – even though that had disappeared into her overdraft. And the jumper could be one she was borrowing from Monica. Pleased with her creativity, she stepped inside and slammed the door behind her. Anna was singing loudly and tunelessly upstairs. Katie walked into the kitchen, where Pete was flicking through a newspaper; there was a cup of half-drunk tea on the table beside him, along with crumbs that suggested he'd had toast.

'Oh, Pete, why can't you use a plate?' she sighed, picking up the mug.

'Hey, I haven't finished that!'

'It's nearly cold.' She grabbed a dishcloth and started to wipe the crumbs off the table, slamming the lid back on the margarine tub, throwing a dirty knife in the sink. 'Nobody ever clears up around here and it really gets me down.'

'Sorry, I wasn't thinking,' he said. 'I've been out in the garden for hours and I was starving.'

'Me too. I mean I'm sorry too,' she said. 'Look, let's have something nice to eat tonight. I could make those spicy fishcake things you like? It's New Year's Eve, we ought to do something a bit different.'

'That would be great, but just to warn you – my parents are coming round in an hour or so.'

'Not to eat?'

'No, they're popping in for a drink.'

Katie started getting ingredients out of the fridge. The prospect of Alan and Brenda arriving on the doorstep didn't fill her with joy. 'That's fine,' she said, grabbing a chopping board from the side and reminding herself about the shopping bags in the car.

The doorbell rang just as the digital clock on the oven was clicking from 5.59 to 6.00. The people who co-ordinated Greenwich Mean Time could learn a lesson or two in punctuality from her in-laws. Katie wiped her hands on a tea towel and went to open the door. 'Alan, how lovely! Come in. How are you, Brenda?'

Once ice had been clunked into glasses, gin had been poured and mixed with tonic, and crisps piled into a large bowl, they went into the sitting room.

'We've had such a wonderful afternoon,' chirped Brenda. 'We popped into Phil's. Camilla really does Christmas in spectacular fashion. So many twinkly lights!'

'Yes, marvellously twinkly,' agreed Alan.

'As for their tree! Katie, you would not believe how beautiful it looks. Camilla went for a gold and blue theme this year. Inspirational, wasn't it, Alan?'

'Inspirational,' he nodded, slugging his gin.

'Were you there for lunch?' asked Katie.

'Oh no dear, just for a cup of tea. But there were some lovely biscuits.'

'Most tasty,' said Alan. 'Although I could have done with a couple more. We couldn't stay long; they'd been out at lunchtime and had people coming over this evening. They're so busy, such a lot of friends.'

'So busy,' echoed Brenda.

Katie smiled at them over the top of her gin glass. Clever old Camilla had got off lightly again this year.

Pete began to tell his parents about the problems he was having at school, and Katie watched as he talked, surprised by how calm he looked. Compared to the grey-faced, stooped Pete who had come back from his meeting with Sara, this Pete seemed to have had his batteries recharged. He hadn't changed out of the old clothes he'd been wearing in the garden, and his hair was still wind-swept, but there was colour in his cheeks and he was talking with animation, re-enthused by his own determination to integrate Damien and prove the boy's parents wrong.

'It's ridiculous they went to the police,' he was saying. 'It means we've all got to go through a lot of unnecessary red tape.'

'What's going to happen now?' asked Brenda, who had drained her gin and was tapping on the outside of the glass with her fingernails.

Katie needed a top-up herself, so she got up. 'Shall I pop another one in there for you, Brenda?'

When she came back into the sitting room, Alan was braying like a mule. 'Bloody people. Don't realise the value of a good teacher. I can't see you losing your job over this, Peter. You've done nothing wrong.'

'Absolutely,' agreed Brenda, reaching out her hand for the glass. 'And at least Sara is backing you.'

'Clive at the NEU says we need to make sure we keep

proper records of everything,' Pete said. 'Including conversations with the parents.'

This was news to Katie. She didn't know he'd had a phone conversation with the union. Maybe he'd mentioned it last night, but she hadn't been listening properly?

'I think it's sensible you've got those pills too,' said Brenda. 'There's no shame in admitting you can't cope when life gets stressful. There have been times when I would have found it difficult to be my normal, happy self without my Diazepam.'

'What's this?' asked Katie, lifting her glass to her lips.

'I went to the surgery yesterday and had a chat with one of the doctors,' said Pete, turning to her. 'He gave me something to help me sleep. Nice guy, quite new I think. Dr Harvey.'

An ice cube flew out of Katie's mouth and hit the coffee table with a crack, while the rest of her mouthful of gin and tonic sprayed across her skirt, the sofa cushion and the leg of Alan's corduroy trousers.

'Argh!' yelled Alan, jumping up and spilling his own gin onto the carpet.

'Katie, what are you doing?' shouted Pete.

Wiping the liquid from her chin, Katie stood up and brushed her skirt, before turning to do the same to Alan's trousers. His face was puce. 'Sorry, so sorry,' she said. 'I'll get a cloth.' Rushing into the kitchen, she put her glass on the draining board and gripped the edge of the sink with both hands to steady herself. *Breathe*, she thought, *just breathe: in and out.* Her hand shook as she reached for a cloth. What the hell had Pete been doing, seeing Joe? She pictured the two of them, sitting together in the consulting room, Joe leaning forward, listening to what Pete was saying. The two men in her life, inches away from each other. It was so wrong.

Back in the sitting room, Pete was helping Alan mop his trousers with tissues and Brenda had moved along to the far end of the sofa.

'I'm sorry, Alan, that was awful,' said Katie. 'It went down the wrong way. Are you all right?'

'Yes, I'm fine, don't worry,' he said, tugging up the waistband of his trousers. 'It'll be dry in no time.'

Katie scrubbed at the sofa with a tea towel, then threw it onto the carpet to soak up the rest of Alan's spilt drink. They sat down again, avoiding the wet patch.

'Anyway,' said Pete. 'That's all there is to tell you at the moment. I feel much better about everything though.'

'Good for you,' nodded Brenda.

'Let us know if there's anything we can do,' asked Alan. 'Anything at all.'

'Next time you come over, you could bring more gin,' Katie said, brightly. 'In case I spit it out over you!'

Nobody laughed.

42

They ate just before nine o'clock, by which time the fishcakes were dry and burnt, because Katie – having drunk two more glasses of gin after the one she expelled over Alan – forgot to keep an eye on the pan. Later they sat with Anna, watching the inane New Year's Eve TV froth that kept her happy.

'So,' Katie kept her voice casual. 'Why did you decide to go to the doctor?'

Pete shrugged. 'I couldn't believe how depressed I was feeling about it all. When I came home after that meeting, I just wanted to sit and cry.' He glanced across at her. 'I know it sounds ridiculous, but teaching is my life. I don't know how to do anything else. I was panicking, I didn't know what to do if everything was going to come tumbling down around me.'

She put out her hand and rested it on his forearm, stroking it gently.

'I spent hours lying in bed, but I couldn't sleep, and I was so tired I felt physically sick. I thought I'd go to the surgery and see if they could give me anything to calm me down. Or just some advice. You hear about these meditation techniques, mindfulness, whatever the hell that is. I wanted to pull myself out of this before it started. I've seen what depression can do to people – remember that guy, Charlie?'

Katie nodded.

'So, I saw this doctor. Really nice bloke, Dr Harvey. He seems to know his stuff, and he sat and listened – which was probably all I needed, to be honest. But he gave me something to help me sleep, if things don't settle down.'

'So, you did this yesterday?' asked Katie.

'Yes.'

'Why didn't you tell me?'

'Didn't really think about it, to be honest. It's no big deal – I'm not having a breakdown or anything!'

She looked at him, sitting further along the sofa, his face in profile as he watched an overweight woman dressed in pink, singing her heart out in front of a panel of celebrity judges. The shape of his nose, the curve of his cheekbone, the way his hair curled up slightly at the back as it touched his collar: everything about him was so familiar to her. If she'd been blindfolded and told to trace that face with her finger, she would have known Pete from any other man.

His phone kept pinging and he smiled as he read the messages, laughing out loud every now and then. Katie's own phone stayed as silent as usual. 'Who's that?' she asked, eventually, feeling left out. He was angling the phone screen away from her. 'Who's so keen to speak to you on New Year's Eve?'

'Just a bloke I used to see at five-a-side,' he said, putting the phone down. 'I'll put it on silent. Didn't know it was disturbing you.'

'It's fine,' Katie said. 'Sorry.' She felt like she was being a misery again.

Anna wanted to stay up until midnight, but fell asleep on the sofa long before, so Pete carried her up to bed. Suky was at a friend's, where she'd said they'd be bringing in the New Year with pizza and lemonade. Katie rather doubted that, but couldn't be bothered to check if any more bottles had been smuggled out of the cupboard where they kept the alcohol. Suky had also mentioned that Adam would be there. She had been strangely cheerful recently: fewer doors were being slammed, and there hadn't been much deep sighing. She had even sat with them in front of the TV for an hour last night, rather than shutting herself in her bedroom with her phone and laptop.

'Do you think she's in love?' Pete had asked yesterday morning, as their daughter left the house for the bus, off to meet Adam again.

'God, you might be right,' said Katie. 'I wonder what he's like? Poor boy, let's hope he has nerves of steel and armour plating around his heart.'

If Suky had fallen in love, Katie envied her. She remembered how she'd felt when she saw Joe in the library and they'd exchanged that knowing glance. The world had seemed less grey, life's little niggles less onerous, as if someone had grabbed a hypodermic and given her a shot of positivity in the upper arm.

With Anna in bed, she and Pete watched a film they'd both seen before. It hadn't been funny the first time, and the jokes were even more laboured now, but there wasn't much else on.

Where was Joe? What was he doing? Probably sitting with Rachel on their cream sofa, arms carelessly wound around each other, a bottle of wine on the table in front of them, the television on in the corner. She saw herself sitting next to him, watching this same film, laughing at the inanity of it. He would lean forward to top up her wine glass, brushing her knee with his hand as he did so, sending a tingle up her leg. She just wanted to be with him, near him, to run her hand down his arm, feel the muscles tense beneath her fingers.

Pete laughed loudly as the main character blew himself up in a bungled bank raid.

I don't want to be here, thought Katie. *I want to be with you.*

That night they made love for the first time in months. When Katie turned off the bedside light, Pete reached for her shoulder with his hand and she moved towards him. Their lovemaking was calm and familiar; their bodies knitted together with ease. But with her eyes closed it was Joe she saw leaning over her; Joe whose strong arms wrapped themselves round her; Joe whose lips she felt against her own.

'I love you,' she told him, her breath coming jaggedly, imagining him smiling at her in the half darkness.

'I love you too,' said Pete.

43

Now that Fraser was no longer a part of her life – putting her down, sneering, making her feel old and dull – Katie was surprised how much she missed him. What had he done on New Year's Eve? Probably partied himself into one hell of a hangover. She wondered how he was getting on with whoever had replaced her. Despite their differences, they'd worked feet away from each other for three years, so he was bound to find it strange having someone else sit in her chair, tap on her keyboard, stare out of her window down into the yard. She hoped they wouldn't get on too well, Fraser and the New Katie. It would be nice to think he'd miss her. Just a little.

Her mobile bleeped, and she felt a thrill as she read the name at the top of the text: Rachel. *CU at 7 2nite? X*

Why could young people never be bothered to spell out words properly? That was the sort of message Suky would send. Katie replied, taking care not to use any abbreviations: *Great. See you at Mulligans at 7, looking forward to it!*

She read her message again, then added an x at the end. Rachel had sent her an x so she guessed she ought to send one back – she didn't want to sound too formal. It was tricky getting the tone right with texting: Monica always signed off with xx, so Katie did the same when she replied to her. On the rare occasions when there was only one x, or worse still none at all, Katie worried she'd done something to offend her. She knew she was being over-sensitive: Monica had probably been in a hurry.

She had no idea what she was going to say to Rachel. She should probably start by thanking her for her advice in the fitting rooms – tell her how much she was enjoying wearing the new clothes. Although most of them were still wrapped in mauve tissue paper, hidden in the boot of her car. And it seemed odd to be grateful to someone who'd helped her spend £318.75 she didn't have.

This morning she had left the house at the usual time and driven nearly twenty miles to waste a couple of hours in a museum, after which she'd bought a newspaper and sat in a café, taking an embarrassingly long time to drink one pot of tea.

She had to talk to Pete; this was ridiculous.

She'd been on the point of telling him about work so many times, taking a deep breath and steeling herself to start talking. But the words just wouldn't come out, and the longer this went on, the harder it became. She didn't think he'd be angry – or if he was, his anger would be directed at Duncan. But she felt so stupid: unbelievably reckless. With the cost-of-living crisis affecting just about everything, no one with half a brain would take such a slack, irresponsible attitude to work that they risked getting fired. Especially not a middle-aged mother of two, who ought to know better.

Her mobile rang while she was driving home. When she checked later, she was surprised to see it had been the surgery. Why on earth would they be calling her? Unless it was Joe…

She played the answerphone message, desperate to hear his voice. 'It's the Pelham Green Surgery here, Mrs Johnson,' said a woman, tinny and distant. 'Can you give us a ring please?'

Her mind went back to her last appointment – the smell of his skin, his smile as he showed her out. Then she saw herself walking back through the waiting room, being knocked by the child with his sword. In her mind the picture replayed of the vase tipping over, as if in slow motion, the horrified look on the receptionist's face as she leapt up from her chair. Shit, they were probably calling to tell her the whole computer system had gone down, and she owed them for damages. She hadn't thought about it since, but now panic surged through her. This was the last thing she needed. If only that woman had kept her child under control.

She deleted the message. Best to pretend she hadn't picked it up.

'I'm home!' she called out, slamming the front door behind her.

Suky and Pete were in the kitchen, preparing tea.

'I thought I might pop out tonight, just for an hour or so,' she said. 'A couple of the mums from school are meeting for a glass of wine. Would you mind?'

'That's fine,' said Pete. 'We're putting on some sausages – there's enough for you if you want them?'

'I won't, but thanks.'

The two of them were standing side by side, one peeling potatoes, the other cutting up a cauliflower. She stood and watched as they worked.

'So, is he at Overton?' asked Pete.

'No, Minsterworth. That's why he knows Claire: he's there with her brother.'

'What year is that?'

'Year 11, he's doing GCSEs. He's working really hard, he wants to get into the sixth form at Bourne Hall.'

'Good for him. So, what time tonight then?'

'We'll go for the 7.30 showing, so if you can pick me up about 9.30 that would be good.'

They worked on in silence.

'What's this?' asked Katie casually.

'Nothing,' said Suky. 'I'm just going to the cinema.'

'With...?'

Suky sighed. 'With Adam if you must know. I've told Dad about it. Anyway, these potatoes are done.' She threw the knife into the sink and walked out of the kitchen.

Pete turned to her and winked. 'We were right,' he said. 'First proper date, and she's really excited. Haven't seen her so happy in ages.'

Katie tried to smile. 'Good for her.' But she felt left out. 'Right, I'll be off then. Won't be late.'

She shouted goodbye up the stairs to the girls, but there was no reply.

Knowing she'd be drinking, she left the car at home and walked to the bus stop. She was far too early, but it was easier to get out of the house than stay and feel excluded from this new atmosphere of family co-operation and cosiness. Since New Year, Pete had been remarkably upbeat. School hadn't yet started again and, in the meantime, he seemed to be settling into a pattern of parenthood that was new to them all. The bulk of the childcare had always fallen onto Katie. She was the one who nagged about homework and planned what to cook for tea. She picked up coats, scarves and shoes that had been discarded in the hall and returned them to their rightful place; she emptied waste bins and tied up black rubbish sacks to leave out on the pavement.

Or she had done.

Now Pete was doing all that, and doing it pretty well. While she'd been pretending to be at work today, he had shopped for food, pushed the hoover across the carpets, collected armloads of dirty clothes from the laundry baskets and even selected the correct setting on the washing machine. Katie was confused by how redundant she felt: for years she'd resented having to shoulder the burden of keeping house and home together. So why did she now hate having to give it up?

Sitting in the car park next to Mulligan's, she pulled out her phone. It was safe to do this now, Suky had told her how. 'Whenever you call someone, dial 141 first,' she'd said. 'Then your phone number will be withheld.'

Katie had taken back the phone, impressed. How did teenagers know all this stuff?

'Why don't you want people to see your number?' asked Suky.

'Oh, I just don't want to give it out, left, right and centre,' she'd said. 'I don't think it's very safe.'

'Mum, hardly anyone phones you!' Suky had laughed. 'I don't think you're exactly high risk. Who's going to be so desperate to track you down?'

Now, Katie took a deep breath and scrolled through her contacts. There he was: J. After her conversation with Suky, she had saved his number with 141 in front of it, and was quite pleased with herself. She felt a fluttering in her chest as it connected and began to ring. He didn't pick up and after ringing half a dozen times it went to answerphone. His voice was suddenly there again, so close that his lips could have been tickling her ear.

'Hi, this is Joe Harvey. I can't take your call right now, so please leave a message and I'll get back to you as soon as I can.'

'Happy New Year, my darling,' she whispered.

There was a long beep to show she could start leaving a message. With a trembling finger she ended the call, her spirits dropping as the screen went black. Saying the words felt good. But saying them to his face would be so much better.

An hour later, wine was mellowing her mood.

'It's not that I don't have any friends down here, it's just that I'm not as close to them as the ones I've known for years, back home,' Rachel was saying. 'I do get lonely sometimes, and I miss having a busy social life – it sometimes seems as if Joe's never at home. But I'm sure it will be fine, we haven't been here long.'

Katie took a sip of her wine. 'So, what about Joe?' she asked casually. 'Was he already working as a doctor when you met?'

Rachel stared at her. 'How did you know he's a doctor?'

It flashed through Katie's mind that she could say Rachel had mentioned this during a previous conversation. But she hadn't. Anyway, she'd used that excuse before – when they'd talked about the crash over Giardiniera pizza. Rachel wasn't going to believe it a second time. 'The paper!' she said. 'There was an article in the local paper about him speaking at some talk, ages ago, before Christmas.' It didn't add up, she knew it didn't. She wasn't supposed to know his surname: they weren't married. 'It said he was new to the area, a GP, just moved from Manchester. So, I'm putting two and two together and making five! Sorry, have I got it completely wrong – is that a different Joe?'

Rachel was frowning, bemused.

The article hadn't mentioned Manchester, Katie was aware of that – but maybe Rachel hadn't seen it? Or it was so long ago she wouldn't remember the details. Now she thought about it, Rachel hadn't mentioned his surname either; shit, this was all getting messy.

'Sorry, this is typical of me,' she said, grabbing the wine bottle and topping up Rachel's glass. 'I'm always trying to work out how friends go together, what makes them tick, and I often get it wrong. Pete tells me I'm interfering and that I should stop being nosy. But I'm just interested in people, I guess. He gets so angry with me sometimes...' Katie knew shouldn't be doing this. 'He gets wound up about a lot of things actually, and he's not good at controlling his temper. I try to take the flak, because I don't want him taking it out on the girls.'

Rachel was now looking concerned. 'That's dreadful.'

'Oh, it's just how things are,' said Katie. 'We're used to it.' Poor Pete: how awful to use him as a diversionary tactic. 'But I don't want to talk about that. Tell me about your Joe. It sounds like he's got a lot going on in his life?'

'Yes, he's on call at unpredictable times at the moment, because they're sorting out a new rota. The GPs at the practice also do outpatient clinics at Overton hospital. He's training for a half marathon in March, so he goes running several nights a week. It's good for him to have a way to get rid of all the stress.'

In her mind, Katie saw him sprinting along the streets, like the two men she'd seen the other day: pounding up through the park, sweat breaking out on his forehead, his muscles taut, bulging like lengths of rope in his forearms and calves.

'So, he must like it when you do your own thing then?'

'Oh yes. He was pleased I was going out with you tonight.'

Katie's eyes widened. 'How did he…?'

'I've told him all about you,' Rachel chatted on. 'That you came to see me after the crash to apologise, then how we had lunch and you came back to the shop.'

Katie's mind was racing to process this new information. Panic had welled up, like something stuck in her throat, making it hard to breathe. 'So, he knows who I am? I mean… you've told him about me?'

'Of course! And he thinks it's great that we've made friends like this – he's all in favour of reconciliation. He said the other day, he admires the way we've been so grown-up about the whole thing!'

He doesn't know it's me, Katie reassured herself. *When he saw me at the surgery, he didn't make the connection.*

Rachel rolled the stem of her wine glass between her thumb and forefinger as she talked, her cheeks flushed from the wine. 'And I think it's good too, Katie. That we've got to know each other like this. It's nice to have you as a friend – even though we didn't meet under great circumstances!'

Katie forced herself to smile. 'Life's too short to hold grudges.'

Rachel carried on talking. 'Joe tells me I need to get out more, and I know he's right. I don't want to be the one always sitting at home waiting for him to come back. But it's all very well for him, he's got a fulfilling career – whereas I certainly don't want to be working in retail forever! I do sometimes feel a bit sidelined.'

'He wouldn't be the first man to be self-obsessed and wrapped up in what he does!' Katie thought of Pete, hammering away on the computer keyboard in the office in the evenings, not thinking to ask how her day had been.

'I know, but it can be hard to be on the receiving end.' Rachel tucked a strand of hair behind her ear. 'I'm sure I'm over-thinking it all – being a bit paranoid. It's not that there's anything wrong between us, it's just that things haven't been the same since we came down here. I guess it's not surprising – we've been together three years, the excitement starts to wear off, doesn't it?'

Katie's pulse quickened. Was she reading too much into this? The pretty girl in front of her was hinting that her relationship wasn't going well. Could there be a reason for that? She remembered Joe's hand on her forearm in the surgery, the compassion in his gaze. Could *she* be the reason his attention was elsewhere?

Katie glanced sideways towards the end of the bar – just as Monica walked in through the door, unwinding her scarf from her neck and shaking rain off her umbrella. Fuck! What the hell was she doing here? Looking away again, Katie put up her hand to cover the side of her face, pretending to lean on it. With any luck Monica would make her way straight to the bar. The place was packed, so she was unlikely to notice them at this small table, tucked away in a corner.

'But if you and Pete have been together for years, you must know all about this,' Rachel was saying. 'Have you gone through stages where…'

'Katie?'

She lowered her hand and looked up. 'Mon! Fancy seeing you here! How are you?'

'Good, fine. How about you?' She looked at Rachel as she was speaking, and when Katie didn't say anything, she stuck out her hand. 'Hi, I'm Monica, a friend of Katie's. Nice to meet you.'

'Oh, you too. I'm Rachel.'

'Well, hello there, Rachel.' She turned back to face Katie. 'So, out for anything special, or just a girls' drink?'

'Just a drink,' said Katie, seeing Monica's eyes widen as they met her own. 'You know, catching up!'

'Lovely!' exclaimed Monica, looking back at Rachel again. 'So how do you two know each other then, where did you meet?'

Rachel laughed. 'Well, it's quite a funny story really…'

'Who are you meeting here, Mon?' interrupted Katie. 'We don't want to hold you up if you're looking for someone?'

Monica glanced at her and narrowed her eyes before looking towards the bar. 'Naomi,' she said. 'In fact, she's over there. I'd better go.'

She turned to Rachel again. 'Good to meet you.' She turned back to Katie. 'Enjoy your evening,' she said, in a voice that would have sounded normal to anyone else, then turned and walked away.

To her irritation, Katie felt herself blushing and fanned her face with one hand as she picked up her glass with the other. 'Is it just me, or is it warm in here tonight?'

Why the hell had Monica picked this bar?

'She seems nice,' said Rachel. 'How do you know her?'

'Oh, we go back a long way,' said Katie. 'A very long way.'

44

————————

Holding the bank statement, she sank onto a kitchen chair. It couldn't be this bad: maybe some money had gone into the account since it had been sent out? Although God knows where from – she certainly hadn't paid anything in. Katie had never been so overdrawn, nearly £700 now, with charges yet to be added on.

This explained why her card had been declined in the bar last night. Embarrassment flooded back as she remembered the look of disdain on the face of the waitress holding the portable payment machine. 'Computer says no,' she drawled, laughing at her own joke as she handed back Katie's debit card. 'Got another one?'

'Yes, of course.' Rummaging through the receipts and supermarket tokens in her purse, Katie had pulled out her credit card. 'Oh no, not this,' she said. 'Hang on, there's another one here somewhere.'

'Let me get this,' Rachel had said.

'No, I invited you out, so this is definitely on me.' But there had been an edge of panic in her voice, and Rachel had heard it.

'Seriously, Katie, let me pay.' She handed a card to the waitress. 'Put it on there, thanks. It's been a lovely evening and I've enjoyed seeing you. Anyway, you've just spent a fortune on all those new clothes – which was my fault! It's only fair I buy you a couple of glasses of wine.'

Katie had been mortified, but relieved. 'Thank you. My wages should have been paid in by now, not sure what's gone wrong there.'

After her evening out with Rachel she had slept fitfully, her dreams full of the other woman: Rachel smiling at her from a doorway, their arms linked as they stepped onto a train together, Katie wearing the red bolero jacket and ripping off the buttons, one by one.

This morning she had a hangover. And this bloody bank statement wasn't helping her mood. She needed some cash: there wasn't even enough fuel in the car to last another day. She felt sick, weighed down with worry. When her final wages got paid, they'd disappear into a big hole.

Pete wandered into the kitchen, his hair damp from the shower, and she folded the bank statement and slipped it inside a magazine lying on the table. 'Have you got any cash you could lend me? I'm a bit strapped at the moment?'

He looked surprised. 'Yes, of course.' He emptied his pockets and put a couple of twenty-pound notes on the table, together with a handful of coins. 'I'll get some more when I'm out. Will that be enough?'

She nodded as she scooped it up. 'Thanks.'

The girls started back at school again this morning, and Suky was up and dressed without needing to be shouted at; she even smiled at her parents as she walked into the kitchen. The date with Adam the other evening had been a success.

'It's as if she's had a personality transplant,' Katie whispered to Pete, as Suky hummed to herself while she opened the fridge to hunt for milk. 'Is this really our oldest daughter?'

On the way to school, Katie pulled over next to a cashpoint.

'Why are we stopping?' asked Anna. 'You'll make me late!'

'I'll be quick,' she said. 'Just want to check my balance.'

The machine didn't give her a chance. After she tapped in her PIN, a warning flashed up announcing that the card had been declined. Another message followed, telling her she wasn't getting it back.

'Bloody thing!' she yelled, banging on the screen with her fist. The man behind her in the queue was smirking when she turned around, and she glared until he dropped his eyes and moved aside to let her pass.

'What were you shouting about?' asked Anna, as she got back into the car.

'The stupid machine took my card. God, this is all I need – what a nightmare. Bloody bank.'

'It's bad to swear,' said Anna. 'And being angry won't help.'

'Well, thank you for your advice,' snapped Katie. 'There are times, Anna, when grown-ups just can't help being angry.'

She pulled up outside the school and, before she had a chance to apologise for snapping, Anna was gone, slamming the door and dragging her rucksack by the straps, so it scraped along the pavement behind her.

Before doing anything else, Katie went to a garage to pour one of the twenty-pound notes into the car in the form of unleaded petrol. It was good to have the rest of Pete's cash in case of emergencies. Although at the moment, everything felt like an emergency. Now she just had to decide how to spend yet another day of clandestine unemployment. At least she'd remembered to throw her trainers into the boot, so she could go on a walk. Her phone rang as she was turning into the car park near the viewpoint.

'There you are. Why haven't you returned my calls?'

Monica had phoned twice yesterday and Katie had listened to both messages, deleted them, then not got round to calling her back.

'Sorry, it's been hectic. You know, kids and stuff.'

'What are you playing at, Katie?'

'What do you mean?'

'You know what I mean! What on earth were you doing sitting in a bar with that girl the other night? It was *his* Rachel, wasn't it?'

Katie didn't answer.

'Thought so. Let's get this straight... You're out drinking with Rachel, the pretty young girlfriend of the bloke you fancy. But she doesn't know that you fancy him – or even that you know him. So, not only did you break into her house, but you then crashed into her car, and you've been stalking her and her boyfriend. And now you're out together drinking wine as if you're old pals. Katie, what the hell are you doing?'

'It's not like that. you make it sound really weird,' said Katie.

'That's because it *is* weird!' hissed Monica. 'It's so weird I'm worried you're having some sort of breakdown. Why are you doing all this? Why are you making friends with this girl? I'm not sure what's going on inside your head, Katie – are you trying to get close to her because you can't actually get close to him?'

'No, of course not, that's ridiculous. Why can't I just like her as a person and want to be friends with her? You always suspect people of having ulterior motives, Monica.'

'Well, that's because they usually do. And don't try to pretend you like her, I know you too well. The other night in that bar you were smiling, but your body language was a million miles from relaxed – you may as well have been sitting there with a loaded gun behind your back.'

'That's not true, Mon, honestly. I really do like her.'

For a few seconds, neither of them spoke. Katie stared through the windscreen, watching cars drive past on the main road. 'Look, Monica, please don't lecture me. I know what I'm doing, and it's nothing sinister. I just felt bad about what happened with the car, so I went to apologise to her and we got on well, so we went for a drink. That's it. There's nothing for you to worry about.'

'And obviously Pete doesn't know.'

'About what?' she said, playing for time.

'About Rachel.'

'Well no. But there's no reason why he should. It's not a big deal. I don't know about all the friends he goes out with. We're not the sort of couple who keep tabs on each other.'

'That's not what I mean, and you know it,' said Monica. 'This is ridiculous. I'm not going to talk about it anymore, but you're playing a risky game. Sorry if you hate me for saying it, but I'm worried about you. Call me if you need to, okay? Just don't expect me to sympathise if this all blows up in your face.'

The phone went dead and Katie held it in her lap, polishing the screen with the edge of her coat. She'd known Monica would disapprove – which was why she hadn't returned her calls. She couldn't explain why she'd arranged the drink with Rachel either, it just seemed like the thing to do next. Maybe Monica was right: If she couldn't get any closer to Joe, she was trying to get close to his girlfriend. But even if that had been in the back of her mind at the start, it wasn't the case now: Rachel was a sweet girl; she had enjoyed spending time with her.

She jumped as the phone buzzed again in her hand. The surgery's number appeared on the screen: they weren't giving up. She rejected the call, then waited until it pinged and listened to the message, asking her to call back. Katie recognised the voice: it was the receptionist dressed in purple who'd leapt up screaming as the water poured over her. Maybe it wasn't just the computer system that had suffered. Her skirt must have been ruined as well and she was calling to insist Katie pay for a new one.

She threw the phone onto the passenger seat.

Ironically, the one thing her night out with Rachel had done, was take her mind off Joe. But this morning he was creeping back into her thoughts again. It was so hard not seeing him, not being with him. But she felt more positive about it all now, possibly because of the things Rachel had been saying. If Katie was honest with herself, she had enjoyed hearing that the girl's relationship with Joe wasn't perfect.

She wondered how Pete was getting on this morning; the first day of term was always chaotic, and he must be feeling rudderless, stuck at home, unable to be with his class. The stress would be compounded by the fact that the Damien issue was unresolved and he had an official complaint hanging over his head. She'd seen the packet of pills on his bedside table: the ones Joe had prescribed. They were mild sleeping pills, but it didn't look as if he'd bothered taking them after the first couple of nights.

Inside her, the ache grew stronger at the thought of Joe. Was he already at work? He would be arriving at the surgery and pushing open that heavy door, greeting colleagues as he walked down to his room, with the smile that spread further than his mouth, producing those wrinkles at the sides of his eyes. The smile she loved so much, it physically hurt not knowing when she'd next see it.

45

Flushed with the success of their first date, Suky and Adam were going out again tonight. Bowling this time.

'Is that a good idea now you're back at school?' asked Katie. 'Two late nights in the first week?'

The old Suky would have sighed and raised her eyes to the ceiling, snapped at Katie and stormed out of the room. Newly reformed Suky smiled sweetly. 'You're probably right, but we'll only bowl for an hour, so I'll be home by nine, and I've not got any homework. Please say it's okay?'

Pete grinned and dug a ten-pound note out of his back pocket. 'Go on then, but make sure you're not late. Here, my treat.'

Suky took the money and put her arms around his neck. 'Thanks, Dad!'

Katie wasn't sure how she felt about all this: Suky was only fifteen. She herself hadn't had a proper boyfriend until she was seventeen, and then it had been an arrangement of convenience rather than a heart-stopping romance. But for a couple of years before that, her friends had all been talking constantly about sex – Emily Baines claimed to have lost her virginity on her fifteenth birthday to a boy at the youth club, although no one really believed her.

By the time they started in the sixth form, everyone except Katie seemed to be at it like rabbits. She was pretty sure some were making most of it up, but inevitably the banter made her feel left behind. In her imagination she was attractive, popular, with a raw magnetism that made boys fall off their chairs as she walked past. In reality she usually bumped into the chairs: she was awkward, shy and had never been kissed. So, when a boy called Gareth asked if she wanted to share his can of Fosters at a party, she fell on him with open arms. Literally. Once they were going out, she lied to her friends about the sexual acrobatics they performed at weekends. She didn't mention the fact that his acute teenage boy BO turned her stomach. She definitely didn't tell anyone that they had only properly kissed once, on their first date, but that it was moist and messy and his braces got in the way, so they didn't bother again.

By the time she left school she had moved on from Gareth to Ed Baker – who took her to Brighton for a weekend and relieved her of her virginity. After that there were only a couple of lovers at university, before she met Pete. Was she jealous of Suky, or worried for her? Probably jealous, but fifteen was still too young.

'Last term he changed to Product Design,' she'd overheard her daughter telling Pete last night. 'He's never liked the practical work; he'd rather be doing the designs on a computer.'

'Sensible,' said Pete. 'It's important to enjoy what you're studying.'

'What do his parents do?' Katie had asked casually.

'They're solicitors.'

'Oh really? Any brothers and sisters?'

'One sister. For God's sake, Mum, what is this, twenty questions?'

Yet she didn't seem to mind when Pete asked about Adam.

'When are we going to meet him?'

'Dad, you're awful!' she laughed. 'You will meet him, I promise. I'll ask him over at the weekend, maybe Saturday afternoon if there's nothing else on. But you mustn't ask him loads of questions.'

'Okay, it's a deal,' said Pete, twinkling back at her.

If I'd asked that, thought Katie, *she would have told me to butt out of her life.*

Suky's new sunny disposition even extended to Anna, who sat next to her sister on the sofa, listening in awe to talk of Adam.

'When I grow up, I'm going to have a boyfriend,' Anna had announced in the car this morning, as Katie drove her to school. 'He's going to be handsome and good at sport and he'll have an Apple watch. He'll probably be called Dane or something.'

'Dane?' asked Katie.

'Yes, it's a cool name, Mummy, but you wouldn't know that.'

There was yet another cake sale at lunchtime to raise money for the PTA. Katie hadn't got round to baking anything for this one – how could parents be expected to gear up for fundraising this early in the term? When she opened her purse to give Anna some change, it was empty apart from a handful of coppers. She scrabbled under the seat of the car and found a 20p, covered in fluff.

'Here, take this,' she said, emptying coins into Anna's outstretched palm.

'But that's not enough to buy one cake!'

'I'm sorry, it will have to do. I haven't got anything else.'

A letter had arrived about the store card account Katie had

set up at Rachel's shop, details of interest rates and notification about the first monthly instalment. She had hidden it away in one of her drawers upstairs, alongside the latest letters from the bank. The tone of the first one – about her confiscated current account card – had been vaguely apologetic. That of the second – pointing out the heavy amount of interest she was now paying on her overdraft – less so. When she stopped to think about her financial situation she had palpitations, so she tried not to think about it.

Instead, she thought about Joe. Again. It was now over a fortnight since her last appointment. The article she'd torn out of the newspaper – how long ago had that been? It felt like a lifetime – was still sitting in the side of her handbag. She pulled it out every so often, to read again the words she knew by heart. The paper was creased and the newsprint so smudged and dirty from where she'd held it, that it was hard to see the photograph.

She longed to hear his voice, see his face. Finding herself standing inches from him in the supermarket had been an unexpected thrill, but it wasn't enough. She wanted more. Was it too soon to book another appointment?

He'd been talking about the perimenopause, so maybe she could work with that, google some more of the symptoms. Although she knew she *definitely* wasn't at that stage in her life yet: she was far too young. Okay, she'd had a few more of those night sweats, and her brain constantly felt foggy – she had forgotten her neighbour's name the other day, when they were standing chatting in the street. But that was probably because she had so much on her mind. In other circumstances, it would have been humiliating for anyone to suggest she was menopausal, but actually, it had been useful, because it meant Joe needed to see her again, to reassess her.

No one else need know: he could write whatever he wanted on her medical notes – just so long as it gave her the chance to go back and see him, ask his advice, ensure she was shut in that room with him on her own, until they could find a way to make this thing work.

Katie knew she ought to call the surgery, though. Having ignored two phone messages, she had now received a letter, asking her to contact them. They clearly weren't going to give up on that business with the water damage. It was unbelievable how, through no fault of her own, she was being hounded for it. She wasn't sure how to deal with it and wished she could ask Pete what to do. But that would mean explaining why she'd been at the surgery in the first place. She'd been reading the letter in the kitchen when she heard his footsteps coming down the stairs, so she folded it up and slid it under the toaster.

Ironically, what she needed more than medical advice right now, was financial support. Someone who could suggest a way out of this awful situation. She wanted to know what to say to the bank about her increasing overdraft, how to put on hold the direct debits and standing orders that were making an even bigger hole in her finances. She needed to work out what to do about the store card she'd rashly taken out that afternoon when Joe's girlfriend had helped her choose armfuls of lovely clothes.

A couple of years ago, a man Pete vaguely knew called Charlie had taken his own life; he'd disappeared one afternoon, walked out of the family home without leaving a note. His body was found the next day in nearby woodland; he'd taken many painkillers and drunk himself into a stupor.

It later emerged he'd been in financial difficulties: he'd lost his job, the house was being repossessed, the extortionate fees hadn't been paid at his children's private schools. His wife didn't know about any of it.

At the time Katie had found it hard to understand. 'How could he do that to his family?' she'd said to Pete. 'Leave them on their own to cope. Nothing could be that bad, surely?'

Now she wasn't so sure. Her own – relatively minor –

money worries were taking centre stage, making her scared and anxious, keeping her awake at night, and her stomach muscles contracted every time she thought about the letters from the bank.

Her eyes filled with tears as she remembered Joe sitting across from her in the consulting room at Pelham Green, his head tilted to one side as he listened and nodded, making notes on his computer. His kindness had been overwhelming.

Her phone bleeped. It was a text from his girlfriend.

Still on 4 cinema 2nite? Cd do 6pm show x

Rachel had suggested this the other night, but it had slipped her mind. Why not? She should really go to Pilates with Monica, but felt constantly exhausted at the moment – maybe she was coming down with something? Of course, it could be the stress of lying to her family to cover up the fact that she didn't have a job to go to anymore. Either way, she couldn't face the stretching, tensing and engaging required by Pilates, and she didn't particularly feel like having to answer any more probing questions from Monica either.

As soon as she'd sent a reply to Rachel, she remembered there was something she needed to add:

Just realised I've left my purse at home. Can you pay? My treat next time! x

46

The film had a complicated plot that neither of them could follow, but it was funny, and Katie enjoyed the distraction, piling through the outsized tub of popcorn Rachel had bought. Afterwards they went across the street to a wine bar.

'Just a quick one,' she said to Rachel. She ought to go straight home – she'd been out so much recently and it wasn't fair leaving Pete to do everything in the evenings.

'Sorry about this,' she said again, as Rachel came back to the table holding two glasses of wine. 'I must have left my purse in my coat pocket yesterday. I've been lost without it.'

'Don't worry, it's fine.' Rachel smiled as she sat down. Two men were sitting at the next table, and Katie noticed their eyes drifting to the pretty girl in the red jacket. Katie was wearing the new green cardigan she'd bought at Rachel's shop; as she glanced at herself in the hall mirror on her way out this morning, she'd been pleased with how she looked. Now, bathed in the glow of Rachel's natural sparkle, she felt drab, more acutely aware than ever of the twenty-year age gap between them.

'If they go ahead with the restructure, I may be sent to the smaller store in Minsterworth,' Rachel was saying, her chin resting on the palm of her hand. 'I don't mind, but it would be a shame now I'm starting to settle in here, and I like the girls I work with.'

Katie nodded, watching as a strand of hair fell across Rachel's face, which she swept back and tucked behind her ear.

'There may be more opportunities for promotion at a smaller branch. But it could work the other way – and, if it's quieter, I'd miss the buzz…'

'Have you always had your hair that length?' Katie asked. 'I mean, it's lovely – the cut and the colour.'

Rachel smiled. 'Yours is just like it!' she pointed out. 'Are you okay, Katie? You seem a bit down tonight.'

Katie took a sip of her wine. 'I lost my job,' she said, surprising herself.

'Oh, I'm sorry. That's awful. Did you know it was going to happen?'

'No. Well, I suppose I should have known I was in trouble.'

'What kind of trouble?'

'I wasn't pulling my weight. I was distracted.'

'Had you worked there for long?'

Katie didn't answer. She stared down at her glass, twisting the stem with her fingers.

'Is everything all right at home, I mean is Pete being okay about it?'

Katie looked at her in confusion, before remembering she'd given Rachel the impression that her husband was a bad-tempered bully, with violent tendencies. She felt her stomach twist with regret. 'Yes, everything's fine,' she said. 'Just financially difficult.'

Everything really was fine, that was the strange thing. Pete had come back yesterday buoyed up, reassured by support from his colleagues and by an initial meeting with the police, held in Sara's office. 'They say they're obliged to follow it up, but that Damien's parents need to provide proof with such a serious allegation,' he told her. 'It doesn't help their case that there was an ongoing issue with bullying last term, and that they didn't go to the police until two weeks after I was supposed to have hit him.'

'Thank God for that,' Katie had said.

'I know,' said Pete. 'Such a relief.'

Now Rachel had asked her a question.

'Sorry? I was miles away.'

'I said what will you do?' repeated Rachel. 'Will you apply for other jobs?'

'Not sure really.' Katie suddenly wanted the conversation to be over. She was fed up with lying and with being the Katie she had created for Rachel in this make-believe life. She was also fed up with this girl and her idle chatter, her tinkling laugh and need for friendship.

Weeks ago, she had thought she wanted to be Rachel: she wanted to wear her clothes, look like her, live in her house, make love to her boyfriend. Not able to do any of that, she had engineered the next best thing: a friendship that brought them close, enabled her to share Rachel's thoughts, hopes and fears.

Monica had pointed all of that out, during their abrupt phone call the other day. Now her words rang in Katie's ears. She was right: none of this would have happened naturally, and none of it was helping. What was she getting out of this bizarre relationship with a woman who was half her age and had everything she wanted? A naïve child, oblivious to the fact that the fleshy businessmen at the next table were looking at her out of the corners of their eyes, or that the barman was flirting as he sold her a glass of wine.

What hurt more than anything was that this unlikely friendship had altered the dynamic of Katie's relationship with Joe. Or rather, the relationship she wanted to have with him.

Previously she'd been able to lose herself in daydreams involving just the two of them: Joe and Katie playing house; Joe and Katie on holiday; Joe and Katie making love.

Now she couldn't think about Joe without Rachel popping up somewhere as well. It was almost funny: she'd be imagining herself sitting on the sofa with Joe, their fingers entwined, lips moving towards each other. Then Rachel would ring Joe on his mobile, or open the door and walk into the room, or call from the kitchen, asking if anyone wanted a cup of tea. Making her presence felt in a private moment, and reminding Katie that she shouldn't be doing whatever she was imagining herself doing. Definitely not the bits where she had no clothes on and was running her hands up and down Joe Harvey's naked body.

'I know something else will turn up for you,' Rachel was saying now. 'You just have to stay positive.'

How can you know that? thought Katie. *You don't know anything about me and you have no idea how good or bad I was at my job. You're just starting out in life, so you don't know what it means to have responsibilities, a family, money pouring through your hands before you have a chance to register the fact that it's there. You're churning out platitudes to make me feel better.*

'I'm sure you're right,' she said, avoiding Rachel's gaze. Why wasn't she sitting opposite Monica right now? She longed to be looking at that familiar face, to hear Monica's take on this situation. She knew her best friend would have something sensible to suggest. Maybe it was because she was older and had seen more of life? But actually, it was just because Monica knew her so well. The two of them shared years of memories and experiences; whereas she was finding it hard to think of anything she shared with this girl.

Apart from her boyfriend.

'Look I'm sorry, I'm not good company tonight. Do you mind if I head home?'

Rachel's face fell. 'Of course not. You should have told me

earlier, about your job. It must have been the last thing you wanted, to come out with me tonight.'

Stop being so bloody understanding, thought Katie. 'That's really understanding of you,' she said, putting on her coat. 'I'll call. We'll catch up again in a few days' time, when things have settled down a bit.' She leant down and gave the girl a hug, her fingers feeling the bones in her shoulders. Rachel's hair smelt of vanilla, and the skin of her cheek was soft as Katie pressed her own face against it. 'Take care of yourself. Thanks for the wine.'

She pushed open the door to the street and walked back towards the car park, the alcohol no longer buzzing through her veins. She felt so tired, every step an effort. A high-pitched squeal off to the left made her jump, and a cat dashed out and disappeared into a yard on the other side of the road. Reaching the car, she collapsed into the driver's seat and sat in the darkness for a while, getting her breath back.

She took out her phone and clicked to wake up the screen, the familiar photo of her girls smiling out at her. Scrolling through the list of calls, she found the number she was looking for and dialled it, listening as the connection was made. She pictured the phone, sitting on a table or a kitchen worktop – perhaps hanging, temporarily forgotten, in a coat pocket – ringing into the empty space.

'Hello, Joe Harvey?'

She gasped as he answered, jolted back to reality.

'Hello?'

She closed her eyes and held out her hand in front of her, imagining his face inches away, with the phone held to his ear.

'Who the hell is this?'

She fumbled to end the call, watching the screen turn dark again. His voice rang in her head, the thought of him racing through her veins like thinned blood. She was so tired she could hardly think straight. It was another five minutes before she mustered the energy to put the key in the ignition and take herself home.

47

Slotting bread into the toaster the next morning, Katie noticed the corner of a sheet of paper poking out beneath it: the letter from the surgery. How stupid to have left it there, where anyone could find it. There was also her bank statement, tucked between the pages of the magazine on the kitchen table. She retrieved that too, slipping both into her pocket.

When Pete and Suky had slammed out of the front door, she ran upstairs to her bedroom, opening the drawer that contained a chaotic jumble of tights, pants and bras. How did they always get in such a mess? The previous letters from the bank were hidden to one side, and she pulled them out, added the papers from her pocket and shuffled everything into a neat pile. As she was about to push it all back beneath the muddle of underwear, her fingers skimmed across the surface of one sheet, thicker than the others, an embossed symbol at the top. It was the letter from Jane Rivers.

Although she knew its contents by heart, she unfolded it again. She hadn't looked at this for days, and was surprised how calm she felt, rereading it now. When she'd first seen these sentences, they had seemed so blunt and dismissive. She had imagined the perfectly turned-out Mrs Rivers sitting behind her desk, dictating the words in her clipped pitiless voice, then signing it with a flourish, her white knuckles clutched around an expensive fountain pen.

But that seemed silly now. It was just a letter. The tone wasn't particularly friendly, but it wasn't personal either. It was just, as Pete had pointed out, businesslike.

She tried to remember the faces of some of the nurses who had looked after Clara during that last week. There had been a pretty young girl called Rosie, quiet and gentle. A kind, older woman too; Katie wasn't sure of her name, but she'd had a helmet of black hair, held in place with so much hairspray it wouldn't have moved in a hurricane. There had also been a girl from Eastern Europe; she'd had a lovely smile but her broken English was almost unintelligible.

These were the people Jane Rivers would have called into her office. It was the standard of their care and their ability to do the job that would be questioned, and when complaints were made, theirs would be the heads that rolled. St Bernard's itself – the impersonal, efficient institution – would carry on regardless.

Katie sat back on her heels, feeling tears prickle at the edges of her eyes. Those caring women hadn't just looked after Clara during the last days of her life, they'd looked after her daughter too. They had greeted Katie warmly, whatever time of the day or night they saw her; they'd brought her mugs of hot chocolate when she was sitting by her mother's bed in the evening, they'd asked her about her family and her own life while they checked monitors and gently washed Clara's wasted body. They had insisted she go home and rest when she fell asleep in the chair beside the bed. They hadn't been there when Clara fell, but that wasn't because they didn't care. It was because they were busy, being pulled in all directions, dealing with other people's calls and crises.

For their sake, she would drop this.

'Mummy,' Anna yelled from the bottom of the stairs. 'I'm going to be late!'

Katie pushed the letters back into the drawer, and scrambled to her feet.

'You always make me late,' said Anna, stomping out to the car. 'Mrs Hall will do one of her sayings.'

'What do you mean?'

'Time waits for no man!' said Anna, in a deep voice.

Katie smiled and ran her hand across her daughter's hair. 'Well, she's right,' she said.

'No, she's not! Time doesn't wait, it isn't a person. She also says that thing about cleanliness being next to godliness. But that's rubbish, because the vicar who comes in to do assembly on Friday mornings has breath that smells of dog poo.'

Pulling away from the school gates, Katie turned back towards town. She had no plans for being gainfully unemployed today. There was a thick frost on the ground, so she didn't fancy a walk. Maybe she would go to a café first, and she could look in the charity shops on the high street to find a paperback. Nothing too intense, an easy read. Some short stories? Clara had loved those.

For some reason she couldn't picture her mother's face today. Mostly she could visualise her so clearly, smiling or laughing, concentrating on something she was reading, her glasses slipping down to the end of her nose. But there were times when she couldn't really see the face she'd known so well. There was just a sense of a woman with white hair, and the harder she tried to remember her features, the more vague they became. It was the same with her voice. It should have been the most familiar one in her life, a voice that had whispered in her ear, sung her to sleep, told her off, played with her, nagged her, soothed her, laughed with her. So why were there times when she couldn't remember how it had sounded?

Maybe none of this was bad; it was a sign that life was starting to get back to normal. In the run-up to Christmas, sudden memories of Clara had left Katie reeling, knocked sideways by the emotion that came with them. Now they were less intense. The ache of missing her mother was softer; less a sharp stab in the ribs, more a dull swell of sadness.

Pete was right, she needed to move on.

She pulled up at a set of traffic lights, watching the hypnotic flip of the rear wiper of the car in front. When she got home tonight, she would take the letter from Jane Rivers and throw it into the recycling box. It felt good, imagining doing that.

She must also tell Pete about her work – or the lack of it. Keeping up this charade was ludicrous. She had run out of places to go, and she couldn't afford to spend all day out of the house, hanging around aimlessly. Today would be the end of it. When she got to the café, she'd text him: say there was something they needed to talk about. She realised she was smiling, although there was no one to see it. The prospect of finally being able to share this particular secret made her feel so much lighter, as if a weight had been lifted from her shoulders, or she'd suddenly lost two stone. Although, as she sat waiting for the traffic lights to change, the band of the skirt digging into her waist was a painful reminder she hadn't.

48

She answered the phone without thinking.

'Ah, Mrs Johnson! It's Pelham Green Surgery here. We've been trying to get through to you – have you been away?'

Damn, why hadn't she looked at the number first? 'No. Sorry, I did get a message from you. I've been busy at work.'

'Not to worry, I've got you now.' Katie recognised the voice: it was the receptionist, Bridget. The kind one with the pink cardigan, who had been at the surgery on the day Mrs Burns collapsed. 'One of the doctors would like a word, if that's all right?'

'Er, yes, I suppose so.' Katie was confused. Surely a doctor wouldn't deal with this? They were far too busy to bother with non-medical matters. 'Look, I'm sorry about the other day, when I knocked over that vase.' There was silence on the other end of the phone. 'It wasn't my fault – that boy ran into me. It's his mother who ought to be sorting this out really, because she didn't have him under control. But I realise it will be awkward to try and speak to them about it now, so I'm happy to pay for any damage. I hope your computer system wasn't ruined?'

'Our computer system…?'

'Yes, you know, when the water went over the keyboard.'

'Oh, I see what you mean. No, there was no damage. We managed to dry that out.'

Katie was confused. What had they been calling about then? 'So, that woman's skirt. That purple, silky one…'

'Oh goodness, Mrs Johnson, don't worry about any of that. Patsy's skirt was fine, the water didn't do it any harm. How kind of you to be concerned though.'

Katie didn't understand.

'I'm calling,' continued Bridget. 'Because Dr Harvey would like to have a chat with you. As I say, we've tried to call several times and I believe we even sent you a letter the other day.'

Katie's heart thrust forwards at the mention of his name, and she clutched the edge of the table in front of her. 'Really?'

'Yes, did you not get the letter? Anyway, Dr Harvey would like a word. He'd prefer to see you in person if that's possible. He's had a cancellation this afternoon, if you can make it at such short notice?'

She felt dizzy, as if she'd been cartwheeling around the car park. 'Yes, I can do that.' Blood was thundering around her temples so loudly, she could hardly hear what the woman was saying.

'I could put you in for half an hour's time, or is that too early?'

'No, that's fine.'

'Many thanks, Mrs Johnson. We'll see you shortly.'

Katie put down the phone and watched as the surgery number remained on the screen for a second before it went dark. She looked up and saw the woman at the next table was staring at her.

'Are you all right? You look a bit shocked.'

'Yes!' she laughed, a bark that sounded strange even to her own ears, relief mixed with excitement. 'Yes, thank you. I'm great.'

The woman was frowning at her. 'You've gone very red,' she observed.

'Yes, I'm sure I have. I've just had some news, that's all.'

'Not bad news?'

She smiled at her. 'No, actually I think it's good news. It's wonderful news.' She stood up so quickly her chair fell over with a crash, and people turned to look. She'd only sipped at her tea, it was a waste to leave it, but she didn't care. She put on her coat and ran out of the café, heels clattering on the polished floor. The car wasn't far, but she needed the fresh air, so maybe she would walk to the surgery? She was finding it hard to catch her breath. What on earth must she look like? She dragged her fingers through her hair, combing out the knots that had worked themselves up since she'd brushed it earlier that morning.

As she walked along the towpath, she suddenly realised what a glorious day it was – the sun beating down on her cheeks was almost warm, although it was only January. Even the water in the canal didn't look as murky as usual.

After all this time, she could hardly believe it. What had changed for him? Why had he suddenly decided he could see her now? Maybe something had happened with Rachel? No, it couldn't be that. She'd only been sitting opposite Rachel in the wine bar last night; if she and Joe had had a row, surely she would have said something?

If it wasn't to do with Rachel, it must be about her. He'd finally realised he couldn't fight this thing any longer. He had to see her and be with her. Katie remembered the missed calls and the messages left on her answerphone – why hadn't he phoned her himself? She would have replied immediately, dialled his number before she'd even finished listening. How ironic that she'd wasted so many days trying to dodge calls she now desperately wished she'd answered. Katie laughed out loud at herself. But no, of course he wouldn't call her. It was safer like this – he had a reputation to think of, a girlfriend, a career. He was doing things by the book in asking the receptionist to arrange an appointment. This way, no one would have any suspicions.

Was this really it, after so long? There was a sudden uncertainty beneath the excitement: a trembling fear. A little voice inside her whispered, *what are you doing, Katie?* But a louder one screamed out his name, so it whirled around in her head. *He wants to see me, to speak to me. He wants me in his consulting room, just the two of us. Alone.*

An elderly man came out of the surgery just as Katie reached the door. She held it open, smiling.

'Thank you,' he said. 'How kind.'

Everyone was in such a good mood today.

As she stepped up to the desk, every inch of her skin was crawling with anticipation. She put her hands in her pockets, so no one would notice them trembling. Patsy was on reception again. This time she was dressed from neck to toe in bright blue. Colour co-ordination was clearly important to her.

'Excuse me. I'm here to see Dr Harvey?'

Patsy looked up and glared. 'Use the automated registration system.'

'But I've just been phoned about an appointment – twenty minutes ago.'

'That makes no difference. If you want to see the doctor, you have to check in, like everyone else.'

Even Patsy's bad temper couldn't ruin this. Katie stepped across to the machine and input her details, beaming at the other patients in the waiting room as she sat down. Pulling a compact mirror from the depths of her handbag, she checked her make-up, rubbed a smudge from her cheek, licked her lips to make them shine.

Her phone started to ring, making her jump: it was Pete. She pressed the button to reject the call; she'd phone him back later.

49

She was sitting facing the corridor, which meant she saw him as soon as he came out of his room. He was wearing a dark blue shirt today, tucked into chinos. He'd had a haircut since she bumped into him in Sainsbury's, and it made him look younger. He seemed slimmer as well – it must be all the running Rachel had said he was doing. Katie sucked in her own stomach, wishing she'd held back a little over Christmas.

'Mrs Johnson? This way please.' The smile was there; his special smile just for her. But maybe there was a shadow behind it today, something she couldn't quite put her finger on. He must be nervous too. But that wasn't surprising: things were finally happening – after far too long – but it was a big step they were about to take, a momentous leap into the unknown.

As she followed him down the corridor, Pete's face popped into her head, laughing with Suky in the kitchen. She pushed the image away.

When they went into his room, Joe shut the door and signalled to the seat beside his desk. 'How have you been?' he said in that rich, deep voice.

She smiled. She couldn't trust herself to say anything yet,

and for some reason she was still out of breath – ridiculous, it must be nerves.

'Thanks for coming to see me at such short notice. Sorry we haven't been able to get hold of you before now.'

She knew she was grinning like a child but couldn't help it. It was so wonderful to be back here. He was facing away from her, reading something on the computer screen, tapping his biro absently against the desk.

She reached out her hand, moving it towards his shoulder where the shirt was stretched taut, a hard knot of muscle pushing through the material. Her fingers were inches from him.

'It's about those blood tests. I'm afraid I need to take another couple of samples, because there's been a mix up at the lab over the holidays.'

She was only half listening. Who cared about the blood tests?

'It means we're having to recall several patients and submit their samples again. There's nothing to worry about, it's just a nuisance.'

Her hand moved forward, and suddenly she was touching the cool cotton. She spread out her fingers and felt his upper arm move. It was so solid, harder than she'd expected, the muscles tensing beneath her fingertips.

He turned around and looked down at her hand on his arm.

'Joe...' she whispered. She could hardly hear her own voice, above the pounding of her heart. She was reaching out with her other hand, but it didn't seem to belong to her. It was like she was watching a film. She was still smiling; laughing now. Her fingers touched his face, resting softly against the skin; the stubble on his cheeks prickling her like pins, tiny jolts that made her nerves tingle.

He was looking straight at her. That handsome face, closer

than he'd ever been before. 'I love you,' she whispered. How many hundreds of times had she imagined herself saying these words, being so near to him, taking his body in her arms and pulling it towards her. Now it was actually happening. At long last.

But there was something wrong. He wasn't smiling; his eyes were wide.

She was moving towards him, lifting herself out of her chair. There were inches between them, when he pulled back, jerking his face away from her fingers, wheeling back in his chair. Katie's hand, the one that had been clutching his arm, fell away uselessly as he stood up.

'Mrs Johnson!'

'Joe…'

'What are you doing?' There was an odd expression on his face, his mouth slightly ajar as if the muscles in his cheeks were frozen in place. She couldn't work out what was going on.

'Joe, I've been waiting so long for this…' her own voice echoed inside her skull, sounding strangely disconnected. She stretched out her hand again.

'Please sit back down.' He looked flustered, and ran his fingers through his hair, pushing the fringe out of his eyes.

'Joe, I didn't mean…'

'Just sit down.'

This was all wrong. Why wasn't he smiling back? 'Joe…?'

'I need you to step back and sit down, Mrs Johnson.'

Katie collapsed into the chair as he picked up the handset of the landline on his desk and pressed a number. 'Bridget, can I have a chaperone in my room, please – immediately?' His voice was clipped, hard. This wasn't right at all.

He sat back down but pushed his chair further away from her so there was distance between them. Four feet that felt like a million miles.

This couldn't be happening.

'Mrs Johnson, can I get you a glass of water?'

She realised she was panting, gasping for breath. The roaring in her ears was louder than before and her heart felt like it was pushing through the wall of her chest.

You bloody fool, screamed the little voice inside her head.

Looking at him, her brain tried to process what had gone on between them over the last few seconds, what had gone wrong. All she wanted was to see that gorgeous smile spread across his face, watch the laughter lines radiate out from the corners of his eyes. *Come on, Joe, smile at me, throw your head back and laugh. This is a joke, isn't it? You know why I'm here, you've always known.*

But he wasn't smiling. He was just staring at her.

There was a knock, and she turned to see Bridget stick her head around the door. 'Is everything all right in here, Dr Harvey?'

50

The house was in darkness, but from the glow of a nearby streetlamp she could see outlines of the furniture in the sitting room: the top of a sofa, a rectangular picture frame on the back wall, the irregular shapes of book spines slotted into shelves on the corner unit. Without anyone at home to light it up, the room looked cold and clinical.

Katie had no idea how long she'd been sitting here; she hadn't checked the time when she arrived. But she was freezing, and her legs were stiff. It had started to drizzle, then to rain more heavily, the raindrops clattering onto the roof of the car. It was more than three weeks since the shortest day, but the evenings didn't feel any lighter, and winter was still a heavy shroud in the air.

She had subconsciously been expecting Rachel to walk up the hill, as she had that evening before Christmas, one of the other times when Katie had parked her car and waited on this lane. She could picture the figure trudging towards her, head down against the wind, a plastic bag of shopping in each hand.

But suddenly, a white Fiat was turning in front of her and

pulling into the parking space outside number 15. The lights went off and the driver's door opened. Katie wound down the window on the passenger side.

'Hi, Rachel!'

The girl turned and smiled when she saw Katie, before confusion flashed across her face. She walked over. She was wearing the red jacket, and had a long scarf of the same colour wrapped around her neck.

'What are you doing here?'

'I was just passing,' said Katie, knowing how ridiculous that sounded. 'I thought I'd come and whizz you off somewhere. Come on, get in.' She put up the window, turned the key in the ignition and leant across to open the passenger door, giving Rachel no chance to carry on the conversation unless she got into the car.

'But I don't understand. What…?'

'Hop in!' She smiled, keeping her voice light. 'Let's go and grab a drink.'

'Well, I'm not keen to go out tonight, to be honest, Katie. I've had a really busy day at work and…'

'I won't keep you long, promise. Come on,' Katie swivelled round to reach for the seat belt, so that Rachel, by now bending to look through the door, was left standing out in the rain. She clearly wasn't sure what to do. Katie's heart was forcing its way up into her throat, and she was relieved when, after a few seconds of hesitation, Rachel got into the car.

Katie accelerated away from the kerb, the sudden movement forcing the passenger door shut.

'Hey!' Rachel was struggling to pull the seat belt across her body. 'Katie, slow down.'

Katie revved the accelerator as they went down the hill towards the main road.

'But… hang on,' Rachel sounded confused. 'How did you know where I live?'

Well, let's see. I've followed your boyfriend home, written to him at this address, broken into your kitchen through the back door, met your cat, walked into your sitting room – oh yes, and I've spent several nights sitting in my car outside, spying on you both.

'You must have told me at some stage,' said Katie.

'No, I never did. I'd remember.' Rachel now sounded more worried than confused.

Katie could sense the girl staring at her. 'Well, anyway, it doesn't matter,' she said brightly. 'Where shall we go? What shall we do? Let's just get away from it all for a bit.'

'Katie, I'm sorry but I don't want to go anywhere,' said Rachel. 'I'm tired and I've got a lot to sort out at home tonight. I'm not sure why I got in here, but please can you stop the car and let me out again?'

Katie had braked at the bottom of the cul-de-sac, where it met the main road, and now pulled out quickly, into a gap in the traffic. She didn't say anything, not because she didn't want to, she just couldn't think what to say. A memory flashed through her mind: her car, hammering into Rachel's that afternoon before Christmas. She wondered if Rachel also remembered the accident, every time she turned out onto the main road?

'Anyway, Joe doesn't know where I am. He'll come home and find the car there, and he'll be worried when I'm not in the house. I'd better text him.' She started rummaging in her handbag.

'No, don't do that,' Katie snapped. 'Look, I just want to get out for a bit, okay? There's no need to make a big deal of it. And if you hadn't wanted to come, you shouldn't have got into the bloody car.'

She heard Rachel breathe in sharply. 'What's the matter with you, Katie?'

'Nothing. There is nothing the matter with me. I'm fine,' she changed gear clumsily and the car juddered.

'Can you slow down then?' Rachel's left hand was curled around the door handle, her right one gripping the bag on her lap. 'This is only a thirty zone, but you're going faster than that.'

'Oh, shut up,' said Katie, unable to stop herself. 'Just shut up, miss bloody goody two shoes. I'm the one driving, so let me get on with it.'

There was a stunned silence. Rachel's hand went into her bag again and out of the corner of her eye Katie saw she was pulling out a mobile phone. Not thinking about what she was doing, she reached across and grabbed it, throwing it over her shoulder into the back of the car.

'What the... My phone!'

Katie took a deep breath. 'Listen, Rachel. There is no need for you to call anyone, we're going on a drive, that's all. You're making a big deal out of this, just sit there, calm down and stop flapping, you're making me nervous.'

'I'm making *you* nervous!' Rachel's voice had risen. 'I don't know what's got into you, Katie, but you sound crazy and you're driving really badly. I don't feel safe, and I'd like you to stop the car so I can get out. Please?'

'Oh, would you? Well, tough.'

The traffic lights ahead were changing from green to amber, so Katie accelerated through as they turned red, swinging the car onto the road that led to the bypass.

'What's this about, Katie?' Rachel's voice was still wobbly, but she was clearly trying to stay calm. 'Is it about losing your job? It's not surprising if you're angry about that. Or maybe it's something I've done? Tell me if I've said anything stupid or... I don't know, if I've done something to upset you? You're scaring me. If you slow down, maybe we can go somewhere and talk.'

The wipers were flipping backwards and forwards across

the rain-spattered windscreen, but didn't seem to be clearing it; Katie couldn't understand why everything in front of her was smudged and distorted and she moved her head from one side to the other, trying to see through the blurred glass. She suddenly realised tears were streaming down her face. They fell onto her top lip and dripped onto her blouse. As she opened her mouth to take a breath, a sob rushed from it, followed by another. With her lungs full of air, she involuntarily let out a strangled cry that sounded – even to her own ears – like the noise an animal might make when it was in pain. She felt Rachel's hand on her arm.

'Pull over, Katie. Pull over here on the side. Come on, slow down.'

She did as she was told, hardly able to see the road ahead, the lights of oncoming vehicles a series of jagged yellow stripes. When the car came to a halt on the hard shoulder, she felt Rachel reach across and turn off the ignition, pulling out the key. Katie was crying so hard she could hardly breathe, her body overwhelmed by the intensity of the sobs. She still had her hands on the steering wheel, braced to drive a car that was silent and immobile, going nowhere.

'Here,' she heard Rachel say softly, and felt an arm going around her shoulders. 'Come here.'

She allowed her head to be gently guided towards the other woman, her rigid arms relaxing as she did so. She closed her eyes and wept, her body resting like a dead weight against Rachel's, her mind empty of all thoughts, the world still dark and bleak, but not quite as terrifying.

They sat like that until her sobs subsided, Rachel occasionally stroking her hair with one hand, holding her tight with the other. Katie had no idea how much time had passed when she finally pulled herself up and leant back against the seat. Her head was pounding, exhausted with the effort of crying, and her face and shirt were soaked. She tried to wipe them, using her sleeve, then taking a pile of tissues Rachel produced from her bag.

'Sorry,' she whispered. It wasn't enough, but she didn't know what else to say. She sat staring straight ahead, the oncoming headlights now proper orbs again on the other side of the dual carriageway.

Rachel shifted in her seat. 'Do you want to tell me about it?'

Katie smiled wanly. There was so much she could tell Rachel, but hardly any of it would make sense. It was all completely insane. 'I'm sorry, Rachel,' she said. 'For everything. I've behaved so badly, and I shouldn't have made you get in the car tonight, I don't know what I wanted to happen.'

'You're obviously upset,' Rachel began. 'Is it losing your job…?'

'No, that's not important. It's more complicated than that.' She turned sideways and looked at the young woman for the first time. 'I've done some dreadful things – to you, as well as to Pete.' Rachel looked bewildered, but Katie didn't have the energy to explain. 'I think I'm going mad,' she said at last, her voice little more than a whisper. 'I fell in love, that's where it all started, but I didn't even know him.'

'Did Pete find out about it? Is that what this is all about? Has he been treating you badly?'

Katie laughed and shook her head. 'No, not at all, he would never treat me badly. I was lying when I said those things about him. I can't believe I told you he'd be aggressive or get angry – I think I wanted you to feel sorry for me. He's a good man and none of this is his fault.'

The car rocked as a lorry rumbled past.

'So, what's the matter then? Is it this other man who's making you so unhappy?'

For a moment Katie thought she was going to tell her; she

opened her mouth and waited for the words to come out. The prospect of talking about it was so appealing; telling someone how she'd felt when she first saw Joe's photograph in the paper, the thrill of speaking to him at the library and then sitting feet away from him in that room at the surgery. The excitement of following him and discovering where he lived, the way her whole body shook with anticipation when she sat in the surgery for the first time, waiting for her appointment to walk after him into his consulting room. It would be so good to share some of that. To tell another human being how the warmth and happiness had worked its way into her world, as she started to live alongside the image of this man that she'd created in her head. How extraordinary it had felt, over the last couple of months, to be leading a double life: physically trapped in the body of Katie Johnson – wife, mother of two, office manager, bored, middle-aged frump – but emotionally existing as a completely different Katie Johnson – girlfriend and confidante, sexy, witty and adored.

'I won't tell anyone,' Rachel was saying. 'You can trust me to keep a secret.'

Katie remembered the hardness in Monica's voice during their last phone call, anger mixed with concern. They hadn't spoken since, and she missed her so much that the loss was a physical ache. How could she expect anyone to understand this, if Monica didn't?

She blew her nose and wiped her eyes again, trying to smile at Rachel, who was leaning towards her. Of course she couldn't tell her. Even if she didn't mention Joe's name, the last person who should be hearing about all this was Rachel: pretty, innocent Rachel who just wanted to be her friend, but had unwittingly played such a major part in this catastrophic collapse of Katie's life.

'I'm sure we can sort this out...' Her hand was on Katie's shoulder again.

From the back seat came a tinny tinkling, and it took Katie a couple of seconds to realise it was Rachel's phone. She waited for the young woman to turn around and pick it up, take the call and tell whoever it was that she needed help.

But she didn't move.

They both sat still until the phone stopped ringing, and shortly afterwards it beeped to show there was a message.

'I thought you had everything I wanted,' Katie said to Rachel. 'But that wasn't true.'

Rachel reached out and took her hand. 'Whatever has happened, I'm sorry it's upsetting you so much. I hate seeing you like this.'

'Please don't be nice to me,' whispered Katie. 'I don't deserve that.'

'Of course you do...'

'No, I really don't. I don't deserve your sympathy.' She turned to Rachel again. The young girl looked so confused. 'Do you love him?' asked Katie.

'Who?'

'Joe,' she took a deep breath. 'Your Joe?'

Rachel looked confused, then nodded. 'Of course. But why? I don't understand why you're asking me that?'

'You look good together,' said Katie. 'The two of you, you make a lovely couple. I'm sure people must have told you that before. You're beautiful people.'

'But, Katie, you don't even know him?' Rachel was frowning.

'No, you're right. I don't know him at all. But it's true.'

Rachel sat back in the seat. 'I don't understand any of this. I've no idea why you're upset, but so much is good in your life, Katie. I envy you!'

Katie laughed and shook her head.

'It's true! There's Pete and the girls, you've got a loving family. You're so lucky, that's what I long to have, one day.'

'You've got Joe,' she whispered.

'Yes, but things aren't perfect,' Rachel said. 'You know that, Katie. Me and Joe, we're just… well, no one's life is all roses.'

Katie shut her eyes and leant back against the headrest.

'I think we should get you home,' said Rachel, holding up the keys. 'Shall I drive?'

Katie had a blistering headache, the sort that would sit above her eyes for hours and send spasms of pain down each side of her face. The sort of headache she deserved. 'It's fine, I can drive,' she said. She saw the doubt on Rachel's face. 'Honestly, I won't do anything stupid.'

As Rachel handed over the keys, another lorry thundered past, the roar of its engine drowning out the sound of the rain lashing onto the windscreen.

They drove in silence along the bypass to the roundabout, where Katie turned and headed back to town. There was barely any fuel in the car, and the orange petrol tank symbol blinked at her in rage. Going into Coopers Lane again, she drove up to the top and saw there were now lights on at number 15, the curtains in the sitting room closed to keep out the world.

Rachel reached into the back of the car and picked up her phone. Turning again, she put her hand on Katie's arm. 'Call to let me know how you are, will you?'

Katie nodded, but couldn't say anything.

Rachel opened the car door. 'None of this matters, what happened tonight,' she said. 'We're both okay, that's the important thing. I'm here if you want to talk about it. Anytime.'

Katie stared at the glowing windows and neat exteriors of the houses in Coopers Lane. She felt drained, as if she'd been running, swimming or dancing for hours, every muscle in her body throbbing and stretched beyond its normal threshold.

Rachel got out of the car and shut the door. Katie

accelerated away immediately, desperate not to be still there, watching, when Rachel walked up to the house and her handsome, loving, concerned boyfriend came to meet her at the door.

She would never call her.

51

She tipped up the bottle. A dribble of golden liquid twisted down, splashing against the sides of the glass before pooling in the bottom. Was that all? She turned the bottle upright, holding it in front of her face – moving it to the light. How could it be empty already? She tipped it up again, but nothing came out.

'Silly me.' Katie picked up the glass and giggled, bringing it to her lips and draining what was left. 'Hey, hello there!' She waved the bottle at the barman. 'Another one of these, please.'

She smiled as he walked towards her. He had short black hair, slicked back against his head with so much gel that it gleamed under the artificial lights.

'Where are you from then?' she asked. 'And what's a good-looking man like you… doing in a dump like this?' She snorted with laughter, falling forward as her elbow slipped off the edge of the bar.

He put both his hands on the wooden surface in front of her. 'I think you've probably had enough for this evening.'

'Oh, don't be ridiculous. I am absolutely fine. Totally fine. I won't have another bottle then. Maybe you're right. Just a glass will do nicely.'

Her phone rang again. It had rung several times: she couldn't remember how many. Each time, Pete's picture had flashed up on the screen and smiled out at her. But now, to her surprise, it was Monica's face on the screen, with her name flashing up beside the green incoming call symbol. She lowered her face towards the screen, studying it intently. 'What are you doing in there, Mon?' she asked the phone, then laughed again. She really was being very witty.

'Are you going to answer it?' asked the barman.

She thought for a couple of seconds, as the phone continued to trill. 'No, I don't think I'm going to do that. But I *am* going to have more wine – can you get it for me please? Pretty please? Customers must die of thirst in this place.'

The phone screen went dark again. 'Bye, Monica!' She folded her arms on the bar and slumped her head onto them, dimly aware that her phone had started ringing again, and the barman was picking it up.

Her head was still aching. The alcohol had lessened the pain somewhat when she first got here, but now the persistent throb was back with a vengeance, hammering in her ears, at her temples, rippling through each eye socket and into her cheekbones.

She'd always wondered what this pub was like. It was a rambling, down-at-heel place. She used to drive past it every week when she brought Suky for swimming lessons at the leisure centre, over the road. She'd never been tempted to go inside, it always looked too seedy. Instead, she'd spent hours sitting on uncomfortable orange plastic seats beside the pool, reading newspapers and drinking milky coffee out of Styrofoam cups, watching her daughter plough up and down at training sessions: backstroke, crawl, breaststroke, butterfly. Years later, she could still remember the smell of chlorine as she walked through the doors; hear the shrieks of laughter echoing from the pool and the clash of displaced water hitting the tiled edges.

She sat up and peered around the pub: the barman was down the other end again and the glass and bottle had disappeared. 'Hello!' she called. 'Can I have some wine please?'

What a shame she hadn't discovered this place while Suky was swimming. She could have spent many evenings sitting on this stool, talking to this good-looking, but rather unresponsive, barman. He was walking back towards her now, carrying a pint glass full of clear liquid.

'Wine?' she asked, realising she sounded pitiful.

'Water,' he said. 'Get that down you.'

He put her phone back on the bar and she picked it up absently, pressing a button that listed all the missed calls. *Pete... Pete... Pete... Pete...* she couldn't quite focus on the times of the calls, the numbers were blurry, but there were lots of them. He'd left messages as well – the answerphone symbol was flashing and when she pressed the button, she heard his voice.

'Katie, it's me. Where are you? We're really worried now. Dr Harvey called to say you were upset when you left the surgery. And I've just heard back from Duncan. He says he let you go last week. Why didn't you...?'

The message cut out and the screen went black, as the battery died.

She took a gulp of the water, then another. As it flowed down her throat, a memory she didn't want to acknowledge pushed its way into her brain. Joe. But not the Joe in the paper: the kind, handsome stranger who had taken her heart hostage. This was another Joe; the real one, sitting beside her.

She didn't want to think about that. She sipped more water.

Then there was Rachel. She could see her saying

something as well, her mouth forming words Katie knew she had heard, but couldn't now remember. She closed her eyes and could see herself resting her head against Rachel's shoulder; there had been the subtle scent of a body lotion, nice but not one she recognised.

'It was all inside my head,' she said.

'What's that, love?' the barman was drying glasses with a tea towel.

'It should have stayed there. It really should have done. It was all my fault.'

He shook his head and wandered away again.

She had a sudden, terrifying moment of sober clarity. How could she ever have thought this thing with Joe would end well? But that was the problem: she hadn't thought about it at all. She had come up with endings – plenty of them – they were just the wrong type: happy ones, where she and a virtual stranger rode off into the sunset together. She'd thrown herself into this fantasy, created a ridiculous double life inside her head. Subconsciously she'd known there would be serious consequences, but she hadn't cared.

How had this special, little secret turned into such a big, dangerous lie?

It had to stop; these weeks of madness must come to an end. But as part of that she must undo some of the harm she'd caused – to Pete most of all. At the thought of him, tears prickled at the edges of her eyes again. Pete, who knew her better than anyone else in the world; Pete, who put up with her grumpy moods and her stubbornness. Pete, who loved her and trusted her. She remembered how they'd stood outside in the dark on Christmas Day, after she'd phoned Monica: the pair of them separated physically by just a few feet, but emotionally by a vast chasm. It wasn't surprising he'd accused her of having an affair; her behaviour had been so erratic, so out of character.

She yearned to see him. The exhaustion she'd felt earlier, sitting with Rachel in the car, hit her again like a wave breaking over her head. Her temples were still throbbing and now everything else ached as well: her arms, her stomach, her legs and ankles, even her fingers. Her eyes itched and, despite the water she was drinking, her mouth was so dry she could hardly swallow.

'How are you feeling?' It was the barman again. He was smiling at her, but it wasn't an unkind smile.

'A bit better, thank you.'

'Drink up then, finish that.'

She had to go home. She couldn't remember getting here, but maybe the car was nearby? She'd drunk far too much to drive though – she'd have to get the barman to call her a cab. Except he'd need to pay for it as well, she didn't think she had any cash; she'd have to ask Pete to lend her some more. How had she paid for the wine? Maybe she hadn't.

God, she and Pete needed to talk about money. Katie closed her eyes and pictured the bunch of envelopes tucked under knotted piles of unruly tights and socks in her drawer: letters from her bank, the credit card companies, the people who ran the store card account. It was overwhelming; she owed so much, but had nothing to spare. Duncan's face flashed before her. She needed to tell Pete about losing her job as well – although maybe he already knew. Hadn't he said something about that in his message?

Staring at her hands around the glass on the bar, she realised she was wearing the green cardigan she'd bought at Rachel's shop. Was that the moment everything began to spiral out of control – when she came face to face with Rachel in that changing room? No, it had all been going wrong way before that. She took off the cardigan, tugging her arms out of the sleeves, balling it up in her hands, noticing how the row of pearls around the neckline glinted through her fingers.

As she dropped it onto the floor beside her stool, she suddenly realised what else Pete had said in the message he'd left on her phone: he had spoken to Joe.

For a moment she couldn't work out why; her brain was fuzzy – there were things she needed to think about, but they were just out of reach, flimsy thoughts floating on the periphery of her mind. Every time she tried to focus on them, they skittered further away. Why had she got so drunk?

She took several deep breaths in and out, focusing her eyes on the rack of inverted spirit bottles in front of her, willing them to stay still. She tried to picture Joe's face, but all she could see were his eyes narrowing as he backed away from her. There was a reason he wasn't smiling.

Oh God.

She suddenly saw her own hand, stretched out in front of her: her fingers stroking the sleeve of his shirt and wrapping themselves around his upper arm. Joe pushing himself away; the confusion on his face. Bridget coming through the door; her eyes moving from one to the other, resting on Katie – immediately understanding what had happened.

She dropped her head into her hands, trying to shut out the memory, feeling shame flare across her cheeks. Had she said anything? She didn't know. She couldn't remember leaving the room, or walking out through the waiting room. She hadn't a clue where she'd gone afterwards, how long it had been before she ended up here. There was something about Rachel, at the back of her mind – she'd been with her.

Looking at the pint glass in her hand she saw it was nearly empty, and knew this was a good thing. Maybe the nice barman would let her have more wine, now she'd drunk the water.

She felt a pressure on her arm and looked down to see a hand resting there. Surprised, she turned to find the body that came with it. 'Mon! What are you doing here? I'm so glad to see you!'

Monica's arms went around her and Katie leant against her friend, overwhelmed by relief, although she wasn't sure why.

'God, Katie, we've been worried sick about you!'

As she pulled away, she looked over Monica's shoulder and saw Pete. His face was drawn and his hair looked ruffled, as if he'd been running his hands through it. Why would he have been doing that? Suddenly she remembered his phone messages. He'd been wondering where she was, worried because she hadn't gone home. Was it late? She had no idea.

As he stepped towards her, she fell against him, her head resting in the curve of his neck, feeling the familiar warmth of his skin, the slight scent of aftershave.

'There are so many things I need to talk to you about,' she said, trying not to cry.

'I know,' he said. 'I know about it all. I know you had a funny turn in the surgery, and that you've lost your job. Why didn't you tell me, Katie?'

Because it didn't really matter, she thought. *The job wasn't important.*

'You should have talked to me,' he was saying. 'You'd been behaving so strangely, I couldn't work out what was going on.'

She pushed herself against him, wrapping her arms around his back and hugging him tightly. 'I'm sorry,' she whispered. 'I'm so sorry for everything I've done.'

When she opened her eyes, she saw that Monica had picked up her bag and the cardigan, and was handing money to the barman. He was leaning forward slightly to talk to her, smiling, warming to her immediately, the way people did with Monica. Not that Katie minded; it was good to see Mon again, she had missed her so badly. Maybe she could get the pair of them together, this slick-haired barman and her very best friend in the world? She giggled at the thought, and tried to move towards them, to hear what they were saying. But as she turned her head, the world span dangerously. She longed to be sober again; why had she done this to herself?

'I'm sorry, Katie,' Pete was saying. 'I've been so wrapped up in work over the last few weeks, I haven't taken enough notice of what's been going on.'

He was wearing an old blue shirt, one of her favourites that he'd had for years. Her head resting against his neck, she noticed the material was starting to fray along the edge of the collar, next to the top button. She would have to sort that out.

She drew herself back and looked at him. 'You're lovely,' she said. 'I don't deserve you, Pete.'

His eyes looked grey under the pub's harsh strip-lighting, but she knew they were actually blue: a pale blue like cornflowers, or the furthest edges of the sky where it clips the horizon on a summer's day.

52

As they went into the car park, Monica tried to persuade her to put the cardigan back on. 'You'll freeze out here!' she protested, as Katie pushed it away.

'Don't want it. Throw it in the bin.'

'That's ridiculous. The car's over there, let's get in before we all get soaked.'

The cold air hit Katie like a smack on the cheek. She staggered as her shoe struck a stone on the ground and Monica grabbed her more tightly under the arm. Pete had gone ahead and was holding open the door.

'Do you want to get in the back with her?' he said. 'In case she feels ill.'

Monica helped Katie into the car, then slid in beside her.

'I'm not going to be sick, promise,' said Katie. She was already sobering up and could now look at her friend's face without it spinning away from her. Monica put her arm around her shoulders and Katie put up her hand and stroked Monica's cheek. 'Thank you for rescuing me, Mon.'

As Pete drove out of the car park, Katie tried to focus on the road ahead: illuminated shop window displays flashing past on both sides, car headlights, figures on the pavement. She was shivering now, and aware she needed the loo.

'Pete's right, you should have told us,' Monica was saying. 'We're both here for you. We'll help you deal with whatever's been going on.'

The heating was starting to work its way through to the back of the car – Katie could feel a reassuring blast around her feet.

'How's she doing?' asked Pete.

'Good, I'm good,' she replied. 'Thank you, Pete. I love you. I love you both, and I don't deserve you.'

Monica laughed. 'I can't believe I'm having to rescue you from a sleazy pub,' she said. 'I haven't had to do that since we were twenty years old!'

Katie laughed too, grateful she was able to take part in this conversation, hear what was being said to her and process it. That pint of water had been such a good idea. 'I'm sorry,' she said. 'I've put you both through so much.'

'Don't be daft,' said Monica. 'You haven't put us through anything. I just wish you'd shared some of the worry with me, told me how you were feeling. You've behaved very strangely over the last few weeks. I didn't know why, I thought...'

Katie opened her eyes and looked sideways. Monica's face was just inches away, eyes locked onto her. 'You weren't yourself,' Monica whispered softly. 'I didn't know what was going on in your head.'

Katie nodded slowly. 'I don't think I did either,' she whispered back.

'Everything okay back there?' asked Pete.

'Yes, we're fine,' Monica squeezed her hand.

They were coming to the outskirts of town. Katie saw the BP garage to her left, the familiar green and yellow signs glaring into the darkness, slightly mottled by the raindrops racing across the outside of the window. The car picked up speed as it headed down to the bypass.

Home. Soon she would be home. Katie pictured the girls waiting for her, maybe looking out from behind the closed curtains, watching for the car. Had Pete told them what had happened when he left to come and pick her up? That he'd traced their mother to a pub in town, where she was drinking herself into oblivion? Hopefully not. She would have to make an effort to stand still and not slur her words when she saw them. It would be fine; she was feeling more sober already. Her head wasn't hurting as badly and she could watch the road ahead without it whipping away from her, like she was being flung around on a Waltzer.

He probably hadn't told the girls about Joe's call, though Suky may have picked up on some of it. Where should she start with all this? In the pub, Pete had said he knew about everything. He'd meant to set her mind at rest, to be reassuring about her irrational behaviour over the last few weeks. But he didn't know about all of it. He thought he did, but the job and her getting drunk in the pub tonight – that was just the easy bit.

As she stared through the windscreen, she saw a smattering of red dots ahead of her: pinpricks that got bigger and glowed more sharply. The car slowed as traffic cones flashed past along one side of the road.

Maybe the easy bit was all that mattered? There was no need to complicate everything by mentioning Joe, or the things she'd done to get closer to him. What she did need to explain away, was how she'd behaved when she was in his office, just a few hours earlier.

'They're always working on this stretch of road,' Monica was saying. She was leaning forward, her hand on Pete's shoulder, peering through the windscreen. 'What is it this time, water or gas?'

Maybe what had happened at the surgery wouldn't go any further? The only people who knew what she'd done were Joe and the receptionist, Bridget. They would talk about it amongst themselves, and it would undoubtedly go around the other staff like wildfire. But would it get back to Pete? Joe wouldn't tell him: patient confidentiality. Maybe Katie could just say she'd felt faint, had a funny turn; she'd rushed out of the surgery because she needed fresh air.

Her head was full of thoughts she couldn't put into any kind of order. Memories from the last couple of months flashed through her mind like clips from a film: conversations with Joe, places she'd bumped into him, watched him, followed him. Rachel in her red jacket, Monica pouring wine, Duncan standing in the door to his office, Pete's name flashing up on the screen of her phone. But it was as if all of it had happened to someone else. The whole thing seemed so crazy now. Not just crazy – dangerous.

The car edged forward.

'Always the same, when you're in a hurry to get home,' said Monica, sitting back and smiling at Katie. 'Don't worry, it won't be long now.'

Pete had turned on the radio, and the soft strains of a piano swept around the car. Beautiful, peaceful music; familiar, although Katie wasn't sure why.

'Wasn't this from that series on the telly?' she asked. 'The one about the couple in New York?' She closed her eyes and began to drift off to sleep, feeling a jolt a few minutes later, as they pulled up outside the house.

Pete got out and walked around the car. Katie's head was lolling against the back of the seat, and she half-opened her eyes and watched as Monica opened the rear door and pushed herself out. She knew she would also need to move, and wondered how she'd make her legs and arms do as she told them. For the moment it was easier to stay here in the warm; wait for them to tell her it was time to go inside.

Monica had shut the door, but Katie could hear her and Pete talking, their voices low. They were standing beside the car, so she couldn't see their heads, just their bodies through the window. She took a deep breath and focused her eyes on the house behind them. There were no lights on and no sign of the girls, thank goodness. Maybe it was so late, they'd gone to bed? She didn't want to see them right now. Or rather, she didn't want them to see her.

Pete laughed softly. 'You always do that,' he said.

Monica murmured something, but Katie couldn't hear what. She turned her head towards them. Everything felt so heavy and she struggled to keep her eyes open. Through the window she watched Pete's hand move forwards and slide down Monica's back, pulling her towards him, so that for a few seconds their two figures merged together.

Katie screwed up her eyes; she didn't understand what she was seeing. The shape in front of her grew wider again, splitting and turning back into two separate bodies, with just the hands meeting in the middle.

Monica mumbled something; again, Katie couldn't hear what it was. Then their silhouettes twisted into each other for a second time and Katie heard an intake of breath. It flashed through her mind that she must still be drunk – so completely pissed that her mind was playing games with her; the world was no longer spinning, but she couldn't be seeing this. It made no sense.

Monica laughed again. Katie lifted her head off the seat, straining to hear, but the words were muffled through the closed window. But, with her head raised, she could see more: she could see Monica putting her arms around Pete's neck, pulling him closer. She could see Pete's arms snaking around Monica's waist.

Katie closed her eyes, then quickly opened them again, terrified by the darkness that flooded in on her from all sides. Although the alcohol wasn't pushing through her veins as quickly, she felt sick and sweat was breaking out on her forehead. What was going on?

The two people she loved most in the world stepped apart, their bodies once more two distinct outlines silhouetted against the house behind. Monica turned around and opened the car door. As cold air rushed inside, Katie heard her whisper: 'Text me.'

Pete replied; Katie couldn't catch his words, but they both laughed. These voices were so familiar, so much a part of her life. Through the shock and disorder in her brain, she suddenly realised there was also an ease between them. These two voices were used to being together, to talking like this; the conversation they were having was natural. What was happening here, had happened many times before. It was nothing new.

Now Monica stepped back as Pete bent down towards the car. Katie shut her eyes and dropped her head back onto the seat, keeping as still as possible and trying to breathe normally, despite the fact that her racing heart was forcing its way up her throat.

She felt Pete's hand on her arm.

'Right,' he was saying. 'Let's get you out of there and up into bed.'

53

S he must have slept, but it felt as if she'd been lying awake
all night. She vaguely remembered Pete lowering her onto
the spare bed and throwing the duvet across her, then he'd
gone out and pulled the door shut behind him, not even
bothering to pull off her shoes. At some stage during the night,
by that time more sober and shaking with shock, Katie had got
up, staggered to the bathroom and retched into the toilet. Back
in the spare room, she'd felt another hot flush blasting through
her body and had wriggled out of her clothes and slid down
beside the bed until the fire passed and she was able to crawl
back under the duvet, her stomach churning, head pounding.

As she lay there in the darkness, all she could think about
was Pete and Monica: their two bodies moving together; their
laughter, their familiarity. However drunk she'd been, however
exhausted and over-emotional, Katie knew what she'd seen.
There was no mistaking it. Bizarrely, she was more upset with
Monica than with Pete – although she knew it should be the
other way round. But the fact that her best friend could have
done this to her hurt so much it was like a physical pain in her
gut. When she pictured Monica's face, fury boiled up inside

her, followed by confusion, disbelief and an overwhelming wave of self-pity.

But when Katie thought about Pete, she just felt sad and empty. Their relationship had been so strained recently; it felt as if they'd fallen out of love a long time ago. If what she'd seen last night meant the end of her marriage – which seemed likely – she wasn't as surprised or upset as she might once have expected to be. The man who'd come to find her in the pub last night wasn't the man she'd married all those years ago. They'd drifted apart and stopped caring about and for each other. Katie knew she had to take some of the blame for that: even before she'd risked everything by her senseless obsession with Joe, she hadn't been as loving or as attentive a wife as she should have been.

But it wasn't *all* her fault: while Katie had been obsessing over a complete stranger, Pete had been having an affair with his wife's best friend. How long had it been going on? Should she have picked up on it? There were bound to have been signs she'd missed, the odd comment that should have seemed strange, the occasional glance between them. But Katie had noticed nothing, probably because her mind hadn't been on her marriage.

As she lay wide awake in the spare bed, she went over everything that had happened in the last few weeks and months, trying to work out when the three of them had last been together. It was so long ago, she couldn't remember. She had got into the habit of seeing Monica on her own, away from Pete and the girls. Clearly, so had he. But despite that, the two of them must be damn good liars to have conducted this affair without her having the faintest idea.

But who was she to judge? Katie herself had become pretty good at lying.

Suddenly, the chaos of the last twenty-four hours seemed irrelevant. She didn't care that she'd humiliated herself in front of Joe or that Rachel thought she was insane – although she did feel bad about scaring Rachel and forcing her to go with her in the car. Nor did it matter that she'd drunk herself into a stupor in a seedy pub or Pete had found out she'd lost her job. Her obsession with a man who barely knew she existed, suddenly seemed totally insane – almost as if it had happened to someone else. Katie's world had come crashing down around her, and she knew it was no more than she deserved. But what she tried to work out, as the hours ticked by, was how she was going to deal with it.

54

It was still dark outside at 6.30am – the sun wouldn't rise for another hour or so at this time of year. Katie sat at the kitchen table, her hands around a mug of black tea. There was no milk; restocking the fridge with basics was yet another thing she'd forgotten to do for her family. She hated herself for being so preoccupied and self-obsessed.

Pete turned on the light as he came into the kitchen, and stopped when he saw her. 'You're awake!' he said. 'I didn't think we'd see much of you today. Why are you sitting here in the dark? Head not quite up to it?' He laughed and walked across to flick on the kettle, reaching into the cupboard for a mug.

She watched as he unscrewed the coffee jar and fished a teaspoon out of the drawer. He was wearing a T-shirt over a pair of pyjama bottoms and his hair was flattened against his head on one side, where he'd slept on it.

'Pete,' she said. 'I know.'

'You know what? Jesus, why is there never any milk in this place.'

'I know about you and Monica.'

He froze, his back to her, his hand suspended in mid-air as he reached for the kettle. She could see the muscles going rigid in his arm. After a pause that was a fraction too long, he turned slowly around, his brow furrowed. 'Sorry?'

'I know you and Monica are...' she could hardly say it. 'I know you're having an affair.'

She later realised she'd witnessed several emotions flash across his face in the space of two seconds: surprise, fear, then anger. When he'd walked into the room, just half a minute earlier, this was the last thing he'd been expecting. She saw him take a sharp breath in. 'I don't know what you're talking about, Katie.'

'Yes, you do. Please don't pretend it's not true. I saw you both, last night while I was in the back of the car. I heard you, Pete. I heard you talking.'

'You were so bloody drunk last night, you don't have a clue what happened!' Pete shook his head in disbelief. 'Give me a break, Katie. What is all this? God, even for you, this is ridiculous. I actually thought that the first thing you might do this morning is apologise but instead you're coming out with some fucking cock-and-bull story to cover your own back! You've got a bloody nerve.'

'This isn't about me...'

'You're joking!' Pete barked out a laugh. 'This is *all* about you. Monica and I were both worried about you yesterday because you went AWOL, and we were trying to track you down, which was just as well considering where we eventually found you. What were you thinking? When I got that call from Dr Harvey, saying you'd had some kind of funny turn, I had no idea what you might have gone and done! Then I called Duncan to see if you'd gone back to work, and he told me he'd sacked you, last week! Jesus, Katie, I felt like a bloody idiot – why the hell didn't you tell me you'd lost your job?'

'I was going to, but...' Katie's head was thumping and she

was feeling nauseous again. 'Pete, don't change the subject! Okay, I know I owe you an apology, I behaved really stupidly and I'm sorry.' She suddenly realised she didn't know exactly how much she needed to apologise for. Was she just trying to explain her disappearance and drinking yesterday, or did Pete know about everything else? He knew she'd got the sack, but did he know about Joe? Did he know about Rachel? Her brain was too fuzzy to think it all through properly, and she had no idea which of her secrets her best friend might have passed on to her husband as pillow talk. 'But this is about you as well, you and Monica. I have a right to ask you what's going on!'

'Oh, you have a right, do you?' Pete snorted. 'Fine, let's play this your way. You apparently have a right to accuse me with some insane theory of yours, but I don't have a right to ask you why you've been behaving like a madwoman? For months you've been a right bloody pain in the arse, Katie. You've been miserable and bad-tempered, you've snapped at me and the girls – talk about mood swings! You've not been interested in anything that's going on with us or our lives.'

'Pete, that's not true!'

'It's as if you've gone all-out to wreck our lives, Katie. The way you've been behaving, the way you've been so self-obsessed.'

'I never meant to hurt you or the girls.' Even as she said the words, they felt hypocritical. She hadn't meant to hurt them, but she hadn't taken them into consideration either.

'You've also been milking your mum's death for far too long now.'

Katie breathed in sharply, as shocked as if he'd smacked her in the face. 'That's so cruel,' she whispered.

'But true,' he said. It was almost a snarl.

She looked up at him, feeling tears smarting in her own eyes, but seeing nothing in his, apart from dislike. She stood up, realising she was shaking. 'I've done a lot of stupid things recently, and I've behaved very badly. I know that and I'm truly sorry for it. I should have told you I'd lost my job, but I didn't want to burden you with that because you had problems at school.'

'Don't try to blame it on me!' he yelled.

'I'm not!' she screamed back. 'I'm just trying to explain!'

Standing feet away from him, Katie could hear her own breath rasping and, despite the fact that the heating hadn't had time to warm up the house, beads of sweat were breaking out on her forehead. She wiped away the sheen with the back of her hand. 'But whatever I've done, however stupid and reckless I've been, it's bloody unfair of you to say that I've milked my mother's death.' She was trying to glare at him, but was crying now and saw a softening in his expression. 'I miss her, Pete. I miss my mum and it hurts not to have her here. Can you understand that?'

He made as if to move towards her, but she took a step back. 'No, don't. And please don't change the subject again. I was talking about you and Monica.'

They stood in silence at opposite ends of the kitchen, staring at each other. Katie swiped at her wet cheeks with her fingers. 'This is all such a mess,' she whispered.

He nodded. 'I know.'

She pulled out a chair and sat at the table and, after a few seconds, he sank into a chair on the opposite side. She looked at him, but he was staring down at the table, twisting his fingers together. She couldn't read his expression – it was strange, for years she'd thought she knew everything about this man: what he was thinking, how he was feeling. But he seemed closed to her now.

'The irony is,' she said, laughing suddenly. 'You asked me if I was having an affair, on Christmas Day. We were standing outside and...'

'Yes,' he said. 'I remember.'

'And in a way, although I flew off the handle, I didn't think it was unreasonable of you to ask that, because I *had* been behaving strangely. I knew that. But all the time, you were the one who was having an affair. You and Monica.'

Pete finally looked up at her. 'You can't claim the moral high ground,' he said. 'I know about you and that man. I don't know who he is, but I know you've been lusting after some bloke. Monica told me.'

Katie nodded. 'Yes, I expected she would have done.'

'Is it anyone I know?'

Katie shook her head. 'No.' It was yet another lie, but she didn't feel guilty about this one – Pete didn't really know Dr Joe Harvey, any more than Katie herself knew him. 'Nothing happened between us,' she said. 'It was only ever in my head. I know that doesn't excuse it, but he never even knew.'

'But you got in touch with his wife and pretended to be her friend?'

'She's not his wife…'

'Whatever. Mon said you've been out with her, but she doesn't know what's going on. It's all fucking insane, Katie. Even you must see that?'

She did see that. As they sat there, deafened by another awkward silence, it occurred to her how strange it was to hear him shortening her best friend's name. Katie had been the only person who ever called her that. But 'Mon' tripped off Pete's tongue easily and naturally.

'So, where do we go from here?' he asked, eventually.

Behind him, Katie could see the sky starting to lighten through the kitchen window; somewhere in the distance she could hear the familiar rumble and metallic scrape of the bin lorry starting its slow trawl along the street outside.

'I don't know,' she said, softly.

EPILOGUE

Nobody enjoyed sports day: the kids were tired and bored, the teachers were stressed, the parents resented having to take time off work while pretending to enjoy watching their children run, jump, pass batons and throw themselves into sandpits.

They stood together, arms linked, slightly back from the crowd, watching Anna launch herself at a high jump for the third and final time, her leap so half-hearted that her chest smacked into the pole and sent it skittering across the grass. Mrs Hall blew a whistle and pointed to the benches, but Anna refused to walk, crossing her arms and puffing out her chest. 'Why do I only get three turns?' they could hear her yelling. 'That's rubbish!'

After a few seconds of heated debate, during which Mrs Hall's neck went very red, Anna stomped back to join the rest of the class.

'She's never been good at losing,' said Katie.

Beside her, Suky laughed. 'She'll go far in the world.'

Katie still felt uneasy at school events. She'd only plucked up the courage to come here today because Suky was with her.

A handful of other parents had said hello, and clearly wanted to ask questions, but only PTA Fiona had enough front to do so.

'Nice to see you, Katie!' she'd squealed. 'You look fantastic. You've lost so much weight!'

Katie had just smiled.

'Is everything else in hand?' Fiona ploughed on. 'All nearly sorted now?'

'Yes, everything's fine,' Katie had said.

'So… Pete still sees the girls?'

'Yes, Fiona, he sees a lot of them.'

Fiona stood, waiting to hear more, but Katie wasn't going to give her the satisfaction. 'I'd better watch Anna in the next race,' she said. 'See you later.'

As Fiona moved away, Suky squeezed Katie's arm. 'Nosy cow,' she muttered.

Katie smiled. 'I don't blame her. I'd want to know the lowdown too.'

One of the younger mums, standing over by the gate, had her hair piled up into a messy bun on the top of her head – it was what Rachel used to do with hers.

For weeks after it all happened, Katie had lived in fear of running into Rachel or Joe. She'd imagined seeing Rachel buying a ticket by the machine in the car park, or finding herself behind Joe in a queue at the cashpoint. This town was too small to avoid them forever. Katie didn't know what she'd say; which of them would be the easiest to deal with. Joe would have no idea what had happened after she fled his consulting room that day, and must have wondered what on earth had led up to those awful few minutes. Rachel would be hurt and confused that Katie had stepped out of her life and never returned her calls. For different reasons, both would judge her – without knowing their other half had reason to do the same.

Katie had once thought she saw Rachel in town: a young

woman had come out of a café on the other side of the road: her head down, searching for something in her bag. She was the same height and build as Rachel, her hair was the same colour. Katie's heart had smashed into her ribs like a bullet; but then the girl looked up – it wasn't her. The relief was overwhelming and, walking on, Katie had realised she was shaking, her legs weak.

That had been just a couple of weeks before she found out about Joe. She'd been queuing to pay for fuel in the garage and the latest issue of the local paper was stacked up in a pile on the floor. Katie's mouth fell open as she read the headline: *Pelham Green GP suspended for misconduct.* 'Bloody hell!' she said, before she could stop herself.

'I know, isn't it terrible?' said the woman in the queue behind her. 'I went to see him once, about my hernia.'

The paper had used that picture again: the one with Joe in a purple and white striped shirt, standing with his arms crossed, leaning slightly forward as he smiled into the camera. Even after everything that had happened, Katie's stomach still jolted at the sight of him.

'Apparently, he was having a thing with one of the nurses at the surgery,' the woman was saying. 'She was quite a bit younger than him, but they were carrying on behind everyone's backs. Or behind closed doors more like! I hear they got caught in the act.'

Katie was only half listening. The words swam on the page in front of her. *Dr Harvey suspended by the GMC... investigation into allegations of professional misconduct...*

'Rumour has it, he was a bit of a flirt,' said the woman behind her in the queue. 'I've heard it wasn't just that one nurse. Honestly, you can't trust anyone nowadays, can you?'

Katie's shock at this news was made worse because there was no one she could discuss it with. Part of her was desperate to learn more, but she was also terrified about what she might find out. She was finally beginning to come to terms with what had happened and make peace with herself about her actions. She knew she'd been delusional and accepted this was an unrequited obsession with a man who had done nothing to lead her on. But now it sounded as if Joe wasn't all he'd seemed either.

Katie had fleetingly considered calling Rachel, but there was no point. What would she say? Offer sympathy about the fact that her boyfriend had been playing the field? She was sorry for Rachel, and she *had* liked the girl, but too much had happened for any kind of friendship to resume. She imagined Rachel's hurt expression: *What the hell happened to you, Katie? You said you were my friend, then you kidnapped me, had a weird breakdown and I never heard from you again.*

The only thing Katie had done, after seeing the article about Joe, was allow herself to make one last detour up Coopers Lane. There were no curtains now at any of the windows of number 15, and a new *To Let* sign speared the small lawn. She had put the car in gear and driven away again quickly. Poor Rachel; what a bloody mess.

Sports Day was drawing to a close and Mrs Hall was running through the house points over the loudspeaker. Anna was glaring at her and, when her class was sent to get ready for the final race, she zigzagged off at an angle to go past where Katie and Suky were standing. 'This is my best one!' she shouted as she ran past. 'I'm really good at it, so I'm going to win this!'

'Just have fun taking part!' called Katie. But Anna was already running away towards the start line, head down, elbows pumping manically.

'Not much longer, thank God,' said Suky. 'This has been hard work.'

She was probably referring to having to watch 200 primary school children race up and down a field. But Katie had found just being here hard work. She still didn't feel welcome amongst these fellow parents. But now she and Pete had found a buyer for the house, she only had to keep her head down for a few more weeks. It would be good to be away from here. The new house she was planning to rent in Minsterworth was small, but Suky was happy because she'd be five minutes' walk from Adam's, and Anna was so excited by the laptop Pete had promised to buy her, that she didn't seem worried about the move.

After having no contact with her for months, Katie had bumped into Monica at the weekend, literally bumped. Monica was looking down at her phone as she came out of a bookshop. They'd both stopped and stepped back; stared into each other's eyes for a second before moving on.

She's probably texting my husband, thought Katie. The possibility didn't hurt as much as she'd expected it to. If the last six months had taught her anything, it was that the old saying about time being a great healer, was one of life's truisms. She wasn't fully healed yet – none of them were – but they were getting there. Monica wasn't living with Pete; it would probably happen, but at the moment she was still in her little terraced house and he had found himself a flat, nearer to his school. Katie had heard, through Suky, that Damien's parents had dropped their complaint against him and he was in line for promotion to deputy head; she was pleased for him. But it was a relief he hadn't moved in with Monica straight away; they all needed time to adapt to this new way of being, especially the girls.

Outside the bookshop, Katie had watched Monica walk off briskly, realising she still felt a pang of love for the friend who had meant so much to her for twenty years. She missed her – possibly more than she missed Pete. As Monica disappeared around the corner, Katie turned and pushed open the door of the bookshop. She was after the latest novel by Maggie

O'Farrell, but it wouldn't matter if they didn't have it in stock – her new book group was more laid-back than the previous one and no one would care if she hadn't managed to read it by the next meeting. She'd been invited along by a lovely woman she'd met at the call centre where she was now working. At this book group, there was no discussion about plot arcs and character motivation; these women spent five minutes discussing the book and the next three hours drinking wine and putting the world to rights. Katie loved it.

A whistle blew, and parents started yelling as a row of children began to run up the field balancing tennis balls on tablespoons.

'Come on, Anna!' shouted Katie.

'Run!' yelled Suky.

They both stopped suddenly, breathing in sharply as Anna threw out her free arm and pushed the girl next to her so violently, that she fell sideways and sent several others crashing to the ground. As whistles blew, children screamed and teachers began to run towards the carnage, Anna sailed over the finishing line, tennis ball still on tablespoon, her fist punching the air.

Katie clamped her hand over her mouth. Other parents were turning towards them and glaring. Suky was trying to stop herself laughing, and Anna was parading around the field, holding the ball and spoon aloft, like Olympic trophies.

'Sorry!' mouthed Katie to a group of parents on her left. 'Problems at home,' she said apologetically, to a mother on her right. 'It's been a tricky year.' But amusement was bubbling up in her gut and, beside her, Suky's shoulders were shaking. They looked at each other, and exploded into snorts of laughter.

'Disgraceful…' she heard a man say.

He was right, of course he was. But at this precise moment Katie didn't care. Let them think what they like, these proprietors of the moral high ground. If they thought Anna was behaving badly, they'd be appalled if they ever found out what her mother had been up to.

Thank God that was never going to happen.

She beckoned Anna over and grabbed Suky's hand.

'Come on, girls,' she grinned. 'Let's get out of here.'

THE END

ACKNOWLEDGEMENTS

This book started life several years ago and has gone through many tweaks, rewrites and edits along the way. An early version won the inaugural Katie Fforde Contemporary Novel award at Stroud Book Festival, and I remain indebted to Katie, Caroline and all the other wonderful Gloucestershire authors who have supported me and my books over the last few years.

I must also thank Sophie Wilson, Amanda Saint and Liza Bewick for looking at various versions of this story (such a long time ago, they've probably forgotten they even did it!) and telling me what worked and - more importantly - what didn't. Sometimes you get so caught up in writing a book, that it's easy to lose sight of what you're trying to achieve, which is where early readers - who aren't afraid to give an honest opinion - are essential, and greatly appreciated.

Thank you to Betsy, Clare, Tara and Abbie at Bloodhound, for getting *The Bad Wife* out into the world, and also to Mat, Sam, Maddy and Jess for their ongoing love, encouragement and general tolerance.

Finally, authors are nothing without the readers who support them and I'm so grateful to all of you who've taken the time to get in touch and tell me you've enjoyed my books; your cheerleading has been amazing. Jeannie, this one's for you!

If you'd like to find out more about me and my writing, please visit www. sarahedghill.com or follow my Amazon Author page by clicking on any of my novels.

ALSO BY SARAH EDGHILL

A Thousand Tiny Disappointments

His Other Woman

A NOTE FROM THE PUBLISHER

Thank you for reading this book. If you enjoyed it please do consider leaving a review on Amazon to help others find it too.

We hate typos. All of our books have been rigorously edited and proofread, but sometimes mistakes do slip through. If you have spotted a typo, please do let us know and we can get it amended within hours.

info@bloodhoundbooks.com

Made in the USA
Columbia, SC
15 July 2023

20514767R00200